The Tragic *Flaw*

Strebor on the Streetz

The Tragic Flaw

CHE PARKER

STREBOR BOOKS

NEW YORK LONDON TORONTO SYDNEY

Strebor Books
P.O. Box 6505
Largo, MD 20792
http://www.streborbooks.com

ISBN-13 978-1-59309-126-2
ISBN-10   1-59309-126-5
LCCN 2007923863

First Strebor Books trade paperback edition September 2007

Cover design: www.mariondesigns.com

10   9   8   7   6   5   4   3   2   1

Manufactured in the United States of America

For information regarding special discounts for bulk purchases,
please contact Simon & Schuster Special Sales at 1-800-456-6798
or business@simonandschuster.com

Tragic flaw *(n)* 1913: a defect in character that brings about the downfall of the hero of a tragedy

Dedication

This book is dedicated to my friend
Oshun "O.G." Garner
rest in peace

Acknowledgments

Thank you to my mother, Shelley, and my aunt Onyta,
the best *consiglieri* a young man could have.

Thanks to my father, Robert Parker, without whom my
education would not have been possible, rest in peace.

And to my stepfather, Archie "Bobby" Miller, for providing
for us and eventually kicking me out of the house.
You will never know how much I needed that.

Chapter 1

Youthful laughter permeates the old neighborhood on an unseasonably sultry winter day. Three-story homes and greening arbors line the streets on either side. The homes' aged and stately appearances clash with the sounds of adolescence. Older model cars dot College Avenue here and there. Most are well kept, washed and waxed, and parked close enough to the curb as to avoid the all too infamous sideswipe. Others lack hubcaps, or sport more than one tone—black and taupe, for instance—certainly not what the manufacturer intended.

Still others lack tires, or have been clasped with city-owned clamps that prevent them from doing what they're meant to do. Of course they're American made. Names like Buick, Ford, and Oldsmobile are commonplace. More than one flatbed truck lives here, and is used here, often to haul in bicycles that require assembly, or to haul out sofas when excuses no longer dissuade eager landlords.

The gold and red masonry of the homes stands strong in the face of frail innocence. The dwellings are seemingly paternal in essence, standing watch over tomorrow's dearest. Visible black bars of iron cover nearly every window on the ground level, hinting at unforeseen perils and dangers that might thrive in this community.

Most sidewalks are well swept, but a few could use sprucing up. They very often resemble the tidiness of the vehicles parked just in front of them. Wrappers with words like Coca-Cola, Jolly Ranchers, and Coors, and other colorful plastics with various titles are seen in gutters, not everywhere, but more than enough.

A single ringing gunshot is heard while children are at play. Nothing uncommon for this neighborhood, so the youth continue their games in the thick humid air. Some, mostly girls, are tossing rocks on quadrangles and hopping on unsteady feet. Others, sweaty boys in T-shirts and dirty blue jeans, thrust outstretched hands toward still others, boys and girls who flee as if their pursuers wished to transmit smallpox or leprosy. Several girls, not quite nubile, twirl opposing ropes as a single entrenched participant leaps in a battle against the encircling cords. Her laughter is infectious, as her beaded locks frolic about and sweat drips from her brow. They're clad in cut-rate shorts and tank tops with waning hues of pink and lavender, and off-white sandals that have had their fair share of rope jumping and inner-city jaunts. The other two partakers giggle with her and against her. They're not new to this game; they have played it many times. Each time it is pleasurable. The summertime weather beckons, even though it is only February. Another gunshot rings out, echoing against the urban edifices. There's still no reaction from the playing preteens as they chuckle and skip.

They have songs and chants and rhymes that usually accompany their rope exercise, but not this time. This time it's more serious. The middle combatant is a champion, and her compatriots wish to dethrone her. Even still, her feet seem to be magnetically repelled by the ground and the ropes. They smack the hot turf methodically while avoiding the merest brush with the composite twine.

A graying grandmother exits her front door and comes to sit idle on her stoop, observing the ever-changing world through wise, time-tested eyes. She has been a witness to Jackie Robinson's first base hit, lynchings, riots, and space travel. She's seen the persecution of quadroons and conversely, the invalidation of age-old taboos. She, perhaps unlike others her age, has no fear of dying.

Her faded floral housecoat and matching slippers appear as aged as she, and her brown, wrinkled, and calloused hands offer a glimpse into the difficult life she has led. Lovely roses of all colors begin to bloom in her yard, fooled by the early ninety-degree day. She has diligently tended to these flowers for years.

The glowing sun fights through the scattered clouds. Baby blue occupies the sky. Undeterred yellow beams of light strike the pavement. It is un-doubtedly a beautiful day.

A beam catches one young lass's light-brown eyes and long lashes, enhancing both, as she twirls her end of the two ropes with coffee-colored hands. Sweaty palms grasp the cordage as she fights to hold on.

Family gatherings bring the aroma of mesquite and charred beef and pork. Third generations are ordered to perform songs and dances for first generations. It's tradition on days like this. And with weather so lovely in the dead of winter, all wish to take advantage of it.

A badly lit mom-and-pop corner store sees a steady stream of at least three generations during the day and well into the night. The neighborhood's rambunctious kids are sustained with consistently stocked shelves of licorice and hot pickles.

Middle-aged and sturdy fix-it men in tattered coveralls stop by for D batteries, seventy five-watt light bulbs, nails, and flat-head compatible screws kept on dusty wooden racks. They chat briefly with the owner about how their home team could go all the way if they just had a decent secondary and some semblance of a pass rush. Well-known rummies fall in for the inexpensive lagers and two-dollar bottles of *vino* stored in lukewarm refrigerator units.

A cool breeze blows. A crackle of thunder interrupts the melodic chuckles, yet the play goes on. The flow of business at the bazaar is uninterrupted. A burnt-out drunk with a hardened face pours worthless suds from this empty beer bottle onto the sidewalk. He then asks the neighborhood's young hustlers for spare change, and they in turn laugh at him, as always. The abodes, while casting a regal shadow of protection on the area's most precious resource, hide a secret.

For just a few feet away, one turn to the left, a few paces down, and yet another swivel the opposite way, then down an alley where vermin reside and slime and sludge congregate, lies a dying shell. It is the shell of a man. The dying, bleeding shell of a man. That ringing shot was no accident. It has hit its mark.

Key aspects of his chest are absent. Maroon solution cascades down the side of his torso in a slow waterfall of despair and anguish.

Yet the children's laughter is still heard, ignorant that it fills the ears of the perishing, who is in no need of its sardonic prodding. The burgundy life force pools just beneath its reluctant spring. The giggling intensifies and is ubiquitous as the clouds open and it begins to rain. A mad scramble is made to every step, stoop, doorway, door, foyer, and elsewhere.

The stray yellow beams of light have been overwhelmed by the dark gray coming of the rain.

The relentless drops splash in the unsuspecting red sauce, pounding the man's body, which at this point has no say in the matter. Yet, sirens can be heard in the background. There is hope for him, as the rain pours. The sudden precipitation makes an overwhelming *SSSHHHH* sound as it coats everything in what appears to be insurmountable moisture.

The man wears exquisite garb from the Old World. Fine lines, evenly stitched, and thread counts in the hundreds, position themselves along sinewy flesh. The stench of forthcoming death lingers as his eyelids flutter. His breathing is weak and faint.

The brilliant powder-blue mainstay of his soaked shirt contrasts sharply with poignant crimson lines that intersect throughout it. Midnight-colored trousers, also of the Italian peninsula, rest comfortably on the drenched and ever more dampening pavement. The man's slip-on onyx loafers lie fixed in a conflicting state, pointing directly at each other in a supple and unsightly way.

Zeus is restless. The rain pounds it all. The man's black blazer now functions as a colander for heaven's tears. His earth-tone hands and fingers, furrowed by the wetness, are bent in awkward positions. The fingers twitch as if communicating via sign language prior to what looks like an inevitable trip to the spirit world. His eyes become securely closed, looking as if he is simply napping as the sirens get louder and closer. The lines on his face display a few years, but not many.

He would look peaceful, if it weren't for his contorted posture and weather-beaten exterior. His frame becomes cold, losing any inkling of heat or energy. Rivers of waste and other remnants are washed to the man by the driving rain.

Rubbish, like shattered glass held together by sticky labels, begins to gather near his feet. Used condoms collect fittingly near his midsection; his body locked in a fetal position. All things urban are flushed toward this once proud man, who now finds himself a filter for a city's precipitation and refuse.

And still, the blood pours. It gathers, and then is dispersed by the rain into several streams that flow down the black glossy alleyway in an artistic display. It is fluid artwork that has decorated ghettos the world over. This medium, unlike colored pencils or pastel chalk, is the medium that keeps Hell engorged with uncaring youth and malevolent adults.

An expiring heart pumps faintly in a rain-soaked alley.

But blaring sirens near. All is not lost.

Chapter 2

Bullion barbs, approximately one hundred symmetrically aligned, millimeters in width, protrude from a focal point of gold. The entire mass rotates and reflects the radiant sunlight of the cloudless day.

The twenty-four-inch disk is accompanied by three clones in flanking positions, as they all support the weight of a large, pearl-white sport utility vehicle and its driver, currently en route.

The rotation of the SUV's Ohio-made rims is hypnotic. Nothing that big should be that gold. The oyster exterior is luminous. Not a speck nor smudge defiles its brilliance.

Its large black tires hug the Thirty-First Street concrete intimately, as if a love affair had been brewing since the new model left the showroom floor.

The driver is ever vigilant of potholes, swerving carefully to avoid them.

The scenery is bleak. Urban blight festers. Names crossed out in graffiti mark the deceased. On any given day, gunplay can make this place look like the Gaza Strip, or some Israeli settlement on the outskirts of the West Bank, except there's no "Breaking Coverage," no Wolf Blitzer, and no international outcry. Regardless, cashaholic militants carry out an assortment of transactions and will not hesitate to let Teflon-coated lead fly with the fervor of religious zealots. They'll die for this shit.

Corner after corner, someone's uncle chugs cheap wine and cheaper beer in an attempt to drown his sorrows, but in the ghetto they know how to tread water well. This while someone else's sister solicits every other blue-collar Joe and white-collar Jonathon.

"Hey! Hey, baby!" one clad in cherry hot pants screams to the SUV's driver, trying to flag him down. Her hazel eyes and delicate skin are appealing, but he's focused, and her call goes unnoticed.

The driver's path is fixed. Avenue after avenue, he continues without making a single turn, avoiding stray dogs and children fresh from summer school on this late June day. Empty brick buildings with broken windows abound.

There are signs of commerce, though. Aside from the open-air cash dealings for illegal narcotics, liquor stores, fast-food restaurants, pawnshops, pager shops, and check cashing businesses flourish here.

Residents of this once up-and-coming middle-class community poison their livers with fermented fruits and vegetables, then continue the self-imposed genocide by poisoning their bellies with high-fat, high-calorie fare. It's readily available and a little too convenient.

And yet the gold rims keep spinning.

The driver, clean-shaven and bald, sips expensive cognac from a red plastic cup. Bass lines from rap music send vibrations throughout the truck's peanut butter leather interior, causing the rear view mirror to shake and shimmy.

His tiny metallic digital phone rings. He grabs it from the center console, looks at the device's caller identification box, notices the number, and decides not to answer it, tossing it onto the passenger seat.

He takes another sip of his aged libation, hints of vanilla and oak escaping from the cup.

"Uuhh," he says, as his full lips curl. The drink is strong, but it's good.

Life in this neighborhood is enough to make anybody drink cordials during the middle of the day, the driver thinks to himself.

After making a right turn on Jackson Avenue and cruising several blocks, the driver pulls in front of a home and stops. He steps out of the truck. His light-blue alligator boots gently kiss the pavement. His blue, short-sleeved Australian-made sweater is intricately woven into eye-catching patterns. It matches his boots to a tee, as well as the picturesque sky above.

He crosses the street and comes before a white, one-story gated house watched by several surveillance cameras. It is extremely clean and well kempt, especially for this part of town.

He pushes a buzzer on an intercom. His diamond-encrusted, European-made watch glimmers in the sunshine. The princess cuts catch and display every color in the rainbow with their many facets. It seems to say, *bliiiing*. The time is 4:06 p.m.

A low male voice answers the driver's page, and asks professionally over the intercom, "Who is it?"

"Cicero," the driver answers, as he takes another sip from his plastic cup.

With a loud buzz, the gate, pulled by a rusty chain, begins to open, retracting to the left.

Cicero slowly walks in, and the gate begins closing behind him, making an obnoxious clanking noise. He takes one last swig of his auburn beverage and discards his red cup right in the front lawn. There's nothing else in the yard, and the cup stands out in the manicured emerald grass.

The electronic eyes follow his progress from the gate to the covered porch. Bars cover the windows.

Men's voices can be heard, muffled, emanating from within the house. The door is unlocked. Knowing this, Cicero turns the brass knob and walks in.

The place smells like a mixture of rancid marijuana smoke and fruity air fresheners plugged into the outlets, but it is immaculate.

White coats everything: white carpet, a white leather sofa and matching loveseat, white stereo equipment, a white marble-based coffee table with a glass top. Yet the stylish purity clashes subtly with the black African art that decorates the walls, not to mention the mannish and outlandish speech coming from a back room.

One rendering, framed in black wood, hangs above the sofa and features a black, bare-chested tribesman embracing his African queen, whose full breasts are exposed. It's huge, running the length of the long white sofa. In the background is the enchanting Serengeti. The chiseled sunburned peaks in the distance further emphasize the softness of the tribesman's bronze female.

Cicero eyes it, as he has many times, and just for a split second longs to be the man in the painting.

A sculpture of a woman stands nearly four feet and is situated to the left of the loveseat near a long hallway. The full figure and bouffant tresses give away the piece's ethnicity as its back arches and its hands are raised toward heaven as if giving praise to the Almighty.

A black-and-white still shot of Billie Holiday with her signature botanical adornment hangs over the love seat. The framed work beautifully depicts the elegant songstress' defined cheekbones, fine lips, and long flirtatious lashes. Her spread fingers, reacting to the heart-pounding offbeat jazz rhythms, make her hands appear to be in flight. Her lace-trimmed blouse is billowy. She is floating.

Mirrors, lined with white accents, are everywhere. The image of the large oil painting of the loving couple is bounced back and forth all over the wide living room, as is that of our elongated inanimate lady.

Cicero bends down and removes his boots, placing them right next to a pair of brand-new sneakers. This Japanese-based tradition of shoe removal, as requested by the homeowner, is a sign of respect. It is also what keeps the carpet the color of pure cocaine. Tan work boots and colorful tennis shoes line the wall to the left of the front door all the way to the towering white entertainment center that holds the state-of-the-art stereo system (also white) and the corresponding flat-screen plasma television.

"Shoot the fucking dice," one man says as Cicero walks down the hallway to the source of the hostility. His white socks blend perfectly into the plush Berber carpet, leaving size eleven footprints in his wake.

Cicero enters a back bedroom that has been converted into a recreation room of sorts. Five men occupy it. Four are kneeling. It's a crap game.

High stakes. Three thousand gets you a side bet. Four thousand gets you in the game.

"Man, will you stop shaking the fuckin' dice and just shoot," one heavily tattooed man says to another who also bears ink, in a frank and quite unfriendly tone. Twin jade serpents intertwine on his right forearm. His hair is tightly braided in straight parallel lanes.

"Chill out, mothafucka," the young dice holder says as he jostles the red die in his right hand. His left supports the weight of his kneeling body. "The sooner I shoot them the sooner you lose your money, asshole, so you better be happy I'm taking my fuckin' time," he says with a sinister smile on his face, exposing the gold and diamonds in his mouth. A Spanish inscription in Old English letters runs permanently down the back of his left arm: *El Hijo del Diablo*.

"Come on, mothafucka, I got shit to do," says another larger man in a black T-shirt, who has an intricate dragon with red eyes and green highlights spanning from his arm all the way up to the middle of his neck. He's extremely overweight.

One man is silently kneeling, looking on with intense eyes, hundred-dollar bills crumpled in his hand. An ink-inscribed name, "V-Dog," written in cursive letters, draws attention to the bulging bicep on his right arm. He has more than ten tattoos: names, abstract patterns, animals.

His dark-blue denim jeans and matching button-down shirt are heavily starched. His creases are rigid. He briefly glances up at Cicero with cold dark eyes, then looks back at the inactive dice holder.

Besides the men, the room is empty; half of it is uncarpeted, exposing hardwood parquet floors. It's perfect for tumbling dice. A very small stereo speaker pokes out of the wall near the door. The underground hip-hop music is tremendously clear, not too earsplitting.

The man with the rhombus crystals obscuring his teeth gives the dice one last good shake, then lets them fly out of his hand. They crash against the bottom of the wall, near the corner, and slide back toward the gambling quartet. One die stops before the other, showing three ecru circles. The second continues to roll, brushes one man's foot, then stops, displaying a total of...

"Seven," the shooter yells with excitement, quickly grabbing twelve thousand dollars and sweeping it behind him into an already large, mint-green pile becoming ever more virescent by the minute.

"Fuck," the large man says, as he reaches into his pocket for a fresh four thousand to get back into the game. The shooter is hot, and his three opponents are down a total of twenty-four thousand dollars.

"I'm out," says V-Dog. He's disgusted and feeling nauseous. He had planned on breaking everybody else and copping some soft. Now he's the broke one, and T.J., the lucky-ass dude with all his money, is talking shit.

"What's wrong, V-Dog?" the fresh-faced T.J. asks. "You all out of dough?" Everyone else in the room laughs.

V-Dog just looks at him, expressionless.

"Check it out, I'll front you four gees so you can stay in the game, V-Dog," a grinning T.J. says, and adds, "with one hundred fifty percent interest, mothafucka!" The room again erupts into laughter.

V-Dog looks unamused, and the other three men continue the game without him.

A fifth, dark-skinned man dressed in all black sits in a white, modern, art-deco half-moon chair. He's the homeowner. He looks up at Cicero and gives him a cool nod.

"Hey, what's up with you, Warren?" Cicero asks with his deep voice as he begins to count out three-thousand dollars so he can get some side bet action.

"Just chillin', man," Warren responds. "Tryin' to maintain."

"I heard that," Cicero replies.

He's feeling lucky, and T.J., his friend, is on fire. So why not bet on him, Cicero thinks.

T.J. rolls the dice again. No seven, but it's still a good roll.

"What's your point ,T.J.?" Cicero asks.

"What's crackin', C? My point eight, and I'm straight," he answers with a smile. His mouth brightens the room in a burst of light and sparkles.

"I bet he hits that eight," Cicero says to Warren, and as he does, he hears a dog barking loudly from outside.

Cicero, looking puzzled, says to the homeowner, "I didn't know you had a pit."

Warren, who isn't shooting dice, just observing, laughs. It's low and brief. He takes a puff from his freshly rolled joint.

"I don't," he says, exhaling a plume of thick cannabis smoke.

Cicero looks even more confused. Surely he has a pit bull, he ponders.

Warren then slowly rises out of his chair with a slight grunt. His potbelly weighs him down, but his jewel-encrusted time-piece makes him look like royalty. The chrome face, with its sweeping second hand, is flooded with yellow baguettes, and aquamarine sapphires surround the perimeter. He gets to his feet and walks out the room, motioning for Cicero to follow.

He does.

They walk through the bare kitchen to a back door. Warren slips on a pair of raggedy, navy-blue house shoes and opens the deadbolt lock with a key retrieved from deep within his jeans pocket.

The light-brown pine door opens and Cicero eyes the most massive canine he has ever seen.

"It's a Presa Canario," Warren declares, smiling proudly. "Fuck a pit bull."

The two step outside and proceed closer. Warren jokingly slaps the dog's huge head side-to-side while Cicero observes from a few feet away.

The animal resembles a prehistoric mammal that time forgot, a distant cousin of the saber-toothed tiger. Its muscular frame looks cartoonish, almost fake. But in its large square, fish-like mouth, reside very real teeth, and enough pressure per square inch to crush a lead pipe.

It snaps at the overly playful Warren, almost removing a finger.

The dog, panting heavily, is chained, but its jaw-dropping physique makes the steel chain seem like an inadequate restraint. Its chocolate coat glistens as white foamy drool flows past its thick black lips and down its chin. Its robust frame helps to conceal dark-red eyes. The ears, set high on its head, ironically resemble flower petals.

"Damn," Cicero mutters in a low voice.

"It's a boy, and I got his papers," comments Warren, who is now on one knee lovingly caressing the beast's head. "I'm looking for a female right now so I can breed 'em."

The dog looks Cicero directly in the eyes, causing him to take a small footstep back.

"Man, if you hear anything about a female for sale, let me know—" Warren says, finishing his sentence abruptly. He's cut off by arguing, and then a commotion, coming from inside his pristine home.

Cicero, hearing the ruckus, turns around to face the house as if expecting something strange or out of the ordinary to appear before him.

Bang! Bang! Bang! Bang! Bang! Five quick shots are heard, followed by the sounds of frantic scurrying. Cicero quickly pulls a nickel-plated revolver from his waistline and heads toward the back entryway. But before he can dart into the house, Warren yells to him, "Look out, C!"

With that, Warren releases the latch from his monster's collar. "Eat them mothafuckas up!" he yells to his instantly fanatical mongrel.

Warren's dazzling watch becomes shrouded in dirt and dust as the beast charges full speed toward the door. No longer barking, the only sounds heard from the creature are pants of rage and its huge paws pounding the earth.

Cicero leaps out of the way, as the beast would have certainly trampled him to reach his target. The front door slams and Warren's loyal animal begins barking loudly from inside the house.

Warren and Cicero cautiously enter. Cicero's weapon is cocked and ready to explode.

The two peer into the back room that several moments earlier was the venue for an urban sporting event. Now a dying body lay facedown on the hardwood floor, blood spewing from several new cavities. It's T.J.

Part of his head is missing. The once intact cranium has been splattered into bloody chunks all over the room, a grotesque ambiance. Active nerves in his body cause it to twitch. It is a disturbing sight.

Warren's loyal dog has his two front paws pressed against the front door, whining. His meal escaped.

"Damn, T.J.," Cicero says in a saddened tone. He looks over at the dice.

One is flat, clearly showing two small off-white circles. The other cube is diagonally propped up, wedged between the wood floor and the carpet, equally displaying five dots on one side, and one dot on the other. The fateful roll was obviously a bone of contention; one that ended young T.J.'s life. He was nineteen.

Blood squirts out of his carcass' various outlets. His white T-shirt now resembles a cape used in bullfighting. His ill-gotten winnings have vanished.

Warren is appalled at the sight before him.

"Look at my fucking carpet," he fumes. The blood has seeped into his flawless floor covering, leaving it a rosy pink. He stoops down over the body and gets a closer look, careful not to step into any of T.J.'s leaking juices.

"Man, why did he have to die like this?" Cicero asks out loud, but to no one in particular. He stands in the doorway.

Attila, Warren's furry companion, has made his way to the back room. The dog is more subdued now. It noses about the room, smelling the corpse and its bloodshed.

Cicero looks to Warren and asks, "You ever wonder how people end up in certain situations?"

Warren just glances up at him, disbelief written all over his fat bearded face. He offers no answer and his eyes return to the body and the blood.

Attila, who has begun to salivate, starts to lap at the blood. His thick tongue twists as it catches the liquid that is now beginning to coagulate on the oak wood floor as well as the white carpet. The beast savors the salty flavor.

"Stop! Stop, mothafucka!" Warren screams to his dog, forcefully yanking on its collar, barely budging the mammoth brute. "Stop! That's some nasty shit, Attila." He's finally successful in tearing his parched dog away from the solidifying pool of blood. Cicero just stares at the scene.

Warren massages the head of his Hershey-colored dog, staring in its eyes. "That mothafucka could have West Nile virus or some shit," he says in a concerned parental voice. "Now you got it, dummy."

Attila's head lowers as if he knows he has disappointed his master. Warren shakes his head, showing obvious displeasure in his canine's choice for a thirst quencher.

Countless thoughts run through Cicero's mind as he continues to gawk at T.J.'s bleeding body. But one sticks.

"You truly are the devil's son now," he says. "I guess."

The bearded Warren, now fully dismayed by the situation that has unfolded in his home, stands to his feet, strokes his face, and walks out of the room toward the front door. Attila trots out of the room and plops down on the fluffy white living room carpet and begins licking his balls.

"A, C, come here," Warren yells to his associate, who is still staring at T.J.'s corpse in the back of the house.

Cicero regains his composure and saunters out of the room. He's focused once again.

"One second," he says as he goes to the kitchen, opens the near-empty fridge, and grabs a cold imported beer with a German-sounding name. After quickly popping the top off the green bottle, he takes a much-needed swig then walks out of the kitchen toward Warren and asks, "What's up?"

"Check this out," Warren says, pointing to the dwindled row of footwear near the door.

Cicero notices just two pairs of shoes remain: his gators, and a brand-new pair of navy-blue sneakers. They would nicely complement a cobalt denim outfit. Apparently, their owner left with great haste.

Enunciating every letter, in a low menacing voice, Cicero confidently says the shooter's name: "V-Dog."

He ponders his next move for a moment, then remembers a booster is coming by his condo with some handmade Swiss timepieces she got with her five-finger discount.

"Yo, I got some business to attend to, Warren," Cicero says. "Be safe. And clean that shit up."

Warren shakes Cicero's hand as he leaves out, then cracks open the cell phone on his hip. He punches one number on speed dial. It is immediately answered.

"Hey, we have a plastic bag situation," he notes calmly.

"I'm on my way," the male voice on the phone says, just as relaxed, if not cooler. He hangs up, cutting off the blaring reggae music in the background.

In roughly fifteen minutes T.J.'s body will never be seen again. The process of dumping bodies is an American tradition, a ritual free of dishonest eulogies, all-black attire, and sobbing mothers. It is a Kansas City tradition.

A dirt hole in the outskirts of town now awaits young T.J.'s remains.

Chapter 3

Back in his iridescent SUV, thirty-two-year-old Cicero increases the volume on his stereo and contemplates his life's beginnings. Why had he been a spectator of murder today, and in the past? As he turns a few corners he recalls one of his first psychology courses, when he learned that everything we are begins in childhood, when we are all tabula rasa, so it is there he looks.

He reminiscences for just a few seconds until one day presents itself as that defining moment that would mold his persona, and inevitably determine which road his soul would take.

Cicero remembers the walls of his room on Highland Avenue were a streaky sky blue. He and his mother, with no prior experience, spent one Saturday afternoon painting them. They lacked the proper equipment, guide rules, new brushes, but went at it anyway.

A huge thirty-two-by-forty-four-inch poster of Nolan Ryan in his red, white, and blue Texas Rangers uniform hung on the left side of the full bed near the corner. Ryan's right arm was fully extended, his left foot firmly planted several feet from the pitcher's mound. The red-stitched orb had just left his mighty rifle. His face showed determination. This game was to be one of seven no-hitters.

Several inches down the wall was a shot of Bo Jackson in his silver and black. Number 34 had no doubt left some unaware defensive back grabbing his freshly bruised chest as Bo galloped toward pay dirt. His large powerfully built thighs bulged through his silver tights. His ripped arms clenched the oblong pigskin in a manner that suggested he was not prone to dropping it. The photo showed it was a sunny day in Los Angeles, as most days are.

Across the room, near the closet door, just left of the window, and to the right of his bookshelf and desk, Cicero decided to hang a poster of the great Michael Jordan.

Jordan is suspended in midair, flying high above the Chicago hardwood court. Fans look on in awe as His Airness leaps like a gazelle from the free- throw line toward the round metal hoop and its awaiting net. His bent arms and legs and red-and-black uniform produce an unnatural human swastika in the arena's sky. The grandeur of this athletic feat has yet to be duplicated.

Toy race cars and impressive-looking robots with moving parts and shoddy craftsmanship lie on the floor. A small, blue-and-white-striped rugby shirt bearing grass and dirt stains has also been strewn on the paneled floor, which could use a good sweeping. It joins the playthings that will surely lose their value soon enough.

Adjacent to the sweaty tube socks and breadcrumbs is one lone forest-green army soldier. Apparently, the plastic infantryman was cut off from his platoon in the middle of a heated firefight. In the confusion of imaginary mortar rounds discharging and claymores being set off, the M.I.A. found himself alone in a little boy's room. The smell from the socks alone has him considering hara-kiri.

Cicero's light-beige bookshelf has all the necessary requirements: the latest edition of the X-Men comic book where

Cyclops proposes to Jean Grey, and the issue of Ghost Rider in which he battles the Punisher. On a higher shelf rests an old copy of *Extreme Lowriders* magazine featuring a new remote-controlled hydraulic system in a 1966 teal Ford Mustang with chrome Dayton wheels. The car's front end is several feet off the ground, exposing its chrome axle and detailed underbelly.

Under a lush, vibrant, orange comforter with diamond-shaped pockets creating a warm quilted veneer, where tiny feathers escape from unseen openings, rests a scrawny child in small yellow shorts.

"Cicero," a honey-sweet voice calls out, ever so gently.

The swaddled child squirms a little.

"Cicero," the woman's voice beckons once again, a bit louder. "Wake up, baby, time for school."

Young brown eyes open and see the world for the first time this day.

A small hand with thin fingers comes from underneath the blanket and, forming a fist, begins slowly and forcefully rubbing the eyes in a circular motion, removing lumps of green crust from the corners.

Sizzling sounds invade his ears. The smell of grilled meat tempts his nostrils. The aroma of breakfast is enticing and persuades him to rise from his slumber.

The shirtless and wide-eyed Cicero, now fully awake, leans up and places his bare feet on the chilly morning floor. His ribs are clearly visible and his bird-like chest is rather pathetic, even for a kid his age.

Heat from a vent near the bookshelf causes the poster of Michael Jordan to repeatedly bulge, sway, and deflate. Bulge, sway, and deflate. Bulge, sway, and deflate.

Cicero peers through a crack in his bedroom door and sees

his mother in her frayed blueberry-colored robe dutifully hovering above the hot kitchen stove.

Still seated on the bed, he takes the opportunity to retrieve a dog-eared magazine from under the comforter. The glossy back cover is blanketed with "900" numbers and voluptuous black women in miniscule bikinis and Tammy Faye Bakker face paint.

The little boy with adult desires smiles at his prized possession, which he firmly grips in both hands while staring at the cover.

"That's what I'm talking about," he mumbles under his breath, as he closes his eyes and pretends to smooch this month's cover model.

"Cicero," his mother calls out without warning.

Startled, he stands up and tosses his smutty keepsake under the mattress, where it joins a woman's pocketbook and a black fully loaded twenty five-caliber automatic pistol. All would be questionable booty indeed if he were not an urban child.

The curly-headed preteen, eager to greet his mother and devour her fine fare, throws on a dirty long-sleeved T-shirt and walks toward the kitchen. The sandy-brown locks that aren't matted bounce as he strolls down the short hallway past the half bath with the toilet that continuously runs and a double-paned window. Falling snow piles up on the sill.

A beautiful woman and a steaming plate of man-sized portions greet the young Cicero in the cozy kitchen.

She smiles, as does he.

"How did you sleep?" she asks.

"Fine," he answers.

He opens the refrigerator door and grabs the pulp-free orange juice. Upon closing it, a tasseled certificate falls to the white linoleum floor. Cicero bends down and scoops the award off the floor and places it back on the fridge door.

It is surrounded by numerous honors, certificates, and awards in all colors of the rainbow, with accolades like top, number one, excellent, best, MVP, captain. Each marks his achievement in either academics or athletics, and features stars, gold stamps, ribbons and stickers. They come in all shapes and sizes with impressive signatures: the principal, the mayor, the state representative, the governor.

The acknowledgments completely cover the refrigerator door, minus several inches occupied by two photographs. One of Cicero and his mother in a warm embrace lies just below another of him and his older sister, the lovely Lucia, standing side by side with enormous grins. Surely they had just said, "Cheese!" with vim.

Cicero takes a seat at the small round synthetic wood table. There are three seats, but only two place settings.

Before him is a plate of grits, bacon, scrambled eggs with American cheese, English muffins and grape jelly, and sliced ruby red grapefruit.

He immediately dives into his mother's specially made bacon. In a move that would horrify any diabetic, she has sprinkled brown sugar on the slivers of swine meat, as she has for years. It's deliciously sweet and crispy. He smiles and begins to hum.

"Where's Lucia?" the eighth-grader asks his mother of the sister he adores.

"She's already gone," his mother replies, even though its merely 6:30 in the morning, somewhat early for a high school senior to be off to homeroom.

The lady of the house begins to wash the dishes she has just utilized to make breakfast, and a few that were placed in the sink overnight by her snacking child. The kitchen is spotless. To the right of the stove is the counter, which extends in an upside-down and backward L-shape along the wall and on which rests a four-slot adjustable toaster that can accommodate the plumpest of bagels.

There's also an exceedingly large microwave that resembles some of the first models made, and an outdated boxy black-and-white television with missing knobs. Pliers from a drawer enable the family to switch from Leno to Letterman.

The walls are concealed in tacky, light-tan wood-grain wallpaper that has become unglued in more than a few places. Ms. Fix It had been meaning to get to it.

Above the table hangs a dark-brown plastic crucifix. It was given to Cicero by his seventh-grade teacher following his baptism. She said a bishop had blessed it. Prior to that, he had always thought she was a racist.

"Did you say grace?" his mother asks as her aging hands work deep in the blistering water under the cover of soapsuds.

With a full mouth he nods yes, even though he didn't, and polishes off the remaining eggs, leaving a huge portion of grits uneaten, and more grapefruit than his mother liked. He was never a big fan of either.

Knowing that her insincere son failed to say his grace, his mother positions the wet glasses and saucers on a yellow rubber drying rack next to the sink and says, "Son, there is a God, and He does watch over your food if you ask Him to. He helped me provide you with nourishment, and in return He just asks for a little respect and recognition. Okay?"

Cicero, reaching for his glass of cold O.J., simply nods in the affirmative again, and takes a prolonged childlike gulp. After wiping his mouth and gasping for air, he asks his hardworking mother, "You're not going to eat?"

Ringing out the dishtowel and turning off the faucet, his mother just smiles. "No, I'm not hungry, honey."

Her son's eyebrows rise in response, but he nonchalantly continues to finish off his jelly-smothered English muffin. As he does, there's a knock at the door.

The diner looks up from his plate in surprise. He glances at the digital light-blue display on the microwave, six forty-five, and thinks that it's much too early for the postman. On top of that, no one ever knocks. Minus one person.

Knock, knock, knock, three more follow. His mother calmly turns from the sink. She knows who raps upon her home's door.

Cicero signals as if he's getting up to answer the door but his mother looks to him and says, "I'll get it, honey." Her son is relieved; he really didn't feel like getting up.

She sashays out of the kitchen, down the hallway, and turns right, through the undersized living room and across the polyurethane floor to the front door. Her full hips swing side to side under her form-fitting robe. Cherokee Indian ancestry comes through in her high cheekbones and the red undertones in her skin, which is accentuated by the light rouge and burgundy lipstick she failed to remove last night.

Just as Cicero noted, only one person knocks.

She opens the door and snowflakes trespass.

A tall man with wide shoulders stands on the front porch delicately powdered in ever-increasing amounts of snow. His brunette brim hat and overcoat complement his dark-olive features and repel the wetness well. His head slightly bowed, he lifts it and grins. It's Daddy.

The mother of his son beams at the sight of him. But it is a response that comes with years of experience with this man, and hard-learned and proven apprehension instantly manifests. Her smile diminishes.

"Hey, Ruth, how ya doin'?" her unannounced guest asks in a heavily accented voice. The chilly air makes his breath discernible. "You gonna let me in?"

"Hello, Antonio," she replies sedately, pulling her robe tighter to protect her neck and chest from the winter nip. "Come in."

He steps in and wipes his expensive wingtips on the welcome mat.

"Cicero!" Ruth calls out. "Your father is here." The multiple bangles on her wrist slide down to her hand as she closes the door.

"Okay, Mom!" Cicero acknowledges from the kitchen.

There is an uncomfortable silence between the former lovers. Antonio looks around the tidy living room. Much of his illicit loot helped furnish it, including the authentic Italian marble coffee table imported from Florence, and the taupe Egyptian cotton window dressings direct from Cairo.

Ruth stares at him with a blank face, thinking about how she fell in love with one dimension of him, with little knowledge of his numerous layers.

"Hey, Daddy, what are you doing here?" Cicero asks as he prances in the room on gangly chicken legs and boat-like feet.

"I came to pick you up; you're coming with me today," his father says with a smile. "Is that alright with you?" He pats his leather gloves together to shake the excess snow.

"Sure, Daddy, but I have school," Cicero replies, "And I have—"

"Look, don't worry about school today," his father says, dusting off his jacket. "You're hanging out with me, end of story, *capisce*?"

Ruth simply looks on. She is repulsed by Antonio's brazen contempt for what she has gone through to raise his two illegitimate children the right way, virtually alone. Sleepless nights. Lucia's sneaking out. Cicero's backtalk.

"Let me get dressed!" Cicero says excitedly, running off toward his room.

"And don't forget your hat and gloves," his mother weighs in as only a mother can.

Flinging open his closet door, the skinny youngster fingers through his jackets and coats trying to find one that matches his father's the closest. In the process he passes by the trusty BB guns he uses to keep the neighborhood cats, dogs, and blue jays in check.

"No, no, no," he says frustrated.

Then, suddenly, bingo.

"Yes," he says, "this will work."

It's black. It's long. It will do.

In the living room, his mother turns to Antonio. Her mindset is written on her face.

"I'll have him back in a few hours," Antonio says. "Don't worry about it. Just goin' to run some errands; get some lunch."

But she has to worry. She needs to worry. Good mothers worry. Especially mothers of little boys with cutthroat fathers. Shyster fathers. Gangster fathers.

"I'm ready," a grinning Cicero says after running into the living room. He fixes his hat upon his head and securely pulls on his gloves, then he pauses. This is the only time he can remember seeing his parents this close together.

"Good, let's go," Antonio says as he opens the door and steps out. "See ya later, Ruth." And just like that Cicero's moment is over. He follows his father out.

"Bye, Mom," he yells as he slams the door shut.

Ruth stands there, staring at the closed door. She says a prayer for her son, that he will return to her safely, and that he will not follow in his father's footsteps.

The inside of his long, navy-blue Cadillac Fleetwood was always warm and welcoming. The swanky black leather interior always seemed to swallow the skinny and awkward Cicero, with the ever-present aroma of cigar smoke and cigarettes lingering.

He looks at his father from the passenger side, and notices how they have the same keen nose. The same sleepy, light-brown eyes.

Antonio noticed the same thing the day his first and only son was born. From that day on he wanted to be a father and a role model to him, but his marriage to a deeply vested Sicilian family prevented that from ever happening. His wife and two daughters needed to see him daily, his father-in-law would have it no other way. Instead, he did what he could. Dropping off cash, birthday gifts, Christmas presents. Calling now and then to say hi, or stopping by and taking his illegitimate son and daughter out for ice cream, or dinner.

Nevertheless, the absentee father knew the Romello name would die with him, and there was nothing he could do about it except ensure that the Romello fire burned inside his affair-born son. His African-American son.

✖✖✖

But this day was to be different.

Ole Blue Eyes croons from a cassette in the tape deck. Cicero looks over at his dad and thinks about how his mom would have played the Staple Singers or the O'Jays. He also thinks about how his mom and dad differ so much. But he knows they both love him dearly.

To and fro windshield wipers fight off big snowflakes, preventing them from sticking. The sedan's large Vogue tires slosh through the dirty urban snowfall.

His dad sings to the music.

"I did it myyy waaay!" he belts off tune, looking over at his son, smiling.

Cicero giggles and his father laughs. His laugh is distinctive, and re-markably jolly, and Cicero couldn't help but think that his dad was cool.

Heading north through the city, from Seventy-Third Street to streets with sequentially lesser numerals, the pair pass liquor stores, homeless men and women bundled up in want of shelter, and money-hungry hustlers looking to dump their product or score some more.

They cruise north on Troost Avenue from where the poor black people live, across the railroad tracks, to where the poor white people live. Mostly old Irish families reside here, along with a few Germans, and more recently some Vietnamese and Laotian families.

Antonio makes a left on Fifth Street, near an old textiles factory, and drives five blocks to the corner where St. Vincent's stands.

The cavernous stone church is festooned on all sides by impeccable stained glass windows. Historical works of art from an era long past allow daylight to pass through vibrant indigoes and vivid scarlets. Snow lightly powders the front stairs as the elder monsignor and his hunched back assiduously sweeps it away.

An enormous mosaic of St. Vincent de Paul, patron saint of

the needy, hovers above three tremendous archways and guards the sanctuary's vast vestibule. On either side of him are depictions of St. Francis Borgia and Leonard of Port Maurice, who is portrayed in a striking manner as the restorer of discipline to the holy orders in Corsica in 1744.

The cathedral and its blessed transoms mark not only a place of worship, but they also denote the edge of *Piccolo Italia*—Little Italy.

Antonio's Caddy hugs the road as it makes a gliding right turn. Cicero immediately knows where he is. Red, white, and green flags hang on the lampposts, outside of homes, and near the park and the baseball field. He had always wanted to play catch there with his dad. But he never did.

They pull in front of a deli and stop where a butcher prepares the day's much sought after *prosciutto* and *abruzzese*. Across the street is a ramshackle pool hall, also claimed as Italiano by a fluttering tri-colored crest. Riffraff, descended from Sicily, Venice, Naples, and other glorious city-states, have staggered in and out of this dive for decades.

"Wait here," Antonio says to his son as he braces for the bitter climate, opens the car door and steps out, slamming it behind him. The wintry air quickly slips in behind him, causing Cicero to tense up and his left eye to water.

Antonio traverses the thick slush near the car, then easily crosses the cleared street and enters the pool hall. Though it's early in the day, Antonio still has business to tend to.

Cicero notices how the street is without snow. It's clean and freshly salted, completely unlike his mother's block, which would often bear snow until it melted on its own accord.

Not naïve to his father's line of work, Cicero daydreams that his well-respected father is shaking down some loan shark, or making some delinquent asshole pay up.

Suddenly, the pool hall's thin wooden door bursts open as his father, followed by two associates, drags a man out by his collar kicking and screaming. The child need not fantasize any longer.

Cicero hastily jumps into the driver's seat to get a better view. His excitement, coupled with the twenty-one-degree temperature, causes the window to instantly fog up. His gloved hand wipes it, and as plain as day, his father begins to stomp this man on the sidewalk. Repeatedly kicking him in the back, head, and face. Back, head, face, and leg. Back, head, face, and arm.

He's in his late thirties, maybe early forties. Blood spurts from his mouth. His overcoat is sullied by the snow and muck. He mumbles fragmented sentences in a futile plea for his safety. The child struggles inside the luxury sedan to decipher what's said.

"I'll pay, Tony, I swear it," the victim screams, throwing up his left arm to protect his face.

Antonio thrusts his wingtip into the man's spine, causing him to wail. The flailing of his arms and legs creates a distressed fallen angel in the snow.

The other two men, both larger and bulkier than Antonio, look on, standing on either side of the pathetic sack of shit in the snow. The goateed pair sport dark leather jackets and slicked-back, jet-black hair. They are portly and unsympathetic. The shorter and younger of the two puffs a cigarette. He stands to the left of the prey, on whom he uncaringly flicks his ashes.

The two henchmen are present to make sure their mark doesn't escape, doesn't pull a gun or a knife, or Heaven forbid, put a whipping on the invincible Antonio.

With a forceful pounce, Antonio's heel crushes the man's jaw. The snow becomes a thick soupy, wine-red.

His victim whimpers.

"I'll have the money!" he mumbles painfully as he attempts to cover the back of his busted head with both arms. A gaping hole allows his red sauce to escape.

Antonio, now winded by his exercise and the cold air, stops his onslaught.

Breathing heavily, he warns the tardy loser, "That's right. I know you will, Gino. I know you will."

Again, Cicero wipes the fog from the window. His eyes bulge in amazement. Falling flakes partially obscure his view, as if trying to shield him from the world of his father.

"If you don't have the money, we're going to give you some concrete knickers and toss your pathetic ass in the Missouri River, you fuck," yells Antonio as he wipes spit from his mouth and clean-shaven jaw line. He's amped beyond belief, his heart racing. "You got that?"

He kicks him in the face one last time for good measure. The ever-weakening man squeals like an injured puppy. Five dislodged teeth, mostly incisors, bedeck the blood-spattered sidewalk.

"Hey, I'll see you guys tonight," Antonio says calmly to his two burly watchmen as he turns to walk away. They remain silent and nod.

Gino, severely battered and hemorrhaging, is subsequently hauled down a nearby alley by the stout henchmen.

The enclosed adolescent again wipes his frosty breath from the window, and he notices his father sauntering back toward his Brougham with a vigorous swagger.

He quickly jumps back to the passenger's seat. The weather, along with what he has just witnessed, causes the thin child to shiver.

Antonio opens the heavy door and sits down. He produces a stained handkerchief from an inside pocket and thoroughly wipes his soiled shoes with it.

Cicero observes his father via peripheral vision. Antonio's wide back and shoulders inflate and swell with each heavy breath he takes as he hurriedly wipes away his stains and his sins.

"Cicero," Antonio says as he swivels to the right, placing both feet in the car. Out of fear and out of curiosity, the young boy's eyes quickly dart to his father. He blushes from the chill.

"Son, you have one life to live," his father says as he slams the driver's side door shut and then stares into his son's eyes. "*Uno*. And so help you God, if you come across a piece of shit that wants to complicate it, you do whatever you have to do to make sure things don't stay complicated."

He pulls the car keys from his overcoat and inserts one into the ignition and starts it. The engine block revs.

"Whatever you have to do," he stresses. "You understand?" His accent is thicker now, similar to how it sounded when he was a younger, more devoted madman.

Cicero nods yes without blinking.

"You *understand?*" his father asks again.

His son nods once more, faster, more emphatically.

"Good," his father says, as he cracks a smile. Cicero's innocence delights his soul. "Always remember, you want to be the one dishin' out the kicks, not receivin' 'em. Alright?"

The child again nods.

"Good. Now, let's get outta here."

Frosty breath fills the car. Fumes spew from the Cadillac's exhaust pipe as the father and son duo is thrust forward by the three hundred horses under the hood.

As Cicero would later learn in Psychoanalytic Theory two hundred twelve, this day would foster the development of his warped superego, and his Freudian-described identification. In essence: Oh, how he longed to be Antonio.

Chapter 4

Smoke from a defiled cigar beclouds the front cabin of a new sports coupe. The signature aroma is that of potent, blue-green marijuana, which has replaced the tobacco once stuffed inside. The smoking passenger coughs.

"You wanna hit this?" he asks the driver. The passenger's mouth is inhabited wall-to-wall by platinum and diamonds. With every word he displays a brilliant eighty-thousand dollar smile.

"No, thanks," Cicero responds. He's coasting steady and sure. Cognac is the only drug he needs. He looks toward his passenger, who playfully tokes his blunt and attempts to blow smoky circles. He fails miserably.

"Man, that shit smells strong. Smells kinda good, though," Cicero states, cracking a smile. He knows such a statement will please his comrade. "Think you smoke enough of it?" Cicero jokingly asks while keeping his eyes on the road.

"Nope," Kam slowly responds as he takes a long deep pull. His voice is Barry White deep. He coughs ferociously, pounding his chest and producing phlegm. His nose begins to run. "Not nearly enough." His speech is early-morning slow. He coughs some more.

The silver German-built luxury car with its independent front and rear suspension slithers and snakes in and out of the slow-poke traffic. Its twenty-inch chrome rims chop the air like shiny Ginsu blades as they pass the city's disproportionately high number of Sunday drivers. Bass-filled hip-hop blazes through the premium sound system and the fifteen-inch sub-woofers in the trunk.

"So where we headed?" Kam asks, as he thumps his ashes out of a tiny crack in the window. Several ambers miss their exit and fly into the backseat.

"To see Brad," Cicero says frustratingly. It's only the third time he's told his drug-impaired passenger their destination.

"Oh yea," recalls Kam as he takes another puff, inhaling for five seconds and holding for ten. The tetrahydrocannabinol is doing a number on his memory. His bulbous cheeks resemble those of a Canadian chipmunk in autumn.

As they drive, the homes begin to get bigger. There's notice-ably less loitering and fewer panhandlers. Streets are wider. There's less litter and cars are newer.

"Man, that still trips me out. A white boy going to a black college. That's tight."

Without warning, an elderly man in an American-made station wagon swerves in front of Cicero, nearly clipping the front end of his one hundred twenty-five thousand-dollar automobile/ chick magnet. Cicero blows his horn and contemplates letting a slug fly in a midday road rage dispute. The perpetrator, with his thick glasses, is unfazed and he continues his route. Kam is so high his face just remains blank as he begins to dig in his nose.

"What did you get your degree in, again?" Kam asks his friend, who's becoming a bit irritated. He checks his finger. Nothing. On to the other nostril.

"Psych—" Cicero starts to say but is cut off.

"Psychology, that's right," Kam utters. His two long Pocahontas-like braids are well oiled and gleam in the sunlight of the partly cloudy day. His goatee beard is well trimmed. "Man, when you going to use that shit?" Kam asks Cicero, referring to his college education. Kam's nose exploration continues.

Unperturbed, Cicero makes a smooth left turn on Metcalf Avenue, his vehicle's independent suspension riding like a dream. His response to Kam's inquiry: "I'm an overman, baby. I use it every day."

Kam begins to snicker and cough at the same time, producing thick phlegm. His window drops and projectile mucous takes flight.

"I heard that," Kam says with a smile as he tosses the remainder of his blunt out the window. His gemstone-rich mouth shimmers.

The two make yet another right and drive several more blocks. Cicero then suddenly stops in front of a coffee shop that's part of a worldwide chain. They passed seven others on the way to this one. Even though at rest, Cicero's twenty-inch rims continue to spin, similar to four chrome ceiling fans.

"Hey, wait here for a minute," Cicero tells Kam, who has finally stopped digging in his nose. He nods slightly in response.

Cicero, dressed casually in loose-fitting blue jeans, a bright yellow Australian-made sweater, and the same color alligator boots, leaves the car running, steps out, and closes the car door behind him. Cars and trucks zip by on the busy thoroughfare. He looks all around, checks his gold-trimmed, black-face timepiece, then carefully steps onto the sidewalk and into the coffee shop. In his hand is a Saks Fifth Avenue bag containing a pillow-sized package wrapped in a brown paper sack and fastened with clear tape. Less than one week after T.J.'s murder, the ever-hustling Cicero is back on the grind.

Seated comfortably on the supple gray leather upholstery, Kam grabs his two-way from his jeans' pocket, pops it open, and begins entering letters at a slug's pace. He has an austere look on his face.

After about three minutes of struggling, Kam proofreads his message, which he has chosen to type in all caps. "I JUST WANT YOU TO KNOW MY DICK IS BURNING, YOU STUPID-ASS BIIIIIITCH!!!!!!!" Satisfied that his point will get across, he contently hits send.

With the lunch-hour rush having passed, traffic has subsided, which is why the movement of a wide-bodied vehicle on the opposite side of the road catches Kam's attention. It's the color of rust, but without the oxidation. It's polished, new, buffed and waxed, miraculous rust. Exorbitant rust.

The modern hand-crafted English sedan comes to a silky stop adjacent to Kam's position. His view of the opulence is superb.

"Damn, that's clean," mutters Kam who, even though he's stoned, still recognizes a piece of modern art when he sees it. His disposition and head-to-toe black ensemble makes him look like funeral material. "That's what I'm talking about."

This mode of transport is a rare and refined gem in a sea of lusterless rhinestones, so Kam ogles it in awe. Its three hundred thousand-dollar price tag puts it far out of reach of the common laborer. Out of the imperial stagecoach steps a well-dressed, middle-aged man. His professionally styled salt-and-pepper hair budges not in the light breeze. His tailored pinstriped Armani suit fits without a flaw.

He carries with him a shiny black briefcase as he crosses the street and glides into the coffee shop.

A few moments later, the Armani-clad driver emerges with a latte in one hand and a very familiar Saks bag in the other. Grand Prix-ready, the twin-turbocharged rust-colored sedan purrs, and in a matter of seconds disappears over the suburban horizon.

Just as Kam is getting over his vehicular crush and subsequent breakup, Cicero steps out of the coffee shop with an espresso and a shiny black briefcase.

He hops back in the car and tosses the briefcase onto Kam's lap and instructs him to "count this."

He mashes the gas pedal as Kam grabs the briefcase without hesitation, slides the two brass latches simultaneously, and begins to count the neatly wrapped bundles of cash.

After about two minutes, Kam looks to Cicero and says, "Fifty G's."

Wednesdays are lucrative: it's the only day that Cicero moves product. And he is expressionless. The money is right and that's all that matters. Had Kam said forty, or even forty nine thousand, nine hundred and ninety nine, there would have been a problem. But Cicero has never had a problem like that. There's a drought on product in Kansas City, hence the thirty-five thousand-dollar profit margin. Besides, it wasn't even pure.

Suddenly, Mozart's "Concerto number five in A Major" begins to play. The violin solo is lucid and invigorating. It's a programmed personalized ring on Cicero's phone. Kam looks surprised. Cicero's other personalized tones are generally hip-hop, maybe jazz.

"It's Brad," he says to Kam, sensing his interest.

"Hello, Bradley," Cicero says with a grin, in his most professional voice. It sounds natural and unrehearsed. As he focuses on the road, his grin diminishes, and his language changes. "*Blanco*.

Gundle is sick. Johnson had a good game, even though Sanders retired." His smile returns and he begins to laugh, exposing his pearly whites.

"I heard that. That Orca is sick! You know we do it," Cicero says to his colleague. Kam just sits in the passenger seat interpreting. He knows every word of this made-up patois.

"Keep it, Febreeze," Cicero adds before hanging up. He closes his phone shut and looks over at Kam. "Yeah, I thought you knew I was a fucking Windtalker," quips Cicero. They both laugh.

Within a few minutes and after several turns, the pair reach a secluded business compound deep in the heart of suburbia confined by a tall black iron barrier and full, lush pine trees. Cicero's ultra-sexy coupe pulls to a main gate next to an intercom and digital monitor.

"Yes, how may I assist you?" a woman's voice asks.

After turning down his thumping stereo, Cicero answers, "Good afternoon, I'm here to see Bradley Micheaux."

"Yes, Mr. Day, he's expecting you," the woman says as the gate silently splits down the middle and opens inward. The two enter the sprawling 175-acre campus and are engulfed in its man-made forest and emerald milieu. Its recently paved black tar drive still smells fresh. Magnolias, chrysanthemums, and azaleas line an assortment of diverging walkways and bike trails. Hand-carved wooden benches have been positioned in front of ponds for trouble-free feeding of the company's house-bred geese and mallards. Shadows pass over the company's enormous sculpture-like logo as the sun is blocked out and dark clouds begin to roll in.

"What the fuck does Brad do again?" asks Kam, who is clearly amazed by the affluence of his surroundings.

"He designs organic-based computer systems, or something like that," Cicero answers. He's been here enough times to be unimpressed.

"Damn," Kam says in response. They've been driving for several minutes and still have yet to reach the main building.

"Yea, he was a double major," Cicero continues. "Chemistry and computer information systems. All A's too."

He pauses.

"And he's from the South, a real country boy."

Kam grins and his carats shine.

"So don't believe that bullshit about people from the South being stupid. It's just that his dad used to beat his mom's ass, you know? He went through shit just like us."

"I feel you," Kam says in agreement, as he once again begins digging in his nose. This time he's successful in his exploration. He slides his window down and tries to discard his finding.

"Yea, when I was in school I had a roommate from Houston who came from a similar background, and he was real smart too," says Kam. "Yea, he was fluent in English and Spanish."

"Oh, for real?"

"Yea, he was Mexican though," Kam utters.

Cicero doesn't respond. Kam continues to flick his slimy trophy from his finger, but it fails to depart.

They finally reach the main building and enter a circular drive that leads them to dual towering steel doors accented by fine cherrywood. The edifice is made entirely of glass, with steel columns and accents for style. The new-age architecture is aesthetically pleasing, and its one hundred or so solar panels make it energy efficient and environmentally friendly.

After securing the fifty grand in the trunk, the two reach the massive double doors, which softly swing open. Cicero dumps his untasted coffee in a garbage receptacle. They're soon greeted by a grinning young man of Asian descent wearing small round glasses and a button-down plaid shirt.

He extends his arm and firmly shakes Cicero's hand.

"Hello, Cicero."

"Hey, how have you been, Omar?"

"Fine. Fine," the smiling Omar says in a strong Calcuttian accent. "Thank you for those tickets to the game. My girlfriend and I had a wonderful time."

"No problem, Omar," Cicero responds. "Anytime." He turns to Kam and adds, "Omar, this is my good friend Kameron, we went to junior high and high school together." Kameron, who is yet to rid himself of his gelled nose content, shakes Omar's hand firmly and with gusto.

"Hey, what's up, Omar? Nice to meet you."

"Same here, Kameron," Omar responds, realizing something is out of kilter with this handshake. He smiles, then winces.

"Brad is right this way," says the tainted Omar. "After you."

They enter the complex's expansive lobby where priceless statuettes abound, and pass a beautiful former model who after a rocky transition is now an okay receptionist. She smiles, as do they.

Omar, feeling something is amiss, looks at his hand and nearly barfs at the sight of another man's booger. He hastily pulls a facial tissue from the receptionist's desk and thoroughly wipes his hand.

The three men venture forward down a short flight of stairs from the mezzanine overlooking open office space chock full of computer terminals, thirty-something I.T. grads, and oddball knick-knacks and video games the employees have brought from home.

Impersonal silvers and grays cover the walls and high vaulted ceilings, but are offset by warm palm trees growing in company-mandated Feng Shui locations throughout the multiplex.

Unconcerned technology whiz kids dressed in jeans or khakis, T-shirts, and sneakers carelessly loaf around, with the exception of one young man exerting more effort than all of his co-workers combined. Cicero, Kam, and Omar amble across the spongy cream-colored rubberized floor and greet the diligent, blond-haired Brad.

Hearing Kam's distinctive laughter, the clean-cut Louisiana boy saves the project he's working on to a mini diskette, and pivots from his ergonomically enhanced desk and smiles.

He stands and shakes Cicero's hand and then gives him a hug.

"How's it going, Bradley?" Cicero asks.

"Good, C. How's life treating you? Good, yeah?" Brad asks with a strong Cajun accent. His deep-blue eyes contrast stunningly with his bright-white button-down shirt.

"Hey, I can't complain," Cicero answers.

"What's goin' on, Kameron?" Brad asks the thirty-one-year-old, who just finished laughing about what he gave Omar.

"Not too much, man," Kameron responds. "Just holding on like a loose hubcap in the fast lane."

"I hear ya, man," Brad says. His rimless spectacles make him look studious, but his lean muscular frame keeps him from looking nerdy.

"You ready to get this late lunch?" Cicero asks as he checks the gold hands on his expensive watch. It's 1:30 p.m.

"Oh hell yeah, let's go, ya'll," Brad answers as he grabs his key card and jacket. The three head back toward the lobby as Omar sits at one of the gray desks and begins typing.

"Alright then, Omar, stay easy," Kam shouts.

"You guys have a good lunch," Omar yells back. After they're out of hearing range he thinks about Kam's handshake and he mumbles to himself in a low breath, "Asshole."

✖✖✖

The aroma of fresh baked bread and the enticing perfume of chocolate pervade the quaint brasserie. Elegantly designed, Café Noir has been a favorite watering hole and eatery for the university-educated Brad and Cicero for quite some time. If it were up to Kameron, the group would have simply gone to one of Kansas City's many barbecue spots.

Lace curtains adorn the many windows, and a rare Pleyel grand piano crafted in mahogany and rosewood welcomes the patrons at the entrance and further establishes the Parisian atmosphere.

There are few diners, so the threesome is immediately seated at their candlelit table by the lovely hostess and they begin perusing the undemanding one-page paper menu. A Hector Berlioz aria hums in the background over the house sound system.

The *assiette de charcuterie* has received scintillating reviews, but the famished gentlemen wish to partake in more fulfilling fare so they skip the hors d'oeuvres.

"Yea, I keep hearing the beignets are really good here," Brad says as he eyes the salade niçoise. Its fresh seared tuna, tomatoes, anchovies, and vinaigrette sound delectable, and he decides on that. Cicero chooses to go with the trout almandine sautéed with almonds, parsley, and lemon juice.

Kam, on the other hand, is undecided. He's torn between the five-ounce filet mignon smothered in a truffle red wine sauce and the *boeuf bourguignon* drizzled with a light brandy cream remoulade.

As Kam debates his choice, a waiter saunters over and asks if the gentlemen would like to view the wine list. The group declines the bistro's superior Riesling and Chardonnay and orders their meals instead. Cicero requests the establishment's finest cognac as Kam decides on the filet mignon, medium rare.

After placing their orders, Brad breaks the silence with an intriguing question: "You guys want to hear a crazy story?"

The other two nod yes and listen with piqued interest as Brad begins.

"Now I normally don't date women I work with, you know, for obvious reasons. Ya dig? But I decided to go to dinner with this young lady in our accounting department. She's smart, kinda attractive, and kind of conservative."

Kam takes a sip of water and Cicero samples his cognac as the waiter walks away and they continue to listen.

"Anyway, we had a really good meal, even though the conversation wasn't at all stimulatin', and we head back to her apartment," Brad explains. "Well, I was just going to drop her off and head home, so I could still catch *The O'Reilly Factor*."

Cicero grins. Kam is at a loss. "The what?" he asks, talking slowly.

Brad ignores Kam and continues, "But when we get there, she invites me in for a coffee. I say, 'Sure, okay.'"

"Can you please get to the point," an impatient Kam butts in.

"I'm getting there, just hold on, Kameron," Brad reassures him. Cicero remains silent and attentive.

"So we go in and have a seat on her divan," Brad says. "Then the next thing I know, we're kissin' and huggin'. Just goin' at it!"

"Finally!" Kam yells, throwing his hands up.

"Yea, this is good stuff, man, and she's aggressive too," Brad says. "So then, she grabs my hand and leads me to her *boudoir*."

"Her what?" Kam blurts. The candle's flame flickers and bounces off one of his two-carat baguettes, lighting up the room.

"So anyway, she sits me on the bed and tells me to get undressed," Brad continues. His Louisiana accent is thick. "And I'm like, no problem, honey. It's been a while, if you know what I mean."

Cicero and Kam both chuckle. They don't know what he means. They're constantly fighting women off.

"While I'm unbuttoning my shirt she goes into the bathroom and comes out a few minutes later in this unbelievable ruby silk negligee," Brad ex-plains. "Just as I'm about to pull my loafas off, she says, 'No, leave them on.'"

Kam and Cicero look taken aback.

"Yea, now I was a little perplexed by this, because here I am in briefs and dress shoes," Brad says.

The two-member audience laughs.

"All of a sudden, she bends over on this freaky black leather bench in the corner and tells me to kick her in the ass as hard as I can."

The drinking Kam spits water from his mouth, dousing the table's candle.

"Are you serious?" Cicero asks in astonishment.

"What the fuck?" Kam adds.

"Yea, I couldn't believe it," Brad responds. "This quiet, petite girl asks me to kick her in the ass with my shoes on. And I'm kind of a conservative guy, so this is simply unbelievable, man."

At that moment the waiter returns with two piping hot plates and Brad's salad.

He immediately digs in without waiting for the freshly crushed pepper. Kam and Cicero frustratingly stare at him, eager to hear his story's dénouement.

Sensing their eyes on him, Brad looks up with a mouth full of vinaigrette-smothered tomatoes and immediately resumes his tale.

"Oh, so after I kick her in the ass like sixteen times—" Brad says before he's interrupted by Cicero's and Kam's uncontrollable laughter.

"Damn, Brad, sixteen times?" Cicero asks.

"Yea, I counted, man," Brad answers in a staid tone. "But anyway, all of a sudden she freaks out and tells me to leave."

His two listeners continue to laugh; Kam's nearly in tears.

"I've seen her at work once or twice since then but we don't speak to each other," Brad says, shaking his head. Cicero takes a bite of his trout as the waiter refills their water glasses and says, "You're a wild man, Bradley."

"Hell naw, you're a sick bastard," Kam says and he again bursts into laughter. "But fuck it. I would have kicked her in the ass too."

Thirsty from his laughter, Kam squeezes juice from a lemon wedge into his water and goes to take a drink when he notices something adrift in his goblet.

A winged insect, about the size of an infant girl's earring, floats lifeless in his glass.

Kam, remaining calm, gets their server's attention. The thin, middle-aged waiter leisurely strolls over from near the bar and snobbishly asks, "Yes, sir, how may I be of service?"

"Yea, there seems to be a bug or something floating in my water," Kam states as politely as he can. "Can I please get another glass?"

The waiter laughs, and Kam is dumbfounded.

"You must be joking, sir. We don't provide *that* type of service here," the waiter says with conviction. "You must have put something in your water."

"What?" a flabbergasted Kam asks, struggling to suppress his anger. Brad and Cicero sit and observe the situation, listening carefully.

"Yes, what are you trying to do, get a free meal or something?" the waiter says. "Please don't force me to escort you to the door, sir."

"That's ridiculous, man," Brad weighs in.

"Thanks, Brad, but I got this," Kam assures him. "Look, mothafucka, I have enough cheese to buy ten of everything on this fuckin' menu," Kam tells the waiter, his voice now louder. "I just want another glass of water. Are you going to get it?" Kam stares at him with unflinching eyes.

The waiter shrugs and begins to walk off. Kam looks at Cicero in bewilderment. Cicero's face is blank. Brad looks uneasy.

Kam immediately leaps up from his seat and grabs the waiter by the back of his collar. Brad stands up in shock, while Cicero sits peacefully and continues to enjoy his meal.

Enraged, Kam uses his strong six-foot-two-inch frame to easily swing the feather-light waiter around, who is completely stunned, and slams his face on the group's table. Cicero grabs his snifter so his precious cognac doesn't spill. The face-to-table action makes an amazingly loud crashing sound as saucers and salad forks clatter, a glorious accompaniment to the French words being belted from above.

"*Ah! qui pourrait me résister? Suis-je pas né pour la bataille,*" the baritone resonates, as Kam slams the arrogant waiter's face into the table again and again, and then begins driving it into his plate. Truffle red wine sauce runs down his battered face. He yelps in pain.

"*Malheur à qui m'ose irriter! Malheur surtout à qui me raille*," the words go, functioning as a score for an urban gladiator's offensive.

"How you like that, mothafucka?" a ferocious Kam yells. The restaurant's other diners watch the ensuing mêlée. Several call 9-1-1 on their digital phones.

"Please! Please, stop!" the waiter begs. He's using his arms as a buffer between him and the plates and table.

Realizing this, Kam yanks the man up and begins dragging him through the bistro toward the kitchen. Some customers, as well as employees, are horrified and run out of the restaurant.

Cicero downs the rest of his drink and drops three hundred dollars on the table to cover their meals and any inconvenience or psychological damage the afternoon beating may have caused. He and Brad then follow Kam through the kitchen and out a back door, which Kam has courteously opened with the waiter's swollen mug.

In the rear of the establishment is a repulsively filthy alley, and Kam tosses the beleaguered waiter to the pavement, face first. He hits the ground with a hard thud and begins to squirm.

"Please, sir, I apologize!" he cries. "Please, sir, I'm sorry." His pedigree-engrained politeness and professionalism are now absolute non-factors.

Wanting to really get through to the maître d', Kam pulls a black Saturday night special from the small of his back and begins to pistol whip him.

Brad is visibly nervous. The magna cum laude grad never envisioned being an accessory to murder.

"Are you going to stop him?" he yells to Cicero. He's on the verge of panicking. Cicero is a bit more concerned now, but he doesn't intervene.

Kam grabs the man by his hair and strikes him over and over in the temple, forehead, and face. Blood squirts from his head, staining Kam's outfit and the concrete. He pummels the man until Cicero steps in and grabs his thrashing arm. He instantly stops. His face, hand, and torso are splattered with blood. Chest heaving, he looks like an animal.

"I hope you didn't have anything planned for the weekend, mothafucka!" Kam yells as he spits on his victim.

The barely breathing waiter knocks on death's door, but does not enter.

✖✖✖

Back at Brad's job without further incident, booming thunder is heard and it begins to rain.

"You alright?" Cicero asks his friend. While Brad doesn't necessarily fly the straight and narrow, he has never participated in such an event or even seen someone nearly killed.

"I'm cool," he answers. They stand under the column-support overhang avoiding the sky's moisture. Kam rests comfortably in the car on the butter-soft leather, still fuming.

After a brief moment of silence, Brad asks, "Did you take care of that?" referring to some unspoken nasty deed.

"Yea," Cicero answers.

"*You* took care of that?" Bradley asks, stressing disbelief in his friend's involvement.

"No, not me. The Ninja," Cicero clarifies, naming an accomplice by code word. Even though he could, he doesn't point out Brad's outrageous hypocrisy: his mescaline and Ecstasy dealing, his meth lab. The rain suddenly comes down harder, in bigger drops, blanketing the area.

"It was good seeing you, C. I'll have that for you later, man," Brad says with a sly look. He turns to walk in the building, but stops and says with a grin, "Hey, try to stay out of trouble."

Cicero smiles.

Trying his best to dodge the rain, Cicero runs from under the steel awning and hops in his coupe. He checks the caller ID on his ringing cell and ignores it.

Cicero looks like something is on his mind, and Kam, still sporting another man's internal Merlot, asks his friend, "You okay, dog?"

"Chillin'," Cicero responds.

"Hey, dude, I'm still hungry," Kam tells his friend, flashing his diamonds.

Cicero just looks at him, then mashes the gas pedal and leaves the state-of-the-art compound cloaked in a cloud of burnt rubber.

Chapter 5

Five-inch stilettos delicately tap the pavement on a sunny late-September day. It's unseasonably humid, and her fuchsia dress is diminutive, exposing excessive amounts of firm thigh and calf, skin resembling warm caramel.

A light breeze easily makes the airy fabric flow. Full hips and a slim ab-rich midsection sway under it. Passersby, male and female, young and old, ogle this delicious creature in awe.

"Damn, she's fine," one city worker says to another as they both pause and stare, further neglecting that perennial pothole. Tax dollars hard at work.

She traverses several city blocks in the deteriorated working-class neighborhood, suede purse in hand, bosom, angelic. Sycamores line the avenue. Her ethnicity is hard to pinpoint. Spaghetti straps reveal toned arms and femininely soft shoulders, which are partially concealed by long wavy black hair.

"You need to get with me, baby, this is real pimping over here," yells a manager of streetwalkers from his old-school Cadillac with gold trim.

She wears a look of confidence as she turns to her left, up a short flight of stone stairs, into the pristine Church of the Risen Christ.

When the riots of 1964 engulfed everything in the neighborhood, the church and its spectacular stained-glass windows stood untouched. It's rumored that the granite hand-carved statue of Mary, the mother of God, wept on that day in the church's outdoor atrium.

Even though she's inappropriately dressed, the femme fatale pulls one of the large wood doors open as it creaks from age.

She takes several steps into the lofty cathedral before stopping and turning back to dab her forehead with holy water. She pauses for a moment, expecting it to sizzle.

The church, first built to serve the area's well-to-do white community, now serves the elderly black community that once fought to live there. Unfettered sun rays pass through depictions of the Twelve Apostles and the Lamb of God. Golden glass rings denote their heavenly halos and perfectly etched pieces in brown mark their long hair and walking staffs.

Dozens of candles burn near the altar, lit for the sick and dying, and the hardheaded and evil. A few senior parishioners are scattered about, kneeling and praying, holding rosaries. The church smells of incense and faintly of dust.

Her heels are now silent on the carpeted floor as she walks to the front of the church, passing row after row of wooden pews, to where an old woman kneels, just to the right of the altar.

The grandmother's face shows time and love as she looks up at her child's daughter. Her expression changes from reserved, to smiling brightly.

"I'm glad you came, honey," the old woman whispers as her granddaughter genuflects, then takes a seat next to her in the pew. She's delighted to see tomorrow's future.

"How have you been?" she asks with genuine interest.

"Fine," Olivia curtly answers, her eyes looking down.

There's a lull in the exchange. A creak in the floor echoes as a parishioner exits a confessional. A married forty-year-old father of five has been uplifted. The weight of sin, much more than that of the rear axles he's lugged for years at the Ford plant, has been whisked away by the glory of God. He leaves the church in search of purity, and an end to his fifteen-year affair with his brother's wife.

"Have you looked at those admission forms I gave you for Penn Valley?"

Olivia doesn't want to disappoint her, but she truly loathes lying.

"No. I really don't want to go to a community college, Grandmother."

"Well, I know, honey, but it's—"

"And besides, what's the point?" Olivia asks, frustrated.

At that moment an elderly Hispanic woman rises from a pew in the back of the church and saunters to the front near the altar. She lights a candle for recent earthquake victims in her native Peru. The cataclysm measured seven point two on the Richter scale, devastating Lima and leaving thousands dead or homeless. In the tongue of her father and his father before him, she offers a prayer:

"*Dios tenga merced sobre las victimas del terremoto y les enseñale el camino,*" the stout woman prays in a low voice. "*Dale paz y tranquilidad, ahora, en su tiempo de necesidad. Dios, esté con ellos hoy y siempre. Amén.*"

Olivia stares at her and wishes she still had such faith in the unseen. Her grandmother has that faith, and in many ways wishes to reintroduce it to the wayward Olivia.

Aware of her granddaughter's yearning, the wise mother of four looks at her and says, "Olivia, God loves you."

Olivia's face remains blank as her eyes again begin looking downward. Her fresh beauty and lavender rouge stand out against the church's waning façade.

The caring grandmother grabs Olivia's hand, which rests on her bent knee. Pigeons take flight from the church's soaring steeple. The sound of their fluttering wings is piercing and resonates throughout the sanctuary and the empty balcony.

"Kneel with me, Olivia," her grandmother instructs. And she does, reluctantly.

"God will be with you, honey, you just have to have faith," she reassures her. "You just have to have faith. Trust me, you will have a long and beautiful life."

Olivia briefly contemplates what she's heard. Then desperately asks, "Why did this happen to me, Grandma? I'm not a bad person."

"Olivia, no one knows God's plans. No one."

"But what about my plans, my future? I can never have a family now, or be married."

"I know. I know, but—"

"And Grandma, you even liked him," Olivia vents as she begins to become emotional. "I mean, how was I supposed to know he was…" and she stops. Her heart sinks. Vibrations in her purse signal a new text message has arrived on her credit card-sized communicator. She grabs the device and flips it open.

The small rectangular screen reads: *"Carne. Favre."*

Olivia checks her pink, ruby- and diamond-encrusted wristwatch. It's three forty-seven p.m. She composes herself and stands to her feet.

"I have to go, Grandma."

Her grandmother rises, then sits in the pew, as she watches

the beautiful Olivia sashay out of the house of God and into the world of the pagans and idolaters.

✕✕✕

"This is him," Cicero tells Olivia as he slides her a wallet-sized photograph. They're in a small midtown coffee shop. The clientele is an eclectic mix of old businessmen and women in suits, and young slackers with dreadlocks and baggy pants. Conversations range from why the T-bond market tanked to astonishment regarding Tony Gonzalez's retirement.

The shop is dimly lit with low-wattage track lighting. Splashes of pumpkin and cardinal red adorn the interior of the cozy little spot. Ficus trees repose in unconventional spaces.

Olivia and Cicero convene at a corner table securely out of sight and earshot. They've sat here many times before, and the employees know not to disturb them.

Olivia studies the photograph closely, examining every detail and making mental notes: small scar over his right eye, chipped front tooth, sinister smile. Tattoos.

A long curly lock falls from the top of her head and lands to the right of her thin nose. It captivates Cicero for a brief moment.

Olivia is silent, but finally nods yes. She looks a bit hesitant. Cicero notices, but doesn't inquire. Roasting coffee beans and seasonal gingerbread yield an aromatic bouquet.

A couple of wasted stoners wander over to the conspirators' secluded section with café lattes in hand. Their unwashed, loose-fitting cargo pants drag along the Spanish-tiled floor. Young guys, probably part-time college students taking less than five credit hours, had spotted an open table next to Cicero and Olivia in the crowded shop and decided it was fair game.

But Cicero thinks otherwise, which is why he calmly lifts his cream-colored cotton sweater and flashes a black forty-caliber pistol at them and says, "This area is occupied."

Sobered fast, the younger of the two turns one hundred and eighty degrees and speed-walks out the front door while the other puts up both hands and stutters, "It's cool, man." He promptly does an about-face as well and follows his friend out.

Cicero looks at Olivia and says, "Cold steel is often an antidote for intoxication." She simply grins.

He lowers his sweater and pulls a thick brown envelope from under his slacks and milky ostrich boots. Cicero passes the package under the table to Olivia, whose hand is there waiting for it.

"It's all there. You can count it later," Cicero tells her. She nods again, this time with a more determined look on her face, as she sips her mochaccino.

Chattering voices flood the cozy coffee shop as Cicero stands and drops a fifty-dollar bill for their coffee and walks out with his espresso. Olivia pulls out a torch of a lighter and incinerates the photograph. It catches fire and immediately turns to ashes. A deliberate breath blows from her mouth and the ashes disperse. She sits there a few moments, idle, five-thousand dollars richer, and deep in thought. After taking a few more sips of her coffee, she walks out of the shop with much on her mind.

Chapter 6

Repetitious bass lines filter out of a nightclub. Twelve days after her meeting with Cicero, Olivia has tracked down the man who has crossed her employer. Velvet ropes block the entrance as an ethnically diverse line forms halfway down the block.

Faux fur coats and micro-miniskirts constitute much of the attire worn by anxious partygoers who have chosen to deal with the October chill on a Sunday night. Banging techno music and one-dollar pineapple martinis draw a nice mix of paraprofessionals and posers.

The wide Mexican bouncer at the door thoroughly checks IDs. After an underage girl left the club drunk and slammed into a state trooper leaving his wife a widow, the club goes the extra mile to avoid liability.

Olivia strolls past a slick, clean-cut Chinese crew, a couple of Armenians in silk shirts and black leather blazers, and a clique of Hispanics with intricately designed facial hair. Her skin-tight little black dress and tall boots get the attention of each and every one of them.

"*Que pasa, mami?*" one *vato* blurts. Cold air escapes his mouth. She smells of jasmine and fine oils.

Ignoring the multilingual cat calls, Olivia and her black full-length fur greet the bouncer, who is busily eyeing an out-of-state identification that doesn't exactly match the description of its owner.

"Hey, Manny," Olivia says to the bouncer. "What's the cover tonight?"

He smiles and removes the latch from one of the purple velvet ropes and motions her in.

"Oh, hell no," screams one pissed off sista who's watched Olivia bypass the entire line. She's been waiting to get in for nearly an hour.

Olivia passes under a bright pink neon sign reading *Chocolate City*. Another man opens the door for her and she is overwhelmed by the pounding music. *Boom, boom, boom, boom.*

The club is dark and densely packed. Its dance floor moves in waves like the Indian Ocean. Amber sconces decorate the walls. Behind the bar to the right, mirrors and premium liquors run the length of the wall, where groups of women down tequila shots and Jägermeister. They giggle as one spills the black Jäger down the front of her white lace blouse. Her friends don't care; it's after Labor Day and she shouldn't have worn it anyway.

Olivia eyes every male face. Many wink in response to what is perceived as her interest in them. Fifty or so simultaneous conversations inundate the part-time nightclub and restaurant in indiscernible babble. A few feminine outbursts of laughter break the monotone sound of white noise.

Techno continues to rock. *Boom, boom, boom, boom.* The low decibels knock. Undulating bodies brush against each other in this passionate venue of urban mating rituals. Olivia slyly maneuvers the crowd, careful to avoid spilled drinks and scuffs on the fourteen hundred-dollar, Italian-made boots she got on a trip to Milan.

Her mink glistens when the lime-green and baby-blue laser lights hit it. *Boom, boom, boom, boom.* She checks her crocodile-strapped timepiece. The oval onyx face shows it's a little after eleven p.m., plenty of time for her to complete her objective.

She glances to the rear of the club where satiny mint-colored sofas and rosey track lighting encourage networking and pick-up line delivery.

"You're beautiful," an inebriated man wholeheartedly slurs.

"Thank you," Olivia says without looking at him. She feels another enticed partier tug at her minkened arm, an oft-used practice she hates, which is why she immediately yanks it free without looking at the guilty fellow.

"Oh, it's like that?" the sub-six-foot twenty-one-year-old asks. His question and his cheap cologne are ignored. Unbeknownst to him, a plot has been hatched, and the one he pursues is in pursuit of another, with potentially life-altering consequences.

The suitor allows Olivia to pass minus further harassment and grabs another, less-attractive woman who happily joins him on the overcrowded dance floor.

Olivia forces her way through the throng and finally comes to the entranceway of a rear lounge area. Liquid crystal television screens hang along the perimeter like neoteric Picassos. Cubism at its finest. Drunkards view the latest mini DVDs and play virtual reality video games.

Boom, boom, boom, boom.

Olivia scans the room and notices from a distance what she thinks is a familiar face, so she edges closer.

"Excuse me, miss," a well-dressed man blurts out. "I see you're not drinking. Is it a religious thing or what?"

He catches Olivia off guard and she smiles, so he continues.

"Well, if it's not, can I buy you a drink?"

She agrees with his appearance and dark skin, so she responds in the affirmative. "Sure."

They walk over to a smallish, less-stocked bar in the corner where an interracial couple enjoys the unborn spawn of a beluga sturgeon. He orders a bottle of overpriced champagne in an unsuccessful attempt to impress the one he wants.

Miniature, hidden JBL speakers rock: *boom, boom, boom, boom.*

"So I take it you're here alone?" the debonair bachelor asks. But before he can pop the cork, Olivia spots her mark across the room. She stares at him intensely, like an eagle stalking a field mouse. His cursive written tattoo gives him away.

"Excuse me, it was nice meeting you," Olivia tells the gentleman. He's speechless. Her mark dons black glass headgear. He's engaged in a heated game of virtual football with the Latvian fellow next to him.

The quarry is dapper, wearing an all-midnight outfit and a matching wristwatch with black diamonds on the bezel.

Olivia steps closer to him. She is stunning. The unwitting man, glancing out the side of his headgear, soon notices her gaze. She stares at him. Her almond-shaped hazel eyes are enchanting. She smiles at him and makes her way to a nearby bar, still within eyesight.

She orders a blueberry martini as the mark follows her with his obscured eyes. His loss of concentration is costly, and his opponent scores a crucial last-second touchdown. Game over.

"Fuck," he yells as he tosses the headpiece to the carpeted floor. Disappointed, but not too, he slides over to the bar and stands next to Olivia, who turns away from him as if no longer interested.

Boom, boom, boom, boom. She's nonchalant and scopes the room, dismissing his presence.

"That's fucked up," the guy says. His skin is ink rich.

"Pardon me?" Olivia sassily inquires, batting her long eyelashes.

"You all in my grill and l lose five-hundred dollars," he spits. One arm rests on the bar as he leans on it. His breath smells of beer and vodka. Olivia is silent.

"You wrong for that," he tells her.

"Oh really?" she responds as she sips her drink. *Boom, boom, boom, boom,* the techno bass is nonstop. "You can't stay focused?"

He grins. "I'm focused now, and that's real talk." They begin eyeballing each other, making bedroom eyes.

"Well, I got something worth more than five-hundred dollars," Olivia explains, playing her ace. "And you'll never be the same afterward."

"Oh yeah?" the man asks as he strokes his face. The motion causes the short sleeve on his sweater to shrink, revealing the ominous name, V-Dog. "Well, I'm broke now, so can I put it on layaway?"

Olivia laughs, then downs her drink. She takes him by the hand and leads him through the jabbering crowd and past the champagne buyer who has watched their entire exchange in gut-wrenching disgust.

They reach a unisex bathroom and upon locking the door behind them, begin ferociously kissing as if there's no tomorrow. Olivia's beauty is irresistible, and V-Dog's ego shoots through the roof.

She loosens his silver belt buckle as he removes her mink and tosses it on the counter. His pants drop to the floor. His manhood is erect. Their tongues dance in each other's mouths. Up and down, side to side, lips smacking. V-Dog squeezes her firm breasts and she moans in pleasure.

Eager to have him inside her, Olivia eases her tight black dress up to her hips. V-Dog becomes profoundly horny when he sees she is panty-less, shaven, and soaking wet. *Boom, boom, boom, boom.*

Without even considering stopping to grab a condom, V-Dog inserts himself into Olivia's hot vagina. She sits on the sink and wraps her gorgeous legs around his waist as he thrusts in and out with powerful strokes. She screams in ecstasy. Her tight love embraces his thickness.

"Fuck me! Fuck me!" she insists, squeezing him close with both arms and legs.

"You like that? You like that?" V-Dog asks as he breaks into a sweat. He thrusts and thrusts.

He pounds her over and over again. His facial expressions show unmistakable lust. Olivia moans again. The pleasure of pain is so good. A few moments later, V-Dog releases his fluids inside her, and lets out a loud groan.

"Oh yea, baby, let it go," Olivia demands as she begins to rub his face.

V-Dog completes his act, and removes his penis from inside her. Olivia immediately turns to the sinks and begins to wash herself. V-Dog wipes his sweat with a paper towel, and pulls his boxers up followed by his slacks.

Olivia puts on her mink and fixes her hair and checks her makeup. Flawless. The good stuff doesn't run. V-Dog tucks in his shirt and fastens his belt. He feels like the luckiest dude on Earth.

Olivia turns and walks to the door and unlocks it, but before parting ways she turns toward him and whispers, "God bless you."

V-Dog looks confused by her comment, but just shrugs it off and grins. Not by chance, but by design, he has bedded a new millennium black widow.

Olivia makes her way past the dance floor and heads toward the front door of the club, now packed beyond capacity and violating the city's fire laws.

As the minx leaves, two women behind her get into a fight, throwing punches, scratching each other, and cursing. It's a significant contrast to her clandestine method of warfare, less effective and much more visible.

Boom, boom, boom, boom. Yet another victim has fallen for Olivia's sinister Kabuki. *Boom, boom, boom, boom.*

❌❌❌

"Hail Mary" is spelled out on Cicero's digital text-message communicator. He takes a quick look at the message, acknowledges its significance, and then deletes it.

He is expressionless and without reaction as he drives his pearl-white SUV through the inner city; titanic tires turning. Kam rides shotgun, once again blowing big blue weed smoke. Today's crop is dipped in embalming fluid, and Kam's being nosy.

"Who was that?" he asks as he inhales deeply.

"Olivia," Cicero answers in his deep tranquil voice.

Kam looks as if he is thinking, trying to jog his memory. A light bulb comes on and he exhales.

"Oh! That bad-ass broad you be meeting in the coffee shop," Kam decides. "She's killin' 'em," he says in his deep, sluggish speech pattern. "What's up with you and her?" he inquires before taking another long puff of his marijuana-stuffed cigar.

"Nothing," Cicero responds as he sips cognac from a red plastic cup. He's nicely dressed in a black blazer with matching T-shirt and slacks. His face and head are freshly shaven. His Italian loafers are well polished.

"Nothing? Shit, ya'll be kickin' it all the time, right?" Kam prods. He wears a similar all-black outfit with matching alligator boots. His dark ebony skin is smooth.

In the past, Cicero has kept his lieutenants in the dark regarding each other's activities, and he's pleased to see these operational details are exquisitely esoteric. He takes another sip of cognac.

"We have a business arrangement," he tells Kam, who is high.

"A business arrangement?" Kam asks as he exhales and fills the SUV with skunk-smelling plumes of smoke. Hip-hop blazes through the sound system.

Cicero looks somewhat bothered, but at this point, he figures Kam no longer needs to stay in the dark. His questions reveal to Cicero that he has interest in Olivia, so Cicero chooses to enlighten him, and possibly save his life.

"I pay her to know my enemies," Cicero states, "in the Biblical sense."

Kam appears confused. He knows what Cicero means, but he can't understand why. He takes an extremely long drag from his blunt.

"Well fuck," he weighs in, "how do I become one of your enemies?" He laughs and playfully punches Cicero in his arm, causing him to almost spill his drink.

Cicero takes another sip and ignores the comment. There's

a long moment of silence, then for Kam's sake he states, "She has AIDS."

Kam's eyes widen and his jaw drops. His face goes from showing glee to showing obvious disbelief. Cicero makes a gliding left turn on Twelfth Street, narrowly missing a homeless man pushing a shopping cart. Cicero thinks to himself that their destination cannot wait on some disenfranchised piece of shit to cross the street, even if he is a Vietnam vet.

Kam slowly leans back in his seat, allowing the leather to engulf him as he takes a long pull from his blunt before tossing it out the window.

In a subdued voice, Kam asks, "How'd she get that shit?"

"Her boyfriend in college," Cicero answers. "He played on the football team, came from a good family. She told me he was even on the Dean's list." He looks over at Kam. "You know, good grades and shit."

Cicero takes another sip of his cognac and begins feeling the effects of the one-hundred-year-old, oak-aged libation. Kam glares at him, listening intently.

Cicero continues, "So needless to say, he was getting a lot of ass thrown his way, male and female. And he was happy to hit both. No one knew." He pauses to take another drink. "That is, until he got sick."

"Damn," Kam blurts in amazement. "He was a damn sodomite, with a hottie like that?" His cell phone vibrates but he ignores it.

"Yea, after he found out why he was sick, he told Olivia to get tested," Cicero adds. "And sure enough, she had it too."

Kam simply shakes his head. Beams from a street light sneak into the truck and brighten the interior after bouncing off Cicero's platinum watch and Kam's teeth.

"Man, they were together for like three years," Cicero says as he glances over at Kam, beginning to slur slightly. "By the time she got tested, that monster was already creeping through her blood vessels, murdering her silently." He pauses. "The ninja."

"So she ain't taking no medicine or nothing?" Kam inquires with youthful curiosity.

"Yea, she is, which is why she needs me," Cicero answers. "She was so distraught and fucked up in the head when she found out her status that she dropped out of school and basically gave up on life. She came back to Kansas City where really nobody knows her. She just felt lost."

"Then you came into the picture?" Kam jumps in.

"Basically," Cicero responds as he takes a sip of cognac. "Since she doesn't work, and the state's not paying for that shit, I supply her AIDS cocktails and what not. The good stuff, you know, so she's able to keep her looks." He pauses. "She can't live without me."

Kam thinks for a moment. "But man, don't they have like a vaccine for that shit? I thought they were working on some shit?"

"Yea, they're working on one, but it's too late for old Olivia," Cicero states. He takes another sip. "Just a little too late, cousin." He takes another quick drink of his cognac, and begins bobbing his head to the fierce hip-hop lyrics.

Kam thinks further. "But damn, so she's basically spreading that shit?"

Cicero takes another sip of his drink and puts his cup down.

"You ever see *Pulp Fiction*? You know that part when Samuel L. Jackson is talking about that shit, that Bible verse he says to people before he smokes 'em?"

"Yea, I saw that shit, but I don't really remember it," Kam says.

"Well, anyway, in the movie he's like, he says it just because it's something sick to say to a mothafucka before you blast 'em. That's how I feel about Olivia, really. It's some cold-blooded shit to say to a mothafucka. Besides, fuck 'em. Them mothafuckas should use condoms."

Cicero picks up his drink and laughs to himself.

Kam glances at his friend and is briefly disenchanted with his sinister words. He then turns his head and looks out the window in silence.

✕✕✕

With enough sodium chloride, even the good mascara runs, which explains the cheetah-like streaks cascading down Olivia's face. She cruises in her cherry-red, two-seater convertible, top up, listening to India Arie.

"*Give me some Stevie, give me some Donny, give me my daddy, give me my mommy.*"

The smooth soulful lyrics comfort her, but only as much as a stranger's voice can.

She passes several women of the night, out soliciting for rent, gold bracelets, or to pad another's coffer. Olivia glances over her shoulder and makes direct eye contact with one, maybe seventeen, getting into a beat-up Buick. The young girl is cute, but her make-up is caked on and tacky. Her platinum blonde wig is bouffant. Yet and still, she looks resolved, as if she's merely clocking in to her nine-to-five desk job.

Olivia wipes her face and turns the heat up in her sixty-thousand-dollar German-made sports coupe. Her Italian boot gently applies more pressure to the accelerator and she further exceeds the posted speed limit. Being cited for a moving violation is the last thing on her mind.

Two hours after her latrine rendezvous, Olivia is full of regrets. She bursts with them. Even the red light before her is not enough to slow her progress and an oncoming driver mashes his horn and swerves to avoid her.

"Watch where the fuck you're going, you stupid cunt," the incensed man yells.

Olivia doesn't hear a single word or even see his car. She continues to head east as she makes a blind left on the right block, College Avenue, just out of years of conditioning. A strong wind blows and shakes her vehicle's light fiberglass chassis.

She pulls up to an aged house, similar to all the others on the east side of town. But this one is well kept, and this is the one she calls home. In the spring, white and yellow roses and tulips and daffodils will bloom in the garden she and her grandmother planted many years ago. Old Mr. Johnson still comes by every Saturday morning to trim the hedges, edge the lawn, and flirt with both women of the house, young and elderly. All he asks in return for his services is a smile and lemonade, perhaps hot chocolate in the fall.

Olivia smoothly exits her sleek coach, and looks all around to avoid rapists and carjackers. For extra security, she keeps a twenty-two-caliber Derringer in her glove compartment. This neighborhood has never been the safest.

After opening the gate and climbing a short flight of limestone stairs, a glimmer of color to the left catches Olivia's eye. She had thought all of the flower blooms had descended to the earth and withered, so she is surprised to see the moonlight illuminate a solitary yellow rose, surrounded by rocks and dead leaves.

It is an intriguing end to her night, but she doesn't ponder the rose's tenacity for too long. Even under tonight's gale, the rose manages to cling to life, for however brief as it may be.

The strong breeze causes the large wood and iron door to swoosh as Olivia turns her key and gingerly opens it, passing the home's four-digit address that lacks two numbers. The two-story house is dark and silent. The only sounds heard are the howls of the wind and the neighbor's malnourished German shepherd.

She gently walks up the staircase as she passes the bedroom of her sleeping grandmother. Olivia is always careful not to wake her; she knows she is a light sleeper.

Last night's tan boots are the only items out of place in her spotless bedroom. Unlike her life, there is extreme order and structure in her nighttime quarters. The room smells of expensive perfume and incense. Her white king-sized canopy bed looks heavenly.

She takes a seat on her paisley-patterned chaise lounge to remove her boots. Olivia is disappointed to see an empty bottle of eye drops on the dresser, because her eyes are once again sore from sorrow. Her misery is worse than that of the inhabitants of Davis Inlet.

"Why me, God?" Olivia questions in a low whisper. Her head is bowed, elbows resting on her knees.

She stands, closes the bedroom door as it creaks, and locks it.

The vanity mirror hasn't reflected vanity in quite some time, and tonight, it reflects Olivia retrieving a coffee-brown glass vial from a drawer as she sits in an armless chair.

Ancient Inca Indians used to chew the leaves for increased stamina and vitality, but tonight Olivia sprinkles the extracted alkaloid onto a mini hand mirror. Derived from erythroxylum coca, the white powder eases her nerves in a spectacular fashion, far better than her prescription Prozac.

She snorts three thick lines, roughly a gram and a half. Hormones are instantly released from her brain's pleasure centers and she cracks a fraudulent smile as new tears form in her eyes. She wipes her face and her nose and continues to smile, disingenuously.

More pure powder flows from the vile onto the glass. Olivia emphatically snorts it. The drug-induced chemical reactions in her brain make her think she feels better.

Once released, the substances in her brain aren't immediately reabsorbed, so for a brief moment, Olivia forgets she has Acquired Immune Deficiency Syndrome. She forgets she lost her academic scholarship when she stopped going to class. She forgets she dropped out of college. She forgets about her desire to have a family and a white picket fence. Her loneliness dissipates.

In the midst of this amnesic episode, Olivia catches a glimpse of herself in the vanity mirror hanging over her dresser, and she stares at it. She loathes what she sees. So she stands and walks into an adjacent bathroom, opens the mirrored cabinet, grabs something, and returns to her seat. A floorboard creaks.

Out of despair, Olivia has retrieved a small orangish-tan plastic bottle of Valium. The wind whips outside, and after some difficulty, she manages to open the junkie-proof cap.

"Take one pill a day," Olivia reads on the bottle, then laughs. "Do not exceed dosage."

Ignoring the warning, she dumps about twelve of the blue V-imprinted pills into her hand. As she eyes the medication, there's a knock at her door.

"Olivia?" her grandmother calls out in a muffled voice. "Are you okay in there?" It's late, and Olivia is usually in bed by this time.

"Yes, Grandmother," Olivia answers. "I'm okay. You can go back to bed."

"Olivia?"

"Yes?"

"Can I come in?"

Olivia thinks about it, but as she ponders her response, the doorknob turns and the door opens. It wasn't locked after all, and her grandmother carefully enters.

Embarrassed, Olivia begins wiping her face and in the process, the pills in her hand fall and scatter across the shiny hardwood floor. Together they make a clear and distinct musical clatter.

Wise and tender, the elderly Juanita glances at the pills, now strewn all over the floor. She immediately grabs her troubled granddaughter and holds her tight, pressing her face into her heart. Olivia can feel it beating with unconditional love, and she breaks down, sobbing uncontrollably.

"God loves you, baby," Juanita says as she serenely begins rocking side to side. "He loves Olivia so much."

The twenty-seven-year-old begins wailing even louder.

"Why?!" she screams at the top of her lungs. "Why?!"

"He has a plan for you, baby," Juanita reassures her broken granddaughter. "You just have to have faith. And baby, you are not alone, I'm here with you."

Olivia's sobbing continues, and is now a low humming buzz.

Her deep sorrow is infectious, and it causes Juanita to begin crying too. She wipes her eyes and cheeks, still holding Olivia tight.

The wind rattles the house as the storm shutters smack against the exterior. And yet, the yellow rose outside remains Herculean.

Chapter 7

Cold wind whirls outside as Brad, Cicero, and Kam sit at a round table in a poorly lit Italian restaurant. For the past week, they've had a series of weighty business meetings, but this is without question the most momentous.

The décor is authentic, but patrons rarely order the angel hair pasta or the sage and basil-powdered bruschetta. More than anything, it's a meeting place. A debugged meeting place. A secure, family-owned meeting place.

"So, Cicero, how's your mother doin'?" the oldest and fattest man seated at the table asks. His mustache is bushy.

"She's well," Cicero responds.

"She was always a beautiful woman," the man says. His Italian accent is prominent.

"And she still is, Jimmy," Cicero adds, smiling.

The restaurant is quiet with the exception of water running in the back kitchen and some dishes clattering. Near the entrance hangs a large oil painting of infamous Cristoforo Columbo disembarking his ship.

Jimmy wheezes. His obesity makes him struggle for every breath. Kam and Brad, both in expensive English-tailored suits, are silent. They're focused, eyes penetrating.

"Your father, God rest his soul, was a loyal man," Jimmy states. "You know that?"

Cicero nods yes.

"Very well-respected," Jimmy continues. "And I hear that you've made a name for yourself. That you've got a lot of your father's good qualities."

Cicero nods again.

Roaring flames crackle in the restaurant's twenty-five-foot brick fireplace while three huge chandeliers made of blown glass hang from the exposed wood-beamed ceiling.

"I also hear you're good with the ladies."

Everyone at the table laughs, including two other Italian gentlemen, one of whom is slender and laughs louder than anyone else.

"Yea, he has an Italian's loyalty and a black man's cock," the thinnest man says. Everyone laughs again, minus Cicero. The thin man's name is Pete, and his face is hard from years of alcohol abuse and stress. The type of stress brought on by federal indictments, warrants, murder, racketeering, extortion, prostitution, Internet pornography, credit card fraud, grand theft, and mayhem in general.

"He can't lose," Pete adds. They all laugh again, and again, Cicero is silent. He eyes the comedian. Kam and Brad sense the tension, as does Jimmy, who jumps in with a timely comment.

"You know, Cicero, it was unfortunate what happened to your father," he says, talking with his hands. "But you know, that does happen in our line of work."

Cicero silently nods.

"And, Cicero, what is this I hear you have a college degree," Jimmy asks, totally switching gears. "I know we've lost contact for a few years, but is this true?"

"Yea, I actually have two," Cicero says, nonchalantly. "A bachelor's and a masters in psychology."

Jimmy pauses and strokes his mustache. Then he looks at Cicero, much like his father or his mother would have.

"Well, what the fuck are you doing here with us?" Jimmy questions. In front of him is a saucer of fresh garlic bread, drizzled with extra virgin olive oil and a pinch of rosemary, and baked portachini mushrooms.

"Jimmy, why should I settle for fifty thousand dollars a year when I can make fifty thousand a week," Cicero says, adding hand gestures to his words. He loves money more than he loves pussy. That, and the fact that he would rather kick, than be kicked, and slap than be slapped.

"Look," the fifty-seven-year-old Jimmy chimes in, "a degree like that is truly an accomplishment, for anyone, black or white. Lord knows my son is a good-for-nothing lazy piece of shit."

Cicero and Kam, who are seated next to each other, both grin as Jimmy continues kvetching about this son.

"Really, Jimmy," the other Italian man asks, smiling.

Jimmy looks toward him and continues, "All he does all fucking day is shove that white shit up his nose, and blow my fucking money day trading and shit. And taking fucking trips to the fucking Ozarks."

Jimmy's voice is deep and booming. It's the voice of leadership. But he calms. His dialogue shows he has feelings for Cicero.

"But, Cicero, you're a grown man, so live your life," he stops, then adds, "for as long as you can."

Cicero frowns.

"No disrespect, Jimmy, but are you finished?" Cicero asks.

Jimmy nods yes.

"Good," Cicero says. "We came here tonight because Brad and I have developed a new product, and with your blessing, we'd like to uh, market it."

The three Italian men look interested, and with that, Cicero looks at Brad and gives him the okay.

Brad's dark-gray suit flows smoothly over his frame as he reaches down and lifts a supple black attaché case onto the table. He pulls a small chrome-like circular disk out and opens it.

In the disk is one small tubular tablet.

"It's a derivative of dopamine, the same chemical released in the brain when someone snorts coke," Brad says, speaking tranquilly and confidently. His accent is not as thick tonight. He slides the tablet over to Pete, and Jimmy immediately demands it, then eyes it, carefully.

Brad continues, "But this has a synthetic element, similar to Ecstasy, that further stimulates dopamine production and blocks re-uptake."

"So what the fuck does all this mean to me?" a skeptical Pete weighs in, snickering at Brad's accent. Pete's incredulous, but his opinion really doesn't matter.

Brad, unfazed, responds, "It means you can get heaven on Earth, Pete, without worrying about hell, ya got me? You see, there are no negative side effects. No coming down from this mountaintop. Not for some hours."

Jimmy grins, still fingering the tablet. Kam sees this and smiles, dazzling the room. His all-black suit almost blends in with his chocolate-colored skin. Cicero cracks a smile as well.

"The best part about it is that it's all natural, and right now, it's all legal."

Now, all eyes are on Jimmy. And he takes a deep breath. On top of the fact that this guy owns three restaurants, two strip clubs, the car dealership where Kam and Cicero bought their cars, and a host of liquor stores, he's very well connected. In fact, Jimmy maintains tax information for Kam and Cicero at a few of his legal businesses, so the federal government thinks they both have real jobs and they're giving Uncle Sam his cut. Paying taxes like good Americans.

"So you guys want to basically unleash a new plague on the Earth?" Jimmy asks.

The air becomes still. No one moves. Cicero had never contemplated, not even for a second, the ramifications of this endeavor, even though he grew up in a time and place where cocaine and crack had ravaged a generation, and left countless youth orphaned, and sons murdered and imprisoned, even on his own block. Friends, neighbors and schoolmates: all casualties in the so-called war on drugs. Still, he had never thought about the potential consequences, the global, epidemic sort of consequences, of this effort. But his mind was made up.

"I guess so," Cicero answers frankly.

Jimmy just nods. And though he has seen many things and is rarely shocked or dismayed, Cicero's unrelenting dark heart, his callousness, surprises the aging Mafioso. And yet, he too, wishes to move forward.

"May God forgive you, Cicero Day," Jimmy states lightheartedly.

"I don't fear myths," Cicero immediately replies. The group is momentarily silent, then Jimmy starts.

"So, how much can you make off this stuff?"

"No, Jimmy, how much can *we* make?" Cicero asks before taking a deep breath. "Well, with your initial financial assistance and national and international connections…"

A mouse in a back storeroom is heard pissing on a cotton ball.

"…billions," Cicero finishes. "It's the new and improved Coca."

Pete and his friend look at Jimmy, who has a straight face, and is still fingering the royal-blue tablet. He then spreads his mustache with a wide grin and begins to laugh.

"With that kind of soldi, I can get some fuckin' liposuction and get head from Jennifer Aniston!"

Everyone at the table bursts into laughter, except Cicero. He wants this too bad to joke about it.

"It's gonna take us a few months to get, you know, things to make the shit and get everything together."

Jimmy nods.

"But, Jimmy, do we have your blessing?" Cicero asks.

Jimmy, in his three-piece hand-tailored suit, struggles to his feet and waddles over to Cicero, who stands up. Jimmy's girth makes his expensive Italian suit look cheap, while Cicero's all-black, single-breasted suit looks miraculous. Jimmy gives him a firm hug. Cicero firmly hugs him back though it is not in his heart. He didn't grow up with a lot of affection, but he loves money. While both his parents loved him dearly, neither regularly embraced him. If they had, his life may have been different.

Jimmy squeezes him tightly, then kisses him on the cheek.

"Look at this kid! You gotta love him!"

Cicero smiles and releases his grasp, as Jimmy follows.

"Of course you have my blessing, and be sure you have my twenty percent," Jimmy adds. Pete and the other gentleman laugh. Kam and Brad smirk, but they knew Jimmy's help wouldn't be free.

"I'll call my guys in Vegas, Chicago, and New York, let them know what's coming, what to expect."

"Cool. It's a deal then," Cicero replies, as he firmly shakes the shorter Jimmy's hand. As he smiles, Cicero thinks to himself that if he had to, he could kill Jimmy, and Pete, and his friend with his bare hands. It's a thought many men have in the presence of other men, but Cicero's thought, and most like it, is never mumbled.

"So, C, you wanna fuck my wife too," Jimmy jokingly adds. Everyone laughs. "'Cause Lord knows, I don't want to!"

Jimmy yells to a nearby waiter to fetch the best wine in the house. The young guido hastily scurries off to a cellar and is gone for several minutes.

As the search for the perfect year and grapes ensues, Jimmy pulls Cicero to the side, away from the others seated at the table.

"Do that for me, Cicero, tonight," Jimmy commands, as he stares Cicero in the eyes.

"It's done, Jimmy," Cicero answers as the kid returns with two rare vintage 1972 bottles of Bernello red wine.

"Good," Jimmy says with a smile. "Let's have a drink."

The two return to the table and Jimmy inserts a long, sterling silver corkscrew into the bottle's top. It's an old harvest, so he slowly removes the cork, then checks it for red streaks. Any sign of veins would indicate leakage, but there are none, so Jimmy pours the fermented fruit into a lead-free decanter. The six men indulge.

The men stagger out of the restaurant a few hours later, after finishing the wine and ordering more drinks and cordials and beer. It's now darker outside, colder. Biting wind whistles as it whips around the corner.

Jimmy and the other gentleman pull their Dobbs hats over their eyes and take in the chilly night air. They wonder if the feds are watching them, equipped with night vision cameras, breaking in their new technology on Jimmy's crew.

Brad, Cicero, Kam and Pete all stagger out of the restaurant laughing.

"So you really kicked this broad in the ass?" Pete asks Brad, astounded. Brad smiles and nods yes.

"Unfuckinbelieveable," Pete adds. "I need to come party with you guys."

Cicero jumps in. "Well, shit, Pete, you need to come with us right now!"

Brad eyes Cicero, who's still clinging to his snifter. Jimmy is a true epicure, and his taste in cognac is superb.

"Oh yea?" Pete asks. "Where you guys headed now?" His voice is raspy from years of Cuban cigar smoking.

"We're going to meet up with these shakers and after that, go to my place to get fucked and sucked," Cicero expounds.

"Shakers?" Pete inquires as the cutting wind blows.

"Strippers, man," Kam clears up before firing up a fat blunt.

"You fucking bullshittin'," Pete asks while grinning.

Shaking his head no, Cicero says, "I'm not bullshittin'. It's going to be wonderful."

Pete, whose blood alcohol content is roughly point three five, thinks about his four kids at home and how is wife resembles Jimmy, just a little bigger.

He then looks over to Jimmy to get the okay, as if he was asking, "Is it okay, meaning safe, for me to hang out with these thuggish monkeys?" Jimmy smiles, and gives a slight nod, meaning, *Yes. You have my word you'll be safe.* Pete grins back, knowing that if Cicero or Kam were to cross Jimmy, they'd never be seen again. Jimmy and the other man slide into a Town Car and quickly leave the scene.

"Let's go," Pete tells Cicero, agreeing to attend the soiree.

"Well, hey, you guys have a good time," Brad says to the guys before hopping in his BMW.

They all look disappointed.

"Come on, Bradley, we'll have a good time," Cicero says. "Hell, you might be able to stick your foot up someone's ass again."

Kam and C burst into laughter.

"Naw, I have a lot of work to do," Brad responds. "You guys have fun. And, Pete, don't do anything I wouldn't do."

"That leaves me a ton of fucking options," Pete throws back. Cicero and Kam chuckle it up and Brad departs without having his balls busted any further.

✖✖✖

All-chrome seventeen-inch wire rims revolve like the moon around the Earth on Kam's classic Chevy Impala. The ten coats of sky-blue paint and three clear coats make it look like a piece of hard candy. Good enough to eat. The refurbishing cost thousands of dollars and hours, including the initial trip to Columbus, Ohio, to pick up the then-rusty piece of junk.

But now it's flawless, and the countless show trophies Kam has picked up over the years are proof of that. The 454 under the hood roars after every stop. It's the king of mechanic beasts in the concrete jungle. And this late at night, the Kansas City streets are always vacant, so Kam opens it up on the empty roads.

After a few minutes of driving, the trio hits the east side of town, where lives are lost over mere chump change. And often, disrespect can lead to T-shirts with photographs on them. Smoke from burning hickory billows from a small family-owned barbecue restaurant.

Regardless of how tough the K.C. mafiosos claim to be, they rarely venture over here, and Pete, who is sitting in the backseat, is a tad concerned.

"Hey, where the hell are we going? I thought we were going to see some, uh, shakers or whatever," he asks.

"Dude, why you actin' 'noided?" Kam asks, talking slowly.

"'Noided?" inquires Pete.

"It means you're acting paranoid. Look, relax, Pete, we're almost there," Cicero reassures, calmly sipping from his snifter.

Kam suddenly then interjects, "Oh! I forgot to get something."

Cicero and Pete both look at him.

"What did you forget," Cicero asks.

"The honey," Kam answers as he checks his Swiss chronograph diving watch. It's 1:59 a.m. "Cool, the l.i.q. is still open."

Pete smiles.

"You guys weren't playing, were you?" he cheerfully shouts. "These bitches must be some true sluts."

Kam and Cicero both smile.

The Chevy glides past Freedom Fountain, which often functioned as a swimming pool for Kansas City's poor black community. Kameron spent many summer days splashing in it, but tonight it is darkly silent and barren.

After cutting a few corners, they pull to a local corner store, and Kam hops out his ride and runs in. Lyrics from an underground Bay Area rapper blast through his fifteen-speaker system and sound crystal clear.

"*I speak another language but I'm not Scottish, got more homies in jail, than I do in college.*"

Cicero looks back at Pete, who's trying not to look too nervous, even though he is.

"Hey, Pete, these girls are freaks," Cicero reassures him in a low whisper. "This one has this trick she does with honey. I'm telling you, it's phenomenal. She's a wild beast!"

Pete cheeses with glee.

"Well, let's fucking get there already!"

Just then Kam returns with a medium-sized plastic bear full of honey.

"Yea! Let's do this," he tells his passengers before mashing the accelerator.

✖✖✖

The three men soon arrive at Thirty-Seventh Street to an old three-story house with recently added aluminum siding. The contractor did a terrible job. Silence fills the block, and the fall nip has caused most of the hustlers to go elsewhere for at least a few hours.

A six-foot black iron gate surrounds the home. A red light bulb beams from the front porch.

Several cars and trucks fill the empty gravel-covered lot next door, which functions as convenient parking for this black-owned crap house and brothel.

They exit Kam's saucy transport and begin walking toward the house. He has the honey in hand. Pete's head is on a swivel, constantly looking over both shoulders for foolhardy stick-up kids and raving junkies. But none approach.

Two digital cameras monitor their position and the gate buzzes as they near it and proceed through.

Cicero takes the lead and knocks on the door, three distinct times.

Knock.

Knock.

Knock.

A very large fifty-something man of African descent opens the heavy door and stares at the faces. He spends more time on Pete's but nevertheless tells the three, "Come on in."

Upon entering, partially muffled music from the "Artist," once again known as Prince, can be heard coming from upstairs.

On the first floor to the left is a huge fifty-seven-inch big-screen television, and to the right, just past the staircase, is a bar complete with drunks and neon Budweiser signs.

A few guys watch the former Kansas City Kings take on the Lakers with a feeling of sick nostalgia. They were never nearly that good when they were in the Show Me State. There's a pool table where a dining room would be, and a jukebox in the space usually dedicated to curio cabinets and fine china.

Cicero motions for Kam and Pete to follow as he makes his way up the red carpeted stairs to the second floor, where Pete is surprised to see three topless women gyrating for customers with dollar bills in hand.

All are topless in different color thong bikini bottoms. One in the distance toward the left is about five feet four inches and caramel; five feet nine when you tack on the five-inch clear plastic platform shoes she has on. Pelvic muscles create an erotic oscillation along her waistline. She's Kam's favorite, and he smiles at her with that expensive grin. She acknowledges with a wide grin of her own. Her face is simple and cute.

The nearest one, milky with sapphire-blue eyes, catches Pete's gaze. Her fiery hair makes her stand out even further in this room of brunettes. And at thirty-six C, her saline-filled faux breasts are superb. She knows the game, so she winks at Pete, and like most tricks, he instantly thinks she likes him. It's the oldest stripper ploy in the book.

"Holy shit!" Pete spits. "How come I never knew about this place?"

Kam and Cicero laugh. Where there should have been two modest bedrooms, the sheet rock has been hauled off and a large stage complete with a shiny brass pole has been installed. Surrounded by mirrors, the third woman dances on the stage alone, as a member of the local United Auto Workers union tips her a ten-spot.

She and Cicero have history. Brief history. Brief-blowjob-on-the-first-night-they-met-in-the-back-of-the-SUV history. She called his last cell phone so much he had the number changed—twice. Regardless of that, she still smiles at him, recalling how he smelled like baby powder. He stares at her long brown legs and flowing curly locks, but doesn't return her affectionate gesture.

They sit at a small four-seat bar that's about five feet long and manned by somebody's uncle.

"Hey, uh, excuse me," Pete says, motioning to get the bartender's attention.

"Yea, what can I get ya?" the older gentleman asks.

"Yea, let me get a gin and tonic."

The man turns and grabs a plastic bottle of gin and pours at least a triple shot into a tall glass. It might be cheap, but you sure get a lot of it.

All the dancers' attention is now focused on the three well-dressed men in suits seated at the bar, and the other patrons don't like that.

A young cat with a mouth full of gold teeth and his boy, who would both typically be out hustling on a night like this, eyeball Cicero.

Cicero notices, and politely flashes the nickel-plated forty-four in the shoulder holster under his blazer. Heat has the tendency to defrost cold stares.

Any other night Cicero might have a gunfight on his hands, because Kansas Citians thrive on respect: for many, it's all they have. But the two punks in Royals jackets are slipping tonight. They're weaponless, so they change their tune and look away from the clean three at the bar. After a few more tips, they leave, pissed off. Cicero remains on guard, however. These young cats are the type to return and light the house up like the Fourth of July.

Hip-hop music rocks as Kam, Cicero, and Pete have several drinks and take a number of quick tequila shots, adding to their buzzes from earlier.

Lyrics from a local artist are powerful and sincere.

"Blastin,' only what the red dot pinpoints. Floor the pedal, then blow dro rolled in thin joints."

Starting to really feel the effects, Pete rises from his barstool and asks, "Hey, where's the fucking john? I gotta piss like a Russian race horse."

Cicero laughs and says, "Man, it's down the hall and to the left."

Pete exits the room and when he does, Cicero reaches into his jacket pocket and pulls out a little off-white eyedropper. He quickly deposits two clear drops into Pete's gin and tonic and waits for his return while Kam gets up and slides a five into his favorite's garter belt.

After draining the weasel, Pete returns feeling like a new man, and immediately walks over to the redhead and places a twenty-dollar bill in her thong.

"Thank you, baby," she says as she rubs his rough face and begins to wiggle her thin frame.

Pete smiles at her like a schoolboy, then slowly saunters back toward the bar. He takes a big swig of his drink, dribbling some down his chin.

"Yea! This place is okay with me," he tells Cicero, who grins at him. "Hey, so which one does the thing with the honey?"

"Oh, none of them, she's in the V.I.P. room," Cicero responds.

"Well, fuck, that's where we need to be!"

They both laugh.

Cicero checks his watch, it's two thirty-seven a.m.

"Okay, cool. Let's go," Cicero says before dropping a fifty-spot for their drinks.

Cicero motions to Kam and he leaves his little stripper as they all walk back down the stairs. Pete is noticeably woozier than the other two, and he nearly falls down the steps before Cicero lassos him.

"Whoa! You okay, Petey Pete?" he asks while chuckling.

Trying to regain his composure, Pete answers, "Yea, I'm okay. I just had, you know, maybe one too many."

"Man, you're fucked up. You sure you still want to fuck with the V.I.P. room?"

"Hell yea! Shit yea!" Pete convincingly slurs. His vision is becoming blurry.

"Okay, come on, it's in the basement," adds Cicero.

"Man, don't be throwin' up in my ride," warns Kam.

They slowly make their way down the two flights of stairs to the first floor, then hook a right past the bar and another right past the pool table. In mid stride, Pete blacks out, nearly busting his head on the corner pocket on his way to the rug.

"Damn, he's fucked up," one older Mexican billiards player

quips with a heavy accent. "Bartender, give me whatever he's drinking."

He and his friend start laughing.

"*El gringo stupido*," his dirty friend mumbles under his breath before taking a sip of his Dos Equis. "*Que idioso.*"

Kam and Cicero carefully lift Pete off the floor. Kam reaches over and opens a door to the right, which leads down to a dark set of rickety wooden stairs.

It's pitch black and impossible to see, but they know their way around down here. After getting down the stairs they walk about twenty-five feet through a lengthy hallway before reaching a reinforced steel door.

Kam removes Pete's arm from around his shoulder and opens the door, exposing a large empty windowless room made entirely of concrete on all sides. A sewer drain and a gray folding chair sit in the middle.

Kam props up Pete's limp body, mouth unhinged and all, on the chair, as Cicero shuts the heavy metal door behind them.

One light bulb hangs from the ceiling in the center. It's cold and quiet.

Kam removes Pete's suit jacket and tosses it to the floor. Then *rip. Rip. Rip.* He tears Pete's white shirt down the middle, buttons popping off. His hairy flabby chest barely moves with each breath. Cicero sips a cognac and stares at Pete, whose eyes are shut tight.

In a devilish manner, Kam grins as he pulls the honey-filled bear from the brown paper bag.

He removes the plastic from the top and, after twisting it open, begins to squeeze the sweet sticky substance all over Pete's passed-out body.

"I can't wait to see this mothafucka's face when he wakes up," Kam says in a whisper, then giggles.

Side to side, Pete's eyes roll in his head. He's in deep sleep, and the mechanism that controls rapid eye movement has kicked in. Quite possibly, he's dreaming of the beautiful redhead upstairs. That he and her are on a hot sandy beach in the middle of the Pacific Ocean drinking daiquiris and tanning.

Slap!

"Wake the fuck up, bitch," Kam says in a sinister tone. His open palm sticks to Pete's viscous face.

Slap! He strikes him again and Pete's body jolts and his eyelids lift.

"What the, what the hell is goin' on?" Pete mumbles. "Where am I?"

"Welcome to the V.I.P. room, Petey Pete," Cicero says.

Feeling his body covered in a strange element, Pete reaches to wipe his face but finds that Kam has bound his hands together behind him with rope, and his feet have been tied to the drain beneath him.

"Hey. Hey. Hey, what the fuck is goin' on here?" Pete yells, regaining consciousness. "What the fuck is this?"

Cicero gazes at him from across the room, then slowly steps over to him, getting just inches from his face, looking at him eye to eye.

"You know what this is, Pete," says Cicero. "This is the end."

Pete's eyes grow huge. His pulse quickens. Sweat forms in tiny beads upon his protruding brow, then descend down the sides of his dark crow's feet.

"What the fuck are you talking about, Cicero?! Untie me!" Pete says, breathing heavily.

Cicero takes a step back and swigs his drink. Kam's smile has yet to leave.

"I know you killed my father, Pete. I've always known it."

"Bullshit! Jimmy had your father whacked!"

"No, Pete," Cicero says in a calm voice. "I remember being at my father's gravesite for his funeral. You remember that day?"

Pete is silent, and sweating profusely.

"Well, I do. I remember I threw up when they began to lower my father's casket in the ground. And some woman, I guess a friend of my grandmother's, led me to the family limousine and told me to wait there. The white part of the family wanted to keep me out of sight. Lucia and my mom didn't even go to the funeral. But anyway, you all knew about us, all of us, I'm sure."

As Cicero pauses to take another drink, Kam slides out of the room and closes the large door behind him.

"So I'm alone, sitting in the limo, and that's when I overheard you talking outside. I'll never forget those words, Pete. I heard you say, 'That piece-of-shit Tony was something to break. We removed every finger, toe and hair follicle, and he still didn't talk.'"

Pete's eyes search the room for a way to escape, then he struggles to free his hands. Recollections of that day are no longer foggy, and Pete knows the inevitable will occur, tonight, now, in the basement of a brothel in the heart of the ghetto.

"And you know the worst part about my father's funeral, Pete?" Cicero asks. "It was on my birthday. I haven't celebrated it since."

At that moment, Pete realizes that only divine intervention can save him now.

"Yea, Pete, when I finally got old enough, Jimmy told me

the whole story," Cicero lays out. "You know why he told me? Because I'm loyal. He saw in me what you dagos claim to be. You talk about loyalty, but I live it. I am it."

An ungodly squeal is suddenly heard coming from down the hall.

Pete's heart nearly jumps out of his chest, and he once again fights to free himself from the cold soundproof room. Once again, his efforts are without fruition.

Cicero continues, "He told me how you and my father pulled a lick together, and how you felt cheated by his cut of the loot."

"Hey, fuck Jimmy, and fuck you too!" Pete screams forcefully, spit flying from his mouth.

Another high-pitch squeal is heard, louder and closer.

"No, Pete," Cicero whispers and he goes to open the door. "Fuck you."

The door swings open and before Pete, standing four-feet high is a starving wild boar.

"Oh my God!" Pete says under his breath as he looks at the razorback, then down at his chest, seeing the syrupy invitation covering his body from head to toe. "Holy fucking shit!"

Reddish-black bristles cover the grotesque beast's meaty frame, as it squeals again. It's a hairsplitting noise. And if it weren't for Kam holding the pig at bay with a chain, it would have already thrown itself upon Pete.

"Yea, Pete, this right here is my baby," says Kam, speaking sluggishly and grinning, sounding like a fanatic. "I love this mothafucka."

Pete is petrified and Kam loves it.

"I bet you're wondering where an asshole like myself got such a fine specimen of an animal. I could tell you, Pete, but then I'd have to kill you." Kam laughs. "Oh yea, we're going to kill you, so I guess I can tell you."

"You fucking psychos!"

Kam ignores his comment and continues. "Yea, Pete, I had just drove to Mexico and picked up three hundred pounds of green, and on the way back, we stopped in this little town in Texas."

The beast squeals. Kam calms her.

"But anyway, we came across this razorback farm, and that's when it hit me," Kam says. "You can keep ya fucking pit bulls and ya Prussian canaries, I'll take Ms. Piggy any day."

Urine flows down Pete's pant leg and into the drain. The smell further excites the beast's protruding snout as it squeals louder and lunges toward him, cloven hoofs tapping the cement floor. Hairs rise on the boar's back as it salivates like a running faucet.

"Petey Pete," Cicero quips. "Kam tells me she hasn't eaten in three days. Do you know that's unheard of for a hog? And she has one hell of a sweet tooth."

The honey aroma is deliciously enticing to the stout-bodied mammal and it longs to taste Pete. She squeals and drools profusely.

"No, please, dear God, I'll…, I'll do anything," Pete pleads.

"Sorry, my friend," Cicero says. "Bon voyage."

Kam releases the chain and the beast dives right into Pete's hairy midsection, gnawing and ripping open his stomach, disemboweling him and spilling his intestines onto the floor with a loud splat. Blood sprays in all directions, covering the hog's snout, face, the floor, and Pete's trousers. Undigested rigatoni and gooey shit splashes on the cement, filling the room with a horrible stench.

Pete screams. Then he gurgles and passes out from the pain before bleeding to death. Blissful shrieks bellow from the swine's germ-infested mouth while it swallows whole chunks of Pete's fleshy tissue and organs.

The sow roots into his torso with her snout and rips out large portions of his liver and spleen, then crunches downward through bone, crushing his pelvis and tearing his genitals into shreds.

Pete's eyelids flutter and his body twitches and shakes as the beast eats him from the inside out.

Kam watches his pet feast with the delight of a proud parent. Squeals and grunts reverberate.

"Good girl! Good girl!" Kam dotes from near the door, smiling.

Tattered remnants from Pete's suit and slices of skin are thrown across the room as the beast ferociously shakes its head side to side savoring the essence.

Cicero stands next to Kam sipping his drink with a blank face, yet fully enjoying the medieval spectacle before him. The foul stench in the room takes him back to his father's funeral, when he threw up near the casket. He thinks about his father's distinct, booming laugh, and Cicero wonders if this act of savage revenge would have pleased him.

As the sow continues to gorge, Cicero, seeing the job is done, turns to walk out of the room, then stops.

"Make sure your baby doesn't leave a crumb."

Kam nods and continues to watch. His baby squeals again, loving her repast.

Chapter 8

prils in Kansas City are inconsistent. One year it might snow. The next year it could be seventy degrees or raining nonstop. But tonight, it's cool out. Lightning waltzes across the late-night firmament.

Roughly five months have passed since Pete's unfortunate demise, and since then, Brad, Kam and Cicero have been meticulously organizing, planning, and formulating plots to get their drug project off the ground.

But all the effort has begun to weigh on the friends, and tonight, Cicero cannot find peace, not even in his dreams.

Three immense rectangular paintings done in primary colors hang perfectly aligned on the living room wall. All are framed in black mahogany. The first from the front door, in ocean-blue, was created using broad horizontal strokes. In the second, created in tomato-red, the same artist employed whimsical circular brush strokes. And the third, in daisy-yellow, was fashioned with firm vertical sweeps. The walls are black.

Lightning strikes outside. Electric-blue arteries charge the sky with energy, then disappear. Frightened children across the city dive for covers.

Three onyx sofas, made from the skin of unborn broadtail sheep, face each other in a sunken living room. Even the king-sized mink bedspread in the next room cannot compare to their softness. At sixty-four inches, the plasma television dominates the sitting area.

Stainless steel resides in the kitchen, wall-to-wall—the Viking stove, the Sub-Zero refrigerator, the two separate self-cleaning ovens. Thunder crackles a few kilometers away.

The world's finest German cutlery occupies only a small portion of the ample countertop space. And in the middle of the unwelcoming *cocina* is a marble-topped island with a built-in cutting board. It's rarely used.

Just past the abortion sofas is a polished ebony, eight-seat dining room table that's never hosted a Thanksgiving dinner, never seen the likes of Manwiches, nor store-bought taco shells or deviled eggs.

Above hangs a hand-made custom Lalique chandelier. Tiny sterling silver loops attach diamond-shaped crystals to larger diamond-shaped crystals embellished on all sides with lady-bug-sized pearls. The light is the way.

Farther to the left, near the sliding door with its Venetian blinds and the awning-shielded veranda, is a tall, lighted rosewood cabinet with a glass door filled from top to bottom with the world's finest cognac.

Cicero typically preferred the local family-owned vineyards with their unblended single estate cognacs from either Ugni Blanc or French Colombard grapes. These brands pervade the brass and gold-trimmed case more than any others, minus a random single-district or single-distillery *eaux de vie*.

Like Gabriel Andreu, one of Cicero's favorites, and Hardy's Fire, with its Daum crystal decanter. On a middle shelf is Louis XIII. And even though it's sixteen hundred a pop, it's easier for Cicero to get than some of the others, so he drinks it like tap water.

Every time Cicero opens his case, traces of chocolate, coffee, and tobacco flee. Hints of eucalyptus and sandalwood present themselves at the second nose. He is truly a connoisseur, and Cicero treasures his collection, which is why he locks the case every night before going to bed.

On the wall opposite the massive flat-screen television, between the half bath and the door to Cicero's bedroom, hang his two framed college degrees. Written in old English, his degrees are authentic, and bear the official signatures to prove it.

A black mahogany bookshelf, nearly twenty feet long and six feet high, features the works of Erik Erikson, Sun Tzu, Niccolò Machiavelli, Sigmund Freud, Socrates, Plato, Aristotle, Albert Schweitzer, Immanuel Kant and Friedrich Wilhelm Nietzsche. On the bottom shelf, a completed Stave puzzle provides the one piece of whimsy.

It was Nietzsche's first title, *The Birth of Tragedy*, that Cicero most favored. Even as the work was criticized by some as assumption-laden and sophomoric, Cicero found it enlightening, and exceptional, as proven by the pages' tattered edges. When Nietzsche proclaimed that God is dead, meaning that traditional values had lost their way, Cicero took it to heart.

God was dead when his father was murdered. God was dead when his boyhood friend drowned. God was dead when crack was unleashed upon his neighborhood. God was dead when Olivia became infected with the AIDS virus.

Nietzsche's concept of the overman, one who is secure, independent, and individualistic, one who feels deeply, but his passions are rationally controlled, further moved Cicero. For Cicero, the overman was one who created his own morality, in which one is liberated from all values, except those he alone deemed valid. And that was what Cicero had done.

Boom. Thunder explodes and rattles nearby homes, but it's not the reason a restless Cicero tosses under his silk sheets and black mink spread. Usually confident, imposing, relentless, C is a little boy again, haunted by troubling night terrors.

The silk sheets make it easier for his muscular physique to flail about as he dreams. Sweat flows.

In this dream, Cicero is grown, sitting at his mother's kitchen table. Everything seems smaller than he remembers. Ruth stands over the stove as she has many mornings, her back to Cicero, preparing the family's breakfast.

Cicero wonders why he's there, naked, in his mother's kitchen.

"Cicero, do you believe in God?" his mother asks.

Her son looks confused, but answers, "No. No, I don't."

"That's a shame, Son," his mother says as she scrambles eggs in that same cast iron skillet.

"Well then, Son, I guess you don't believe in heaven or hell?"

"No. I'm sorry, Mom, but I don't."

He stares out the kitchen window and notices two rottweilers staring at him from the backyard. The day is sunny and hazy.

Ruth shakes her head. Her hair is drawn up tightly in a colorful scarf. Cicero can smell the enticing butter in the pan as it sizzles. His mother then lets out a deep sigh.

"Son, you really should believe in hell," and with that, she turns to look at her son and her face is bloodied and mutilated, eyeballs hanging from the sockets, puss oozing.

Cicero becomes unglued and screams.

"You should, Son! You should!" Worms and maggots dance through her cheeks from one hole to the next. She laughs devilishly and swiftly charges her son with outstretched arms.

Cicero suddenly awakens, frightened and drenched in sweat.

He's shirtless, clad only in boxers. His breathing is rapid, as is his heartbeat. He sits up and checks the digital wall-mounted clock to his right. The large rectangle reads 5:44 a.m. in dull red lines.

Shaken, the avowed gangster and hustler reaches over to the black leather-padded nightstand and dials his mother's number; she was always an early riser.

The phone rings twice, then, "Hello?" Her voice is soothing.

"Hey."

"Cicero?"

"Yea."

"Hey, honey," Ruth says with joy. "Why are you awake so early?" She pauses. "Is there something bothering you, Baby?"

Silence fills the phone for several seconds, as a woman's hand appears from beneath the sheets and begins to rub Cicero's chest.

"Can I come by to see you today?" he asks his mother.

"Of course," Ruth responds. "You know I have to go church, but I can go to the early service. Other than that, I'll be home all day."

"Okay, good."

"Oh, and Lucia is coming by, so you can see her too."

"Really," Cicero tries not to sound surprised. "Okay, cool. Well, I'll see you later on today."

"Okay, Son, see ya later," Ruth says before hanging up.

Cicero gazes over at tonight's companion, she smiles, and he descends under the covers to satisfy both of their primordial urges.

Chapter 9

ater that morning, water runs in one of the black marble double sinks in the restroom. The place is warm and cozy. Cicero sits on a *negro* leather bench in front of the bed buttoning his pale-pink, ultra-soft cotton shirt. It's finely pressed, and matches nicely with his light-gray English-tailored suit.

A newscast blares from the flat screen in the living room on the digital sound system.

"The U.S. Supreme Court is expected to decide tomorrow whether all religious material and historical references to religion, will be completely banned from America's public domain, including schools, libraries, privately owned businesses, and the Internet. Top legal experts close to the matter say the ban is inevitable. For more on the story, we go to the nation's capital..."

Oblivious, Cicero stands and ambles over to a tall, slim, rosewood and glass case that holds his two dozen timepieces. A bright solitary bulb at the top illuminates the case magnificently, highlighting his many Swiss minute hands and bezels, sweeping second hands, multiple complications, one hundred or so total carat weight in diamonds, and over seven hundred and fifty-thousand dollars in gold and platinum. Time is of the essence.

Cicero gazes over the collection for a few seconds, then decides on a plain-face platinum piece with a single flawless carat where the twelve would be. The bracelet is flush and impeccable.

It's Sunday, and since he hasn't shaved in two days, stubble begins to bloom on his face. Shower waters continue running in the restroom. It's 9:18 a.m.

Cicero glides out of his bedroom to his prized cognac mélange, unlocks it, and selects the Louie, pouring it into a simple red plastic cup kept in a cabinet under the glass shelves. The crystal *Trece* bottle is now more than half-empty. Truly the breakfast of victors.

Exquisite dark chocolate appears in the bedroom doorway, fresh from the massaging showerheads. She's five feet eleven without the pumps, and a prime example of what an African queen looks like. She possesses blemish-free skin from face to foot, and tightly wound spiral curls protrude from her head like a God-given crown. Under her towel, her large firm breasts resemble sacred Indian burial mounds.

Cicero looks at her and takes a long sip, thinking, "Damn." His penis jumps beneath his slacks. For a split second he ponders bending her over the sofa and pounding her firm round ass from the back, but decides not to. He's got shit to do.

She strides into the living room with her undergarments and moisturizer in hand, sits on the loveseat, then slides her hot pink thong over her infinite legs. A glimpse of shaven vagina reveals itself. Her lips look like flower petals; eyes set at nearly forty-five-degree angles.

The towel falls to the divan; her bosom, divine. Areola, saucer sized.

"You leaving?" she asks while rubbing cocoa butter on her long stems.

"Yes. You can let yourself out," Cicero says, then takes a swig.

His guest looks disappointed.

The man of the house strolls over to the front door and sits on a mahogany bench where he slides on his Italian loafers.

The mocha queen stands, then turns to enter the bedroom to get dressed, but Cicero stops her.

"Hey," he yells to her.

"What?" she replies with a hint of attitude.

"I need fifty bucks."

She looks stunned.

"What? Um, C, you're ballin', right?" And she smiles.

Cicero just smirks. "How you know I'm ballin'? Let me get that out of you."

His overnight friend goes into the bedroom and retrieves a canary-yellow canvas tote. She walks over to the foyer and pulls out a one-hundred-dollar bill.

"All I have is a hundred," she tells him.

"Cool, that'll work." He snatches it, opens the door and turns to leave, then pauses.

"Hey, on second thought, go ahead and get dressed and leave now."

She frowns. Upset, she hurriedly tosses on her saffron designer dress, grabs the rest of her things, and leaves. Cicero locks the door and heads toward the parking garage and his seductive sport coupe.

Once inside, Cicero places his drink in the retractable cup holder and turns the stereo on. Commercials advertising parties in death-trap locations and rent-to-own centers, seem to be on every station.

Put off, he slides in a CD and increases the volume. The

singer's voice is internationally known, and it helps to calm him. He is still seeing visions of his mother's grotesque appearance.

After exiting the garage, Cicero drives several blocks from his condo, just south of downtown. He passes several Spanish-inspired fountains spewing waters from serpents' mouths and babies' penises. There isn't a cloud in the sky. The music is relaxing, and he takes a swig of his cognac.

Fuck, I need some breakfast, he thinks.

His thoughts then run the gamut: from Olivia to Kam to Brad, to his mother, to his father, and to his sister. He wonders how Brad's work on their new dope is going, and he considers stopping by his house before seeing his mother. As he ponders making a quick detour, he comes to a yellow light and plans to run it, but decides against it, slamming the brakes.

While sitting at the light, he is engulfed in the lyrics of the French African songstress.

"You give me the sweetest taboo."

He feels the tranquilizing melody.

"That's why I'm in love with you."

As he vibes to the slow jam, a moss-green 1968 Camaro pulls up on the left side, but a few feet from the intersection. Cicero glances over and sees only the passenger, a scruffy guy with dirty blond hair.

Cicero turns back to the light, which is amazingly still red. Rock-n-roll thumps from the Camaro and the passenger bobs his head to it. The man then looks over to Cicero, as the sunlight bounces off the coupe's twenty- inch chrome ceiling fans that are still spinning.

The ruffian, clad in a hand-me-down Chiefs jacket, sees his reflection in the rim, and is mesmerized. He grins, looks at

Cicero again, then leans over to his boy in the driver's seat and whispers in his ear. A rear passenger in a filthy peacoat leans forward to hear what they're discussing, then he too looks over at Cicero, then his rims. They're spectacular, and at twelve thousand dollars for the set, they're a liability.

Bored with staring at the light, Cicero glances in his side-view mirror back over at the dudes in the unwashed Camaro, and he notices the sunroof is now open. Cicero is still eyeing it, when the third man in the backseat pops out of the sunroof with a pistol-grip shotgun pointed at his coupe. His bearded face shows heinous intentions. Seeing the weapon, Cicero punches the accelerator and darts through the traffic light that has yet to turn green.

"Come off those rims, bitch," the man in the sunroof yells as he pulls the trigger. The blast shatters Cicero's rear driver's side window, sending glass flying and buckshot into his seat. One grazes the top of his head, breaking the skin.

Cicero's foot is planted in the pedal, cutting corners at breakneck speed. High-performance Japanese tires clutch the asphalt. And even though the Camaro needs some serious body-work, the engine is police chase ready and the driver clings to Cicero's bumper.

"Catch me if you can, you punk-ass bitches," Cicero says to himself in a low voice.

Left, right, straight away. Straight away, right, left, he can't shake the threesome. Since those nights of sneaking out the house in eighth grade and joyriding in stolen cars, Cicero has considered himself an expert driver. But the Camaro's driver is no slouch, and the sunroof gunman fires again, this time taking out the coupe's rear window with a loud blast. Shards of glass spray.

"Blow his motherfucking head off, Stevie," the passenger yells to his cohort. "Stay on his ass, man!"

Driving about eighty miles per hour down a side street, Cicero calmly makes a quick right down a residential block on Forty-Fourth Street. His pursuers follow as an unaware kid rides his bike from the sidewalk toward the street in an attempt to cross it.

Cicero sees the kid out the corner of his eye at the last minute and hits the horn, then swerves to his left, tires screeching. The youngster falls from his bike, but is unscathed, lying safely on the ground between two parked cars. The jackers in the green Camaro zoom by seconds later. They want those rims. They need those rims.

But Cicero's sudden right on the next block and his state-of-the-art German engineering is too much for the American muscle car, which is why the Camaro's driver loses control of the vehicle and it skids to the left, crashing head-on into a towering oak tree. The car's front end is completely crushed, and the engine catches fire. Cicero sees the collision in his rearview mirror and promptly hits the brakes, stopping on a dime. Sade's voice is riveting, and helps keep him composed.

From about fifty feet away, he stares toward the wreckage and observes twitching, movement. They survived the impact. But he is resolved. They deserve to die. They're going to die.

"You mothafuckas wanna try to jack me?" Cicero says to himself. "Okay, I got something for you bitch-ass mothafuckas."

Without missing a beat, he lifts the seat cushion on the passenger side and pulls out a fully automatic submachine gun.

He hops out the silver two-door, seemingly in slow motion. His tailored suit clings to his body.

Seeing Cicero through the engine's flames, sliding to the

left, the Camaro's driver shakes the cobwebs and yells to his armed comrade, "Shoot that mothafucka. He's got a—"

The sunroof gunman stirs, but before the driver can finish his command, Cicero, hunkered down behind a pickup truck, unleashes a flurry of slugs through the driver's side windshield, with a sound similar to a ferociously rolling tongue. Gun smoke pollutes the air, inevitably increasing this midtown neighborhood's asthma rates.

The rounds penetrate the driver's chest, puncturing a lung and chopping his heart, spewing his blood onto the dashboard and out his mouth. He dies instantly.

The passenger, who has just watched his partner take four in the chest, struggles to release himself from his jammed seatbelt.

"Fuck! Fuck! Fuck!" Then, "Yes!"

Finally able to free himself from the restraint, the passenger jumps out of the fiery vehicle and moves laterally to his right, firing rounds from a nine millimeter pistol he had tucked near his navel.

Cicero, not realizing the passenger was armed, is stunned by the slugs that are whizzing by his head. He's baffled, but only momentarily. He's been in shootouts before, which is why he reacts by sliding further to his right, with his weapon's butt pressing firmly against his shoulder. He then lets off three aimed, controlled bursts. The first slug misses just under the shooter's outstretched arm, which is still firing rounds as he moves further across the street.

But Cicero's second slug is successful, and it strikes his target in the middle of his Chiefs jacket, pulverizing his sternum into minuscule fragments of bone, causing him to drop his weapon and yelp. His neck is then aerated by the third and final round, forcing him to gasp for oxygen as blood bubbles in his throat.

Leaking too much necessary fluid, he falls lifeless to the pavement.

Cicero lowers his weapon and stares at the carnage in the street. A few children happen by on bicycles, and gawk in fright at the bloodshed on their block.

"Oh my God, that dude is dead," one points and yells as his friends spin their knobby dirt bike tires faster and disappear around the corner. Unfortunately, these kids have seen dead bodies before.

Slightly embarrassed, Cicero turns to get in his coupe but his peripheral vision catches motion on the right.

The rooftop shooter has regained focus, and he lifts his shotgun toward Cicero, who responds with inhuman quickness and releases nine slugs, Swiss cheesing the would-be killer.

In his mind Cicero hears a voice. It is that of the rounds he's firing. They speak to him: "I am leadened fury. Release me upon thine enemies, oh master, and I shall smite them. My flight ensues, and you shall have your rage enacted upon such transgressors."

At that moment a second thought manifests, seeming to be not his own, "And lo, whilst thee revels in thy triumph, beware of grander vengeance, my master. For your Master is masterless, and he alone claims all rights to vengeance."

Clap. Clap. Clap. Clap. Clap. Clap. Clap. Clap. Clap. Like a Jitterbug dance instructor, the gunman's body trembles and quakes to the steel applause as the hot lead makes his anatomy resemble room temperature margarine.

Cicero dashes back to his coupe, but stops in his tracks when he notices his cognac has spilled on the pavement.

"Fuck," he mumbles, looking at the wasted beverage, before slamming the door and mashing the gas pedal. He hits zero to sixty in 4.6 seconds and is in the wind. Chunks of glass fall from his rear window in large clumps. The single red rear fog lamp has been converted into smithereens.

He heads south up Troost Avenue toward his mother's house, riding his wounded steed. Staring over at his empty cupholder, Cicero is pissed. He decides to pull over at the next liquor store and grab a fifth of Louis.

Sure enough, there's a liquor store on the next block, and he hits the brakes. Glass descends into the backseat. Passersby gape at his vehicle, many in utter amazement. The bullet holes are still fresh. Smoke emanates from several.

Once inside the store, Cicero sees his reflection on a round security mirror. There's a small cut on his forehead from flying glass, and a laceration on the top of his bald head from the near-fatal buckshot. More importantly, Cicero notices he looks...different. Like a sub-humanoid absent of compassion. A person with no inkling of decency, or virtue. A killer.

He ignores it and ambles over to the counter. "You got Louis?"

The Italian behind the counter nods yes, but appears cautious. Cicero looks a mess, and people rarely wander into this ghetto corner store asking for $1,600 cognac. The clerk grips the pistol on his belt as he turns his back to unlock the case holding the requested merchandise.

He sets the crystal bottle on the counter, and Cicero drops $1,600, plus tax, in cash. The storeowner eyes Cicero, and seeing that he had money like that, pretends to be concerned, hoping to establish a rapport with this rich moulie.

"Hey, you look like you were just in a shootout or something," the clerk quips. "You alright there, buddy?"

Cicero just nods yes, and then asks for a cup with ice. The owner retrieves it, then returns and opens his mouth to say, "That will be twenty-five cents."

Cicero frowns. "Are you serious? I just spent over sixteen hundred dollars in here and you're going to charge me for ice?"

"It's not the ice, it's the cup," the clerk states.

Cicero just laughs.

"Fine," Cicero responds, and he throws down another hundred-dollar bill. Cicero quickly snatches his bottle and his cup of ice and heads out the store before the owner stops him.

"Hey, you want a whole bag of ice?"

Cicero ignores him and walks out to his car, cracks open the Louis and, violating cognac rule number one, pours the drink on the rocks. He takes a sip and drives off. Cool breezes and sunshine easily make their way through the auto's newly installed urban ventilation system.

The streets are empty. Only churches, most of them former houses or stores, see steady bustle. Feathered hats and trench coats make their way toward benches and chairs to pay tithes and hopefully absorb the Word. Cicero resentfully stares at the flocks he passes on every other block, sipping his cognac. Some of God's children ogle his fish-netted vehicle with astonishment, and unbeknownst to Cicero, several offer prayers for him during morning services.

The blank-faced man arrives at his mother's house moments later, with a nice buzz, just as his cell phone begins to ring with that unambiguous violin solo.

"Yea," Cicero answers.

"A, man, my stomach hurts," Brad replies from his in-house lab in North Kansas City. Sun lamps and ultraviolet lights illuminate plants behind him, while Bunsen burners heat glass beakers in front of him. Aluminum tubing and blue chemicals conceal the white table where he's working.

"I don't feel like interpreting right now, Bradley. What's the problem?"

"Well, in our initial trial runs with the product, everything was perfect, right?" Bradley asks.

Cicero's end of the line is mute.

Bradley continues, nervously leafing through shorthand scribbled notes and esoteric mathematic equations.

"Well, we've repeated the process, but the compound won't solidify. We've tried everything, but the product is not turning out right."

"That is a problem, Bradley," Cicero responds. A much-needed gulp of cognac slides down his throat. He eyes the cup, and says, "Twenty-five cents," under his breath. "Today has not been my day."

"So what do ya'll wanna do, C?"

Following a deep exhale, C answers, "First, we return J's money, with interest. And then we look over our shoulders for the rest of our lives."

Brad is silent.

"That's going to be a problem too."

"Oh, really, Brad?"

"The money is gone. We spent it all on the chemicals we needed. Equipment, supplies and shit. And your *connect* wanted more money to bring the leaves into the country. Fuckin' jerks. They said some shit about their bosses cracking down on them because of terrorism threats and shit. But anyway, the mixture is damn near worthless, man. Like, we'll have to start from scratch or somethin'."

Cicero pours himself another cup because his ice has melted

and diluted the fine mixture. Sitting in front of his mother's house, he just shakes his head. Early April breezes blow through the vacancy in the rear, chilling his head.

"Well, the money is not a problem, Bradley, just sell the stock in your company, and pay J back his initial investment, plus interest." Cicero's deep voice contains footprints of agitation.

"Stock! Man, are you kidding me?" Brad blurts. "Unfortunately, our young-ass CEO lied to our investors and our stock is pretty much worth shit now."

Cicero pauses before responding.

"Dude, I've known you for a very long time. I trust you. You know this, right?"

"Yea."

"Okay, with that said, get the fucking money," Cicero yells into his phone.

Brad interrupts, "But—"

"But nothing, Bradley. Get J his two point five. Make it happen. Look, dilute the mixture, change it, whatever. I don't give a fuck if you piss in it," Cicero demands, then sips his drink. "Either have the money or the dope. Get your shit together, cuz."

Then he hangs up. He exits the car and staggers up the sidewalk to his mother's front door and knocks.

Ruth is dressed in a lovely white blouse and black skirt when she opens the door.

Her appearance warms his heart.

In less than a second Ruth sees something is amiss, and she hugs her son firmly, holding him for longer than usual.

"Hey, Son. How are you?"

Looking younger than her years, the angelic mother of two

bids her son to enter. He walks past her and Ruth peeks at his buckshot-riddled sports coupe.

"It's good to see you, Son," she says. "You look nice." Her son's suit is the only thing that helps him maintain the ounce of dignity he has left. Ruth frowns as a sliver of glass falls from Cicero's trousers onto her hardwood floor, but she doesn't prod.

"Are you hungry? Have you eaten?"

"Naw, I haven't eaten, but I don't have much of an appetite right now. How was church?" Cicero asks.

"It was nice. Reverend Cleaver delivered the Word today," Ruth says while locking the front door.

They have a seat in the spotless living room, facing each other, with the glass and marble table between them. Over the exposed maroon brick fireplace hangs a framed collage of old and new family photographs. Cicero is without words, but calamity invades his demeanor.

On the table is a large King James version of the Bible. Cicero briefly eyes it, then looks away. Seeing her son's cynicism before her, Ruth inquires, "What's bothering you, Cicero?"

He's silent, then, with eyes to the floor, exclaims, "I had that dream again."

Ruth's lovely face looks troubled.

"What did I tell you, Cicero?

He peers at her sheepishly, then back toward the polyurethane. Even though her son is a bona-fide gangster, he's developing what he's read to be oneirophobia, a fear of dreaming.

"I told you, you had to pray." Ruth's hands are wrinkled and soft, and she rubs them together as she talks. "God will take those nightmares away from you, Son."

She goes on to say something else, but Cicero interjects.

"God. God has the answers, does he?" the skeptic questions. "You wanted me to go to college and get an education, right? Well, I did and I've been taught to rely on evidence, on facts. Not presumptions and wishful thinking."

"Cicero, God is real, and He is loving. Faith is the ultimate venture."

"Loving? Then why was my father murdered? Why was I the product of a sinful affair?"

Ruth is slightly ashamed and without answers, as her son calmly goes on.

"Why do young black children catch stray bullets? Some god you have, Momma. Life is like the weather, unpredictable random chaos. Kneeling and mumbling won't change that."

Since before working for the Kansas City school district, the phone company, and taking computer classes at night, Ruth was never one to complain. It was a trait Antonio also had, and so did Cicero, usually. But today's release was new to Ruth. She never knew Cicero harbored such feelings.

"Well, Son, people have free will," Ruth says. "We decide the paths our lives and our souls will take."

"But what about Olivia? She went to church, didn't smoke or drink, or even curse," states Cicero. "Did she deserve to get AIDS?"

Ruth pauses. She appears tired. Years of sending prayers to heaven for two children have become a burdensome load. She stands and turns to walk toward the dining room, then stops.

"Look, Cicero, I don't have all the answers. Do bad things happen to good people? Yes. Honey, all you can do is be honest, live a moral life, and treat people fairly. And you know what, I will keep praying for you, Son, because I love you."

There's suddenly a light knock at the door.

"I'll get it," Cicero says.

He saunters over and opens the door. His sister has striking natural beauty, but she looks worn out. As she stands there grinning, the baggage under her lovely hazel oval eyes is heavy, aging her beyond her thirty-eight years.

"Well, well, well," Lucia quips. "If it isn't the one and only Cicero."

She steps into the house. In her arms is a one-year-old baby boy. Neatly dressed in a trendy pink velour sweatsuit, her curves are accentuated, but excessive rouge and eyeliner make a failed attempt to conceal many moons of late-night partying and early-morning regrets. Lucia's learned from experience that burnt toast and another vodka tonic are not the magical cure for a hangover.

"How are you, Lucia?" Cicero asks, looking down at his five-foot-six sibling.

"I'm fine," she responds after letting her son stand on his fat wobbly legs. "What the fuck happened to your car?"

"I ran into some knuckleheads."

"Hmm. I bet you did."

The toddler ambles off toward the glass living room table. Lucia is inattentive, as she is with all her kids, so her mother grabs the youngster before he falls and his head is split open on the edge of the glass.

Ruth walks over with baby in hand and shuts the front door behind her daughter to prevent the cool breeze from entering.

"You all want something to drink?" Ruth asks her children. The baby drools on her white blouse.

"I'm fine," answers Cicero, still grasping his cognac-filled plastic cup.

"Yes, I want something to drink. You got some beer?" asks Lucia, smiling.

"Um, no. Well, there may be some beer you left in the fridge from last time," Ruth states. "If not, I have some wine."

"That's cool. Is it zinfandel?" Lucia asks. Her mother doesn't respond as she steps toward the kitchen, and Cicero and Lucia seat themselves in the seldom-used dining room.

"Where's Shaquanda?" Cicero asks of his eldest niece.

"With her father, thank God. She's really starting to get on my nerves. He is too, shit."

There's a brief moment of silence between the two. They haven't seen each other for over three months. They run in different circles with different degenerates. The six-seat table is set, as it always is. Fake aromatic reeds and tulips occupy a sky-blue vase in the middle. Ruth painted it herself one day out of boredom.

Lucia's son is seen stumbling from the kitchen.

"So are you still doing private shows?" Cicero asks his sister. "For the so-called *V.I.P.* crowd?"

"Yep," Lucia quickly replies. "Everybody doesn't have two degrees like you, Cicero."

It doesn't matter to Lucia that his degrees have never earned him an honest paycheck or even a single day's wage.

"Lucia, you don't need two degrees to keep your damn clothes on," her brother tells her in an unfriendly tone. He's usually more cool about it, but faking his dissatisfaction for Lucia's lifestyle takes effort, and today's events have already drained him of that resource. Not to mention he's still fuming about the twenty-five-cent cup.

"Who the fuck are you to talk to me like that?" screams Lucia. "I used to change your funky-ass diapers! Remember that!"

She stands and stomps into the kitchen and grabs the glass of wine her mother has poured. Ruth silently puts away dry dishes that she washed the night before.

Cicero follows his sister into the kitchen.

"You wouldn't be living your life this way if Daddy was around."

"If Daddy what?" Lucia yells. "Look, Daddy already had a family and two daughters. He didn't need, or want, another one. Okay? Especially a black one!"

Ruth's quickly offended and she stops what she's doing to intercede, but Lucia's domineering personality is overwhelming, so she continues to rant.

"And if he already had a son, he wouldn't have *given* a fuck about you either!"

It's suddenly silent. Cicero, in deep thought, peers at the linoleum floor and considers what his sister just said. Then Ruth weighs in.

"Look, you two are family. Family is stronger than anything," she says. "That's one thing your father believed in. Family is stronger than money, and stronger than the streets. You want to argue and fight? Save that for those so-called backstabbing friends of yours. But not in my house."

Cicero's cell phone chirps and interrupts the discussion. He leaves the room and says a few words under his breath. Lucia sips her drink. Her toddler son is nowhere to be seen. Ruth finishes her housework then convenes to the living room for a tension-releasing cigarette. Her white blouse ebbs as she strides.

"Yea, okay," Cicero confirms before ending his call. He slides into the living room and looks at his mother. She's clearly fatigued. Emotionally exhausted.

"I have to go," he tells her. Lucia eyes him from the kitchen and merely shrugs, as her unsteady child tries to make his way up a thirteen-step flight of stairs.

C kisses his mother on the cheek, as he does every time he leaves her blessed presence. She always told him to cherish good-byes, because any one could be the last.

"Good-bye, Mother," Cicero says. He then gazes toward his incensed sister, but she doesn't make eye contact. Drink in hand, he walks back into the small kitchen and tells her in his sincerest voice, "Good-bye, Lucia."

He leans in to kiss her cheek, but she edges away. He's not offended.

"I love you anyway, *sorella*."

Cicero walks out of the house, to be in the wind once again. But before he can get into his battered automobile, Ruth runs outside and catches him.

"Cicero. Wait a minute, Son."

She gets close to him. Close enough to whisper.

"Son, you are not the master of the universe. You need to humble yourself."

Cicero looks at her. Winds blow Ruth's hair into her face and she moves it away with her furrowed hands. Her thin nose and strong cheekbones help her remain as lovely as ever.

"There are forces at work greater than you, and you need to believe that. Call it God, Allah, Yahweh, or whatever, but you need to humble yourself, Son."

He just smiles, then retrieves a knot of hundred-dollar bills from his pocket and slides it into his mother's hand.

"Take this," he tells her, but she's reluctant.

He opens the car door and starts the engine. It purrs.

"Look, if you don't want it, give it to your church. I'm sure the preacher could use another Cadillac."

And with that he drives off, leaving his mother standing there, clutching two thousand dollars.

Ruth saunters back into her home and shuts the door. Crestfallen, she peers at the collage of photographs over the fireplace, then edges closer as a small black-and-white snapshot catches her eye.

Her hair was longer then, fuller and with more sheen. His face didn't yet have the lines that cigarette smoke and scotch provide. She remembers that day, when she and Antonio first met and posed for this photograph. It was one of only a few.

At ninety-five degrees, it was a hot and humid midwestern day. Unleashed energy filled the air, the type of energy that only a Saturday can provide. This is when they met. Purple, red, blue, and green streamers flap from banners when the light breeze strikes them. It was officially titled "Nigger Day": the only day of the year the local amusement park allowed blacks to attend. Ruth's prideful mother forbade her to go as she had every year she asked, but this summer she snuck and went anyway with her best friend.

Generally the piazza was about ninety percent black on this day, with a few European-descended stragglers sprinkled about, still demanding the usual unwritten courtesies and deference typical of this era.

But on this day, Antonio Romello and his crew were among the spread-out minority.

"Come on, Ruth, let's get some cotton candy," her chubby friend Sandy demanded while tugging on her arm. Ruth was always easygoing and eager to please, so she went to the stand where the white vendors looked on with disdainful grimaces.

"What you gals want?" a gruff character asks.

"Two cotton candies, please," Sandy says. The carnie prepares the girls' pink treats with obvious agitation. But their money is green just like that of the white kids who come there throughout the summer, so he serves them nonetheless.

The park is festive. Clowns and streamers and vivid colors are surrounded by laughing kids and cheerful teenagers.

Bobby socks, long straight skirts, French rolls, and straightened hair flood the park. Guys in pressed blue jeans and button-down shirts gaze at the young ladies as they stroll through the crowds giggling.

"Oh! Ruth! We just have to ride the Tornado," Sandy insists with a mouth full of cotton candy, tugging on her friend's arm.

"No, Sandy, I can't. What if we get hurt or somethin'? If my momma found out she would kill me," Ruth says. Her full breasts bulge through the off-white blouse her mother made.

"Oh, Ruth. It's just a little rolla' coaster. And yo momma ain't gonna find out. She's probably at home drunk."

Ruth's face goes red. Her half-Cherokee mother grew up on an Oklahoma Indian reservation where drinking fire water and passing out or fighting was commonplace. And the mother of two carried that trait with her to Kansas City when she ran away from home as a teenager.

"That's not funny, Sandy."

"I'm sorry, girl, but she won't know. Come on, let's ride it."

Bouffant hair bounces and black-and-white saddle shoes kick up sand and gravel as the girls run to get in line for the popular Tornado. Sweat runs down their faces and backs with the sun beaming on them. Their virgin brown skin glistens in the heat.

And that's when they make eye contact. He would tell his friends it was her eyes that fascinated him the most, and she would say the same.

"Jimmy, you see her? She's fuckin' beautiful," Antonio says of the voluptuous Ruth. He's clean-cut in a snug white T-shirt and blue jeans. His black hair is slicked back.

"Who you talkin' about, Tony?" a chubby Jimmy asks.

"That colored chick over there, she's unbelievable. I don't know what it is, but she's fuckin' gorgeous."

His friends laugh.

"Get the fuck outta here. You bring her to the neighborhood and you'll both be runnin' for your fuckin' lives," Jimmy yells. The guys stand in line for the Tornado with Ruth and Sandy right behind them. The park's segregation policy was out the window this day, allowing unheard-of first glances to evolve into affection, passion, and new life.

Ruth notices Antonio's gaze, and she becomes flushed in response.

Not one to be shy, Antonio speaks up first.

"Hey, how ya doin'?"

Ruth and Sandy are shy, and unsure of how to react.

"I'm fine," she answers with a wide grin, looking down. Her teeth are snow-white and perfectly aligned. Since Ruth's family never complimented her on her looks, she fails to realize she truly is beautiful, and a compliment from an Italian boy was the ultimate form of praise, especially in Kansas City. These were the days when a black woman was usually a maid, or a nanny, or a housekeeper. Dolled up in her veiled hat and white gloves, she was docile, but quietly courageous. And often, in the concealed thoughts of others, she was seen as beautiful, by all races.

"Oh yea? So you been here before?"

"No," Sandy butts in. "Ruth's momma won't let her."

Ruth just smiles.

"Oh really?" Antonio asks. A red-and-white pack of Marlboros protrudes out his back pocket.

"So you're a good schoolgirl, Ruth?"

"Yes, I am."

The line moves and Jimmy slaps his friend's arm.

"Come on, Tony, leave them colored broads alone."

Sandy gives Jimmy an evil look, and he turns back around.

"So your name is Tony?" Ruth asks.

"Antonio. But my friends call me Tony."

Ruth laughs.

"So what do you want me to call you?" His interest has unleashed a never-before-seen flirtatious side of her. Sandy is dumbfounded.

"You can call me whatever you want, gorgeous."

The ride's operator opens the gate and motions to Jimmy and his crew to board the ride.

"Come on, you two are riding with us."

Tony pushes Sandy into the two-seater car with Jimmy and he takes Ruth by the hand and leads her to their car.

Jimmy is pissed, as is Sandy, and they frown at each other.

The unlikely foursome spends most the day together. Riding rides, and inviting stares from everyone in the park, black and white. One park employee went as far as to deny them access to the Ferris wheel.

"We don't allow that here," the old bearded man said, meaning interracial mingling.

For years, like many American cities, Kansas City's design was that of segregation. Certain streets were and still are well known as racial barriers. Twelfth Street to the north, Twenty-

Seventh Street to the south. Indiana to the east, and The Paseo to the west. Crossing them could mean jail time, beatings, or filed missing persons reports.

Despite years of master-slave rape and even love affairs such as that of Thomas Jefferson and Sally Hemings, miscegenation was the worst taboo, publicly anyhow. Even cavorting with the olive-skinned Italians and Sicilians, who ironically had mixed blood with the Ethiopians, Egyptians, Moroccans and other Africans for centuries, was grounds for ostracism.

But on this day in the park, Ruth and Antonio fell for each other, for all of the Show Me state to see. He liked her innocence. She liked his charisma. He liked her beauty, she the power he exuded. Jaws dropped at the sight of them together. A few whites contemplated phoning the nearest KCPD precinct.

Jimmy and Sandy were the most uncomfortable, but they respected their friends too much to interrupt their fun, even though the tension was enough to suffocate a small child. Besides, it was one year after Alan Shepherd made his historic visit to space, so an inculpable Ruth thought anything was possible.

A young couple of fifteen or so pops out of a tiny photo booth grinning as wide as the Missouri River. Their snapshots, taken behind the shield of a yellow, orange and red-striped curtain, would be a treasured reminder of the glorious time they had in the hot sun at Nigger Day.

Antonio spots the booth.

"Hey, Ruth, would you like to take a picture?"

She thinks for a moment, then answers with a smile, "Yea, sure." Short bangs hang just above her slanted eyes.

The sixteen-year-olds run over to the booth, take a seat,

then pull the colorful curtain closed, leaving only their lower legs and feet exposed. Antonio drops a shiny dime into the machine, then *flash*.

They laugh.

Flash!

Antonio kisses Ruth's cheek.

Flash!

She blushes.

Flash!

They smile.

Kids of all ages and sizes run freely through the park eating nickel pretzels and hot dogs, toting huge stuffed animals with adult-like arrogance. They cherish this scrap of a day thrown to them.

The four prints come out, and the black-and-white technology helps further distinguish the couples' opposite skin tones.

Sandy steps in. "Ruth, we have to go. It's getting late, and yo momma's gon be lookin' for you."

Ruth looks at her friend and realizes she's right. Lost in Tony's aura, she'd forgotten about her strict mother and that switch she used to tan her hide.

"What are you doing tomorrow, Ruth?" Antonio asks.

"I have to go to church with my momma," Ruth tells him. "My daddy's the preacher." Ruth's father was an uncaring philanderer who was rarely home, but he preached the Word with the enthusiasm of a homebound Israelite. Ruth loved him regardless.

Later that same year, the Supreme Court would decide that prayer in the public schools was unconstitutional, even though just a few years earlier the phrase "under God" was added to the Pledge of Allegiance. But in those days, religion was seen as an indicator of anti-Communism, not a conviction of the soul.

"Well, maybe I'll see you around," Antonio tells the beautiful Ruth, who shines her bright smile at him.

And he would see her around. They would meet every once in a while over the next few months, going on long walks and talking for hours, most of which was done in complete and total secret. Years later, after Antonio was married to his white and publicly acceptable wife, Ruth would become pregnant with Lucia, without knowledge of Tony's nuptials.

By the time Cicero was conceived, she knew he was married, but her love for him was deeper then the Dead Sea. His union was a sham, as many are, but even still, Ruth came to respect it, and their relationship as lovers would fizzle away, against Tony's wishes.

Ruth stares at the small black-and white-photograph, wondering how her life could have been different if she never met the dashing Romello. Maybe her father would have let her stay, maybe she could have accepted one of the college scholarships she was offered.

Lucia's son falls from the staircase and smacks his head on the hardwood floor. His uncontrollable wailing brings an end to Ruth's brief and infrequent moment of self-pity, and she runs to his aid.

Chapter 10

While driving north down The Paseo passing moss-covered fountains, Cicero calls Kam back.

"Hello?" Screaming and yelling is heard in the background, along with dogs barking. He's got seven hundred and fifty dollars on a tan three-year- old pit bull named Yola, known for locking on rear legs, then rolling like an Everglades alligator.

"Hey, you ready?" Cicero asks. Cold air enters unfettered from near the trunk, giving his neck goose bumps.

"Just about, my dog is up next, hold on."

Kam removes the phone from his ear and in seconds Yola has shot for the left hind leg of a thinner, younger, dark-brown pit. This dog should have never been in the ring with the more experienced, more vicious Yola. Moments later the leg has been gnawed, masticated and removed like a scene from a South African shark attack.

"Damn!" Kam yells.

The bloody stump leaks from Yola's jaw as his victim yelps and twitches in utter anguish. Yola's owner steps over and tries to pry the drippy prize from the dog's mouth, and the canine growls in full resistance.

"Yea, C," Kam says smiling, exposing his baguettes and platinum. "Meet me at the crilla."

"Cool," his friend responds before taking another sip of his cognac.

XXX

Running water tingles the sense of hearing upon entering the minimalist's home. Ten-foot ceilings allow ample space for the seven-foot rock waterfall fountain in the corner. The sound is refreshing.

Cream-painted hardwood floors span the loft from wall to wall, minus the tiny kitchen. In the center of the large room is a wood-framed futon juxtaposed to an exact clone. Between the two is a narrow hand-carved pine table with bear's paws for feet.

After Kam takes his sneakers off, Cicero removes his loafers at the door. He knows Kam's house rules.

"You want a drink?" Kam asks, before realizing he already had one, not to mention the bottle. "Oh, I don't even know why I asked."

He'd searched high and low for the authentic Japanese tea set placed on the stone-based glass table behind the futon. For the set to be strictly for show, the search may have been too expansive.

Without a doubt, the focal point of the room is the twelve-foot long, five-foot high, hand-painted rendering of a seaside Samurai battle.

Ancient combat plays out on a picturesque beach. With swords drawn, opposing warriors on horseback converge in a fight to the death. White-caps pound the shore in the background in their own climactic war of nature versus nature. Trademark mustaches and highly animated eyes of the feudal aristocracy make profound statements in this epic saga to decide the fate of the Japanese Empire. The steeds too have a sense of purpose, and mortality, as they are also prepared to die.

For Kam, the depiction defined life on Earth, for it is a scene of conflict. There is no life without conflict, Kam often thought, for it was all he knew. And that's all he ever saw or read, so to escape it, he chose not to own a television. His only source of entertainment or news comes from a bantam high-tech stereo, well hidden in a kitchen cabinet. Wireless speakers are buried in the walls, offering quality as well as discrete sounds.

Freshly squeezed juices and bottled water fill the Sub-Zero fridge. One cabinet overflows with multivitamins, milk thistle, ginseng, St. John's Wort, vitamin B complex, cod liver oil pills, beta-carotene tablets and orange-flavored vitamin C chewables. Even though Kam indulges in liquor and drugs, he does his best to offset the effects. Some shit he heard a rapper talking about.

The trickling sound of the elevated fountain is quite soothing. Kam's loft is one of the only places outside of his own home where Cicero truly enjoys being.

Flames cavort in a gas-controlled fireplace along the far wall. Regardless of the weather or the temperature, the brass-encompassed flames burn. It's a part of Kam's balanced approach to living; at least within his home's confines. Despite his barbarous shortcomings and outward flamboyance, Kameron's living quarters reflect the sensibility of Asian emperors. Some shit he saw in a movie.

Numerous palm trees sprawl out. Kam is careful to water them according to their need. This is the second batch. He killed the first few he had by overwatering them, so now he's more mindful.

"So where's your girl?" Kam asks.

"She just texted me. She's trying to find a parking spot."

While Kansas City is known for its wide-open spaces, Kam's apartment sits in one of the most congested midtown neighborhoods, filled to the brim with transients, weirdos, prostitutes, hobos, and losers.

There's suddenly a succession of feathery rapid-fire knocks at the door.

"Come in!" Kam yells from across the room as he sits on the futon and opens a plastic bag of red-haired marijuana. His deep voice booms.

A petite caramel-skinned beauty enters, carrying two large black plastic trash bags.

"Kam, you need to check those homeless mothafuckas downstairs," the cutie says while removing her altitude-boosting black boots. Her truck driver mouth contrasts with her actress face and her delicate green eyes. "One tried to grab my ass." An eight-button sleek leather coat clings to her defined shoulders and hugs her spherical derrière.

Kam just laughs. The lemon-yellow velour sweatsuit he wears is plush and vibrant.

"You should have smacked him," he tells her.

"No, I should have shot him," she retorts, hair purposely untamed. "Hey, Cicero, how you doin'?"

"Fine. How are you?" he asks, seated in his gray suit at the other futon with his drink.

"Just tryin' to make a livin', you know?"

"I heard that."

She steps into the center of the loft and looks around. The bags appear to be heavy, but with her many hours spent in the gym she has no problem lugging them about.

"So where you want it?" she asks Kam.

He looks up from the table. His fingers vigorously break down the sticky weed without looking at it.

"Right there is cool."

"Okay," she responds, then dumps the two big bags on the floor. Recently stolen designer shoes and hand-knitted sweaters spill out, all in various sizes and bearing authentic store price tags.

Cicero and Kam gaze at the seductive pile.

"Look, those Allen Edmonds were kinda hard to get, but I got a couple pairs," the girl says. Her craft is age old, and she is a tenacious five-foot-three student of the art.

"You got any Thomas Pink shirts over there?" Kam asks. His blunt is rolled and he ignites it, taking a big puff. A small circular terra cotta ashtray captures the embers.

"Yea, there's a couple in here, and some short-sleeved Lacoste in solid colors," she answers. Her voice is sweet and high pitched. She unbuttons her jacket and tosses it on the arm of the futon. A tiny T-shirt exposes her sexy flat midsection.

"What's up with that Patek Philippe?" Cicero weighs in as he searches through the textile mass.

"I'm working on it. Those watches are kinda hard to come by," she says. Thick thighs bulge through her tight low-rise jeans, which allow a scarlet silk thong to see the world. "I'm working on this square cat at Pivoli's jewelry store, so it shouldn't be much longer. But I'll let you know when I get my hands on one."

"That's cool, just let me know."

Kam decides Lana has come across some good plunder, so he inquires about the entire lot.

"How much for all of it? I can give my little cousins the shit that don't fit."

Lana thinks for a moment, then says, "Just give me two."

He immediately reaches into his bulging pocket and pulls out a stack of hundred-dollar bills, and counts out two-thousand dollars and hands it to her.

"Cool," she says, while stuffing the wad in her red lace bra between her firm breasts. "Alright, then, you guys be good." She turns to leave but then stops in her tracks.

"Oh yea, my great aunt died last week," she tells her clients.

"Damn, Lana, I'm sorry to hear that," Cicero says.

"Yea, I know you stayed with her. You need anything? You straight?" Kam asks.

"No, I'm cool, but fuck her. She was mean as hell," Lana responds.

Kam and Cicero chuckle.

She continues, "Shit, I'm taking bids on her social security number right now. Bitch has flawless credit. You know it'll take the IRS like ten years to figure out she's dead and recycle it."

"Yea, I know," Kam says, then flashes his diamonds with a laugh. "You said she had good credit?"

Cicero looks interested. Cascading water flows in S patterns down the stony fountain.

"Man, she had a seven hundred-fifty beacon score," Lana yells with the enthusiasm of a teenager.

"Damn," Cicero and Kam respond in unison.

"Where's the bid right now?" Kam asks. Unpaid schools loans from years ago remain on his scarred credit report.

"Right now it's at like five thousand dollars," she says.

"Is that it? Shit, I'll give you seven thousand dollars right now," Kam tells her.

She thinks about it for a second, then chooses to decline his offer.

"Naw, I'm okay, I'm waiting to see how these bids pan out. I got some Mexicans on the West Side that might really come through with some real money. You know they need work visas and shit."

"That's cool. If they don't come through, come holler at me," Kam says.

"Alright. Alright, C, alright, Kam," Lana says as she opens the door to leave.

"Okay, baby, be careful out there," Cicero says.

She just giggles. "I thought you knew." And she returns to the realm of undercover security guards, five-finger discounts, and attorney's fees.

Kam shovels the clothing and shoes back into the bags and places them near his informal closet; the untidiness is disturbing the tranquility of his loft.

Cicero pours himself another drink, and takes a moment to exhale.

"Man, did I tell you some assholes tried to blow me up," Cicero calmly tells his friend.

"For real?" Kam asks as he tokes his blunt and begins to cough. "What was that shit about?"

"I don't know, but I think they wanted my twenties."

"Damn. They tried to take your head off for your Barry Sanders?"

"Yea, I guess," Cicero answers. "That's crazy, huh?"

Kam hits his weed again and holds it for ten seconds before exhaling. His lips are becoming blacker by the day.

"So I guess since I'm talking to you," Kam says, "it's safe to say you introduced their insides to the outside world?"

Cicero nods in the affirmative.

"That's cool." Kam begins coughing violently, on the verge

of coughing up a lung. Snot trickles from his nose and he wipes it with his sleeve.

"Whoa, this is some good shit," Kam exclaims. "You sure you don't want to hit this, dog?"

"Naw, I'm cool," Cicero says as he takes a sip of his liquor. "But thanks for offering."

"Hey, anytime," Kam says politely. "So you know who they were?"

"Who?" asks Cicero. Just that quick other thoughts have clouded his mind.

Frustrated, Kam says, "Man, the mothafuckas that tried to give your head a permanent part."

"Oh. I don't know. Some sick-ass white boys. Irish cats, I think."

Kam looks as if he's thinking while he takes another drag from Mary Jane.

"Damn. Some white boys? Dude, the economy must truly be fucked up for some white boys to resort to jacking people."

Cicero laughs.

"Tell me about it," C answers.

"I mean, for real, that's generally not their style, you know?" Kam asserts as his high begins to kick in and the philosopher in him takes over. "You know, they might get down with some computer hacking, or maybe molesting some little kids, or somethin'. You know? Some sicko shit. Serial killing and shit. But jackin'? That's wild."

"I know," Cicero simply responds. But he knows people, regardless of race, are capable of anything, especially in hard times. Pressure either crushes, or creates diamonds. The ass-holes who tried to jack him allowed the pressure of greed to place them on an anvil. And Cicero gladly took on the role of the sledgehammer.

"Oh, and just so you know," Cicero weighs in while pouring himself another drink, "the product isn't looking too good."

Kam perks up.

"It's not a total wash. I don't think," continues Cicero, "it's not going according to plan, though."

"Fuck, are you serious?" Kam asks, fingernails clenching the smoldering roach. "Damn. So I guess we can expect drama from Jimmy?"

"Yea. Just anticipate it. You know? Stay on your toes."

"Oh, that's always, homeboy. I thought you knew?"

"But I told you that for a reason."

"Oh, yea?"

"Yea. I need you to do something for me."

"Shit. Just say the word, cuz."

Cicero stands from the futon and ambles over to the kitchen, and returns with a pen and a sheet of paper.

"When you get a chance, go to this address for me, and holler at Bradley." Cicero checks his platinum watch. "He likes playing golf there, usually on Mondays, I think. And check it out, I'm going out of town for a while, hittin' a few spots, so maybe in, like, a few weeks, go holler at him. Cool?"

"Alright. So what's the plan? I mean, what do you want to happen?"

"Just put something in his ear. You feel me?"

"I got you."

Cicero hands him the slip of paper as the fountain's cool waters rush down the sloped rocks.

"Now, Kameron, you know Bradley is my friend. Right?"

"Man, I got you. Not a problem."

Cicero knows sometimes people need that extra push. While he doesn't necessarily want Brad harmed, he does want to kick-start his engine. And Kameron can be one hell of a motivational speaker.

Cicero checks his timepiece again.

"Well, I got to get out of here. I'm fuckin' starvin'. Might get some Gates."

"Yea, I got some shit to do, too," Kam replies, and they both stand, feeling woozy. "And C, why don't you go ahead and take my truck, man. Your shit is fucked up. Your Escalade still getting worked on?"

"Yea. Fuckin' Mexicans fucked up my electrical system."

"For real? Fuck that. But yea, I'll have my guy come pick your shit up and take it to the crusher."

"Yea, okay," Cicero answers. "You still got that plug at State Farm?"

Kam smiles and nods yes.

"Cool. I'm going to write off some extra shit, like that original Matisse I bought in Paris for my mom's birthday."

And they both laugh.

"You know I had one in my backseat," Cicero says with a grin.

"Hey, I'm not mad at you. That's what you're supposed to do," Kam says. "But why you bullshittin'? You know my boy Jacque works at that art gallery on Southwest Trafficway. He could probably hook you up."

"Oh for real? Cool. I'ma go holler at him."

They start to walk out when Cicero's thoughts jump to a completely unrelated topic.

"A, so have you thought about going back to school?"

Caught off guard, Kam asks, "Where the fuck did that come from?"

"Man, I was just wondering."

Kam pauses and looks at his friend.

"Actually, I thought about it. But you know how it is. **Gettin'** this paper now," he says as he grips the blunt, now mere millimeters in length. He goes to take a hit and the cinders burn his lips. "Ouch. Shit."

Cicero starts to laugh.

"No, for real. You should think about that."

"Yea, I know. That's what my Mexican weed man keeps telling me," Kam says. Then in a Mexican accent, he adds, "He says, 'Bro, you should go to school, cuz. These streets are evil, cuz.'"

They both start laughing.

"Well, your weed man might be right."

"Yea, I know. But fuck him. I'm about to start getting all my shit in Canada. The price is right, and it's fire. Like that K-Town."

"That reminds me, I need to call my Mexican snowman," Cicero says.

"Yep, you don't wanna get caught with no product, missin' paper," Kam explains.

"I know."

And they depart from the serenity of feng shui. Waters run and flames burn despite their absence.

Chapter 11

Ropes of burgundy pepperoni, oregano, and marjoram-spiced sausage hang from steel racks attached to the ceiling. Chattering and ringing bells from archaic cash registers happen to drown out the conversation of two important men who are discussing weighty and clandestine matters.

"How the Royals gonna do this year?" a tall man asks his fat boss.

"First of all, they need some real pitchers, that's the first fuckin' thing," Jimmy says. His voice is rough. "A closer. Somebody who can get some saves under his belt."

He points to a wheel of aged ivory-yellow Parmesan and the clerk quickly cuts off about a pound and weighs it: It's one-point-one pounds.

"Yea, but they don't have any power hitters either," the tall man says.

"Well, yea, but that comes second. You don't give up ten hits a game and expect to win."

They walk along the long glass case inspecting the day's meats and cheeses.

"Well, to be honest, Jimmy, the franchise has gone downhill ever since the eight-six season, after they got Bo Jackson."

"Yea, honey, what else can I get you?" a young butcher asks

an elderly Italian donna, who requests an extra slice of shaved ham to get her purchase right at one and a half pounds.

"What?! Are you fucking kidding me?" Jimmy is irate and his hand motions suggest that as they jut back and forth. "Bo Jackson's one of the greatest athletes to ever live."

Herbs and cheeses emit nostalgic fragrances from behind the spotless glass case.

"Yea, but—" The tall man doesn't quite agree.

"No, fuck that," Jimmy says, cutting him off. "This town should be happy he ever played here."

The deli is busy as usual. Baby boomers, with their liver spots and wrinkled faces, bark out orders to the half-dozen hurried bakers and butchers.

"This guy played two major league sports and went to the all-star games for both," Jimmy continues.

The tall man nods in agreement, so Jimmy calms.

"But that was years ago, they need to worry about today. Fucking Martinez and Lopez aren't going to get the fucking job done. I'll tell ya that," he concludes.

"Let me get half a pound of the kosher corned beef," an elderly Jewish man asks, his hands quivering with old age.

"I'll tell ya what, they need another George Brett," the tall man weighs in, causing Jimmy's eyebrows to raise.

"Look, don't get me wrong, Brett was a consistent player, but fuck him. The guy's a fucking asshole," Jimmy exclaims. He stops strolling along the glass case and looks the tall man in the eyes. "Me and Jimmy Jr. waited after a Twins game once. And this fucking asshole comes out and doesn't sign my kid's autograph book."

The tall man looks shocked.

"Really?" His voice is deep and steady.

"Yea. He's a prick. I seriously thought about having him kneecapped, but it was late September and the Royals were just a game and a half back."

The tall man nods again.

"You know what I mean?" Jimmy emphasizes. "What are ya gonna do?" He throws his hands up in disgust, as they begin walking again.

"So what are you going to do about that little situation?" the tall man asks. His eyes are dark and menacing.

"You mean the one involving Cicero?" Jimmy's voice is booming, but no one is listening. They're too busy trying to order the last of the pumpernickel and humus.

"Yea. That needs to be rectified, don't you think?"

Word gets out fast in K.C. Leaks abound. The grapevine is intense. Good gossip is power; underworld gossip is omnipotent. Without Cicero's knowledge, his connects know there's a problem with the product, which means a potential problem with the return on their investment.

"Yea, that's good. And let me get two pounds of fresh mozzarella," Jimmy tells the clerk. "First, two things," he says to his associate as he wheezes. "One, Cicero is a man of his word and a man of loyalty. I used to run numbers with his father, for God's sake. And we did a lot more than that, believe me."

The tall man listens closely. His face is without expression as he keeps his hands in the pockets of his black leather jacket.

"So if there is a problem, I know I'm going to get my money back, with interest," Jimmy continues. Even though he owns numerous businesses, he wants his money. All his money, even money that isn't his.

Foot traffic at the deli increases. The front door swings open every few seconds, inviting chilly winds and WWII veterans and widows inside.

"And two," he adds, "they might be expecting us to act. I would think that if I were them." His camel hair coat hovers just above the white tile floor. "Hey, this time, just two pounds of that sausage," Jimmy tells the butcher. "I'm trying to watch my cholesterol."

The butcher nods and grabs about a foot of links and weighs them before wrapping the meat in wax paper and plastic.

Jimmy turns back to his associate. At that moment, his cell phone rings from his coat's inside pocket. He checks the caller ID.

"Well, well. Speak of the devil," Jimmy says before answering the phone. "Hello, young man. How's business?"

"It's slow goin'," Cicero communicates over the phone.

"That's not good to hear," Jimmy says. "I expect better from you."

Cicero pauses.

"I know. I'll take care of it," Cicero tells him.

"Good. See that you do." And Jimmy closes the flip phone, ending their discussion.

Then he looks up at the tall man.

"Look, we'll give them some time, a couple months. See if they get their act together. I don't want to act impulsively. You know I never have. Learned that from my father."

He willfully stares into the tall man's dark eyes.

"Nothing happens unless I say so. You understand?"

The tall man cherishes his role of enforcer. Cicero could identify him as having antisocial personality disorder, making him cruel and violent, without the baggage of guilt or remorse. But today, he's caged.

"Understood," he assures his obese boss.

He then glides out of the deli, past old men and women, with restrained intentions in his heart.

"Okay, Johnny, what do I owe you?" Jimmy asks the butcher while fingering through a five-inch stack of twenties and fifties.

Chapter 12

Sunday afternoon, mammoth forty-eight-inch tires harass the pavement as Cicero cruises north down Wornall Road in Kam's shiny black flatbed truck. The new four-door model's interior is luxuriously fitted with all the bells and whistles including a navigation system, a DVD player, and five flat-screen televisions.

Cicero takes a sip of cognac and looks around the cabin. His own SUV is still in the shop. Cicero and his like aren't going to drive their vehicles unless everything is perfect. Even after driving Kam's truck for a week, he still hasn't gotten used to it.

"Damn. Kam, do you have enough shit in here?" he thinks out loud. Children of nothing often overdo it when they're finally able to. Subtlety is not in their repertoire.

Plush trees obscure homes of five-thousand square feet and up. Cicero passes estate sales and mini-vans en route to a meeting with Olivia in one of Kansas City's most affluent areas. It is an area of inheritances and judo-trained butlers, where power of attorney is the ultimate power.

Scattered clouds slowly pass overhead as thoughts race through Cicero's mind. Hip-hop knocks through Kam's tremendous twenty-speaker sound system.

As Cicero contemplates why people do stupid shit, a soccer mom darts in front of him, nearly causing him to rear-end her

Swiss-made station wagon. She's late for her daughter's recital, and the au pair is off today so no one was there to remind her. Cicero slams the brake.

"Stupid-ass bitch," he mumbles to himself. His words defy his usually laid-back persona.

Geese fly above in a checkmark formation, headed for their winter sabbaticals.

Cicero passes a woman in her mid-thirties jogging behind her red Irish setter. Five-thousand-dollar obedience school offsets the need for a leash. It better had.

He makes a left into the large crescent-moon gravel drive, eyeing families of four and couples out on first dates. His drink waxes to the left in the red plastic cup.

After parking he steps out of the truck and glances at those in the park. Frisbees whiz through the air while golden retrievers snag sticks and receive congratulations from their well-off owners. These seventy-four acres of trees and rolling hills have seen decades of visits from the upper echelon.

And there on a wood and black iron bench, those dark curly tresses flow with the occasional light gale. Her tan suede jacket stops just before her touchable hips begin to protrude through her snug low-rise blue jeans.

Cicero strolls toward her sipping his cognac, past an intimate red-wine and Gouda-cheese lesbian picnic and a huge French poodle taking a crap. His all-black Italian suit looks somewhat odd in a city park full of fleece and denim.

Olivia sees him and looks up. Her beauty is astounding, but she has become the epitome of sadness, and she exudes it.

Cicero takes a seat next to her, his ebony loafers narrowly missing some kid's chewed bubble gum.

"What's on your mind, O?" he asks before taking a swig of his cognac. She sent him an urgent text message, so he responds with promptness.

"I've been thinking. I, I can't do this anymore. I can't work for you anymore."

Her eyes are in their perpetual state of red swollenness. Olivia has endured much in her young life.

Just two years ago, shortly after she found out her positive HIV status, both her parents died in a disastrous car accident. While pursuing some teenagers in a stolen car across the state line into Kansas, the KCPD slammed into her parents' Ford head-on. Her mother, riding in the passenger seat, wasn't wearing her seatbelt and was decapitated as she flew through the windshield. Her head was found some twenty yards away. The first emergency workers on the scene said she was smiling.

The force of the crash turned the steering wheel into a deadly scalpel and it peeled her father's face like a ripe banana, leaving the space a blank bloody mess resembling a real-life Picasso.

Cicero ponders her words. He looks out over the pond in front of them as two birds fight over a piece of bread.

"You know, Olivia, life is crazy. I've seen the worst of it from as far back as I can remember." The smell of pine fills his nostrils. Olivia's eyes are down as she rubs her manicured nails together.

"And as far back as I can remember, I've kept everything inside. Mostly because real men don't discuss their pain, you know how it is. That's a sign of weakness." He looks over at Olivia. "But I know that pain has festered there. It has grown into this cancer, this disease that lives in me. That's real."

Olivia looks up at him.

"And you know what? I tried to pray about it," Cicero says, then sips his drink. Olivia's eyes squint. She's never once heard Cicero say he prayed, or had any belief in a higher power.

"I used to," he continues, talking with pronounced hand gestures. "It wasn't often, not often at all, for real. After my father was murdered, I just lost faith. I mean, I was an altar boy and everything, did you know that?"

Olivia shakes her head no.

"I was. Yep. I was, I guess, eight when my best friend Gary drowned right in front of me, and about a year later I saw my next-door neighbor murder his cousin, then blow his own brains out." He laughs. "I've seen some fucked-up shit."

Olivia looks a bit relieved, as if Cicero's misery has helped to alleviate her own. Symbolic notations on plaques along the southwestern edge of the park mark the Battle of Westport, where armies clashed and lives were lost.

"You know, I wish there was no such thing as murder, or crime or drugs. I really do. But one day when I was about sixteen, I found myself getting on my knees to say my prayers, and something just clicked inside."

"And what was that?" Olivia asks.

"I just thought, 'What the fuck am I doing?' This is the real world where real bullets fly and good people get turned into a buffet for fuckin' roaches and maggots. And I realized that I could step one foot outside my house and get plowed down at any moment. Just like that."

"But it doesn't have to be that way."

"Yea, but that shit happens every day, so why couldn't it happen to me? It's Murphy's law. I mean really, look at what happened to you."

Olivia appears uncomfortable and she squirms.

"So fuck it. That's why I do what I do."

The chilly winter prevents the four-thousand seedlings in the park's rose garden from breathing new life. Cicero and Olivia's conversation echoes off the circular stone-quarried courtyard, which has been host to hundreds of weddings and joyous celebrations over the years.

"You were innocent enough, not conniving or corrupt, you know," Cicero comments, then takes a swig of his aged brown. "But look at your predicament. I feel sorry for you. I really do care about you, Olivia. You're like my little sister."

He pauses. A new pair of New Balance sneakers pedals by on a mountain bike, followed by a smaller pair of New Balances on a smaller bike of the same color. The blond youngster giggles as he tries to keep pace with his father.

Cicero lets the twosome proceed past him and Olivia, then he continues.

"I'm sure the money I pay you has allowed you and your grandmother at least some peace of mind. I don't think you're worried about where your next meal is coming from, right?"

Olivia shakes her head no.

"It's wrong, Cicero. I was raised in the church, and so were you. We can't go on living like this. It ain't right."

Olivia looks up and notices a large canary-yellow dragonfly-shaped kite soaring in the cool blue sky above. The kite's handler makes it dance and barrel roll first to the right, then counter-clockwise. Twin red tails stream behind the artificial odonate.

She goes on.

"If you believe there's an afterlife—"

"I don't," Cicero interjects. A light breeze flows through the budding trees.

"Well, I believe in heaven and hell," Olivia tells him as she looks Cicero in the eyes. "And when I die, I want to go to heaven. Call me stupid or naïve, but I do."

There's a long pause. She wipes her face in frustration. Cicero takes a sip from his red cup. An elderly man wearing a blue baseball cap strolls before them and tosses some breadcrumbs on the sidewalk. Since the late 1950s, his tattered vest has concealed tons of shredded Wonder bread.

Cicero stands and looks over at Olivia, who has buried her face in her hands.

"Well, I need you, and your grandmother needs you."

She exhales as Cicero finishes off the rest of his cognac.

"And don't worry about it. If your Bible is right, then your God will forgive you."

And he leaves, walking through the murder of birds that part and scatter as the old man tries to offer them more of his pocketed fare.

Olivia sits motionless, staring at the stationary water. A fountain bubbles inside a large veranda nearby.

She eyes the ducks in the pond, majestic above the water, and kicking like hell below. The New Balanced pair has cleared the circumference of the park, and Olivia decides it's time to go. She stands and then traverses a short narrow-planked bridge that arches over a runoff of the pond surrounded by lily pads and ferns.

She looks back over her shoulder at the family of ducks treading water, and she smiles.

Chapter 13

It's a Monday morning, and the infamous Kameron Brown is on a mission. The spokes on his old school rotate beyond the inner city to the outskirts south of town. The long winter has subsided, so dew-covered saplings see new growth and varying shades of green begin to sprout from miscellaneous earth tones. The windows are halfway down as his braided head bobs to the low tones of reggae coming through his elaborate sound system.

Thick purple smoke flees his lungs as he exhales out the window, then coughs ferociously, pounding his chest like a gorilla in the mist. The platinum-framed Cartier sunglasses he wears seem to give him X-ray vision, allowing him to see through the bullshit of half-steppers and to immediately differentiate between a quarter-pound and a quarter-key.

After several years of constantly smoking bomb weed in his six-four, a thin tan film of soot and residue covers the inside of his windows. The detail shop could do nothing for him.

The area is rural, few cars are on the road, and his sneaker-clad foot goes heavy on the accelerator. The four fifty-four howls.

Kameron's black sweatsuit is comfortably unzipped and baggy, revealing the white wife beater underneath. Ashes evacuate out the window as he flicks his blunt in the wind. A platinum-encased second hand sweeps on his left wrist. It's 8:46 a.m., a perfect time to hit the links.

Baby-blue rock candy cuts through the morning suburban air crossing defunct railroad tracks as if launched from a cannon.

The empty road allows Kam to ponder his usual thoughts: "I hope the dry cleaners can get that fucking Hennessy stain out my cream Gucci sweater; man, Larry Johnson is a cold piece of work, but the wide receivers are garbage; Kansas City needs a basketball team, bad; I bet there would be some bitches at those games; man, that bitch Shameeka had some good pussy, she needs to call me back."

He glances down at his silent cell phone, resting noiseless on his hip, and frowns. The weed calms him, so he takes another prolonged hit. It doesn't help him forget his worries, it just helps him not care about them. And even after smoking blunt after blunt, he has no problems driving nor operating heavy machinery, such as AR-15s and Israeli-made submachine guns.

He exhales like the exhaust from his Chevy.

Suddenly, his cell phone begins to vibrate like a metallic bumblebee. He grabs it and checks the caller ID, then answers it.

"Yea?"

A woman's voice mumbles a few words.

"Yea," he responds calmly, before taking another long toke and holding it.

"Yea, well, just meet me and drop it off," he says, then exhales.

"Loch Lloyd. Yea. Out on Holmes." He hits the weed again.

"Alright," he tells the woman on the phone, then hangs up, returning the small cube back to his hip.

Kam's lungs then release the THC into the atmosphere, and his capillaries are grateful.

His load climbs a steep hill and upon reaching the top, a row of tall sycamore trees appears along the horizon. They enclose something.

The steering wheel revolves to the right and that rough grumbling sound peaks as Kam pulls over onto the gravelly shoulder. He sees the sign for his destination—Loch Lloyd Country Club—and he slows a bit and stares at the enclave.

A ten-foot-high black iron barrier, as well as surveillance cameras, surrounds the gated country club. Kameron knows they would never let him or his old school in without a hassle. So he removes his sunglasses and waits.

At that moment, a new Lincoln Town Car arrives from the other direction and pulls to the gate and a small black box on the left. The driver, in his short-sleeve taupe polo and light green sweater vest, looks ready to tee off.

White hair styled to perfection, the sixty-year-old small business owner inserts his navy-blue key card into the black box and the gates smoothly swing inward. Seeing this, Kameron quickly reaches over and grabs another blunt from the glove compartment, then coolly exits his vehicle and jogs in behind the Town Car.

The gates gently close behind him as Kameron places the blunt behind his right ear and leisurely strolls up the gray gravel drive. Pine trees line the path as Kam puts one foot in front of the other, covering his snow-white sneakers in dust.

After walking over five minutes, and having yet to see anything but shrubbery, Kameron thinks about how he should have just put a slug in the Town Car's driver and taken his damn key card.

"Fuck. This is some bullshit," he says to himself. Pebbles crunch under his shoes with every step.

Just as he's pondering turning around and leaving, a steep rooftop appears, followed by an archway, and then glass. The teepee-shaped clubhouse is impressively designed. Its façade features triangular-shaped sunlight panels. To the north of the clubhouse is a vast one hundred-acre lake. Mallards soak up the morning sun.

He stands out. Not like a beautiful blonde in a red dress. No, he stands out more like a curly-mustached rapscallion in a nineteen-ten silent movie, wearing a black trench coat and an elevated top hat.

Once inside the twenty thousand-square-foot clubhouse, Kameron walks over to the front desk and enlists the assistance of the blazer-clad concierge. Oak paneling covers the walls, and the odor of fine cigars adulterates the available oxygen.

"Yea, I'm looking for a Bradley Micheaux," Kameron states with his deep voice. His blinding platinum teeth stun the concierge, who's instantly impressed and repulsed at the same time.

Assuming correctly, the young brown-haired front-desk manager frowns with disdain, then replies, "I'm sorry, but if you're not a member of this club, I'm going to have to ask you to leave."

Upset, but undaunted, Kam replies professionally, "Look, I know I'm not a member. I'm a mechanic, and I was told to meet Mr. Micheaux here with his antique Chevy."

The concierge thinks about it for a second, and it makes sense to him.

The clean-shaven thirty-year-old picks up the house phone and while looking down, asks, "Yes, where is a Mr. Micheaux scheduled to be at this time? Yes. Okay. Thank you."

He gazes back up at Kam, who is impatiently waiting with his back to the front desk. The concierge purposely coughs, and Kameron turns around.

"Yes. Mr. Micheaux is said to be on the driving range," the man tells Kam. He then reaches under the counter and retrieves a laminated map of the grounds and points at it.

"Please feel free to go through these double doors, they'll be on your right, behind me," he tells Kam, who looks uninterested.

"Yea, okay," Kam says before snatching the map from the concierge.

"Sir, excuse me," the startled concierge says. "That's the only map at the front desk."

Kameron looks at it and begins to walk off.

"Thanks, sunshine," he tells the front-desk manager, who looks appalled.

The inner-city native makes his way around the corner and collects stares from the club's pale-faced old money. The city's wealthiest residents lounge on velvety thrones upholstered in dyed camel hair. Stogies defile the premises. Brandies, straight, abound.

Kam passes through dark, limousine-tinted double doors and emerges outside to the rear deck of the clubhouse, facing eighteen holes of manicured excellence.

The day's warm weather permits the town's privileged few to hit the green, and young Bradley Micheaux is among them.

After weeks of schmoozing the old money, he's becoming an expert handicapper, particularly on the less difficult front nine.

Brad's efforts to attain legal funding for his illicit endeavor so far have been unsuccessful. But this round of golf may prove lucrative. Quiet as it's kept, the potential investor has bankrolled some Sicilian and Mexican projects in the past, but they had reputations. Clout.

Bradley, on the other hand, is a nobody, with a mediocre set of hand-me-down clubs, and his golf game needs some work. But to his credit, Brad does have a good understanding of the streets and the street mentality, which will be his only chance of securing some funds and not waking up one day with some burly Italian pouring gasoline on his flannel pajamas.

Kameron's eyes search the expansive greenery. He doesn't know where to begin, so he removes the brown marijuana-stuffed blunt from his ear and sparks it.

Golf carts cruise by carrying fat millionaires and third-generation defense attorneys. They don't hide their arrogance, and they stare at Kam with contemptuous glances.

Kam takes a deep puff from his blunt and intentionally blows smoke toward the carted golfers, then grins widely. Sunlight bounces off his baguettes.

Soon thereafter, the intense purple smoke from Kam's blunt attracts unneeded attention. Over saunters a short, studious-looking man in glasses. He's borderline nerd material.

"Uh, excuse me, sir," he addresses Kam.

Kam turns and looks at him, remains silent, then turns back around.

The vertically challenged guy continues.

"Uh, yea. Is that marijuana?"

Bothered, Kam softly responds, "Yes, it is. Why, are you security or somethin'?"

The man blushes.

"Oh, heavens no." He chuckles, and his potbelly jiggles.

Kameron returns to searching the fairways with his eyes and continues to smoke.

"Uh, well, I was just wondering, if you were willing to share," the short golfer inquires. "Or if you had any extra."

"Sorry, dog, all I got is my personal. And I smoke solo, cousin."

Eager to relive his college days, the short man sweetens the deal. "I'll pay you."

Kam is bored, so he decides to entertain himself, as he takes another lengthy puff from his imported herbs.

"Oh, yea? How much you got?"

The man pulls a thick wallet from his back pocket and leafs through the bills.

"All I have is a hundred and twenty dollars."

"Cool," Kam says, then swipes the money from the man's stubby hands. Kameron turns around and continues to smoke his weed, when his would be customer becomes tired of waiting.

"Uh, where's the pot?"

"What pot?" Kam replies, laughing to himself.

The man catches Kameron's drift, and saunters away broken-hearted.

Still smoking, Kam returns to watching the linksmen, many of whom struggled to make par. Despite the occasional ace, slices and mulligans were the norm.

Kam eyes a new group set to tee off. Clad in green, red, and yellow plaid pants, the man with the honor is also the man with the old black caddy. He's hunched over and obedient. His dark skin is sunbeaten.

Kameron takes a long pull from his marijuana, and even though he's high as hell, he knows he never wants to be that old black man, lugging some white man's shit around.

"Man, fuck that," he mumbles out loud.

The golfer's driver goes back and he swings at the one hundred compression Titleist on the dog-legged course. The tiny white ball soars high near the tree line, peaking over a near water hazard, then descending to land just to the right of a sand trap. The caddy bends over, placing further stress on his aged back, and replaces the huge divot left by his employer's mighty stroke.

"This shit is funny," Kameron says, staring at the golfers' outfits. He pictures himself out there and laughs. "That would be some *real* funny shit."

Kameron would be the one talking while others were taking their practice swings. Even if he were lagging, he would never let anyone play through.

On hole eighteen, out of Kameron's view, Bradley Micheaux was attempting to close a deal that could possibly give him a new lease on life.

"Come on, Bradley, sink this and you've got a deal," the tycoon tells him. Bradley looks to the flag, then back down at his ball on the green. It's only a fifteen-foot putt. His bronze linen trousers and airy cream-colored cotton Polo shirt flutter in the light breeze.

Brad grips his club and focuses on the ball.

"Remember, Bradley, we didn't count that whiff from earlier," the entrepreneur tells him. "That should have been a penalty."

"I know, Mr. Pendergast. You're too kind," Bradley responds sarcastically, trying to suppress his accent. He's nervous on the dance floor, his short game could be better. He swings.

The club connects with the ball and it rolls straight ahead with the grain, before hooking toward the cup. The ball rolls in slow motion before dropping in.

Pendergast frowns, and Bradley smiles.

"Looks like we have a deal, Mr. Pendergast," Bradley says with confidence.

"I guess we do. Congratulations, Mr. Micheaux, you'll soon

be a rich man," Pendergast says while firmly shaking Brad's hand. "You'll make me a richer man too, right?"

"That's what I'm here for," Bradley cheerfully replies.

✕✕✕

Back at the clubhouse's deck, Kam is still choking on his purple broccoli when the short nerdy man returns with a fairly large twenty-eight-year-old Caucasian man.

"Yes, this is the guy, please throw him out," the nerdy guy tells the club's security guard while pointing a stiff finger at Kameron. "Uh, he robbed me, and I want him thrown out and my money returned."

The security guard, who is a bit intimidated by Kam, asserts himself nonetheless.

"Sir, are you a member here?"

"No, I'm not. I'm looking for Bradley Micheaux," Kam says, looking at the security guard on his left through his peripheral vision.

"Well, I don't know who he is, so I'm going to have to ask you to leave," the guard says. His polo-style club shirt is one size too small.

Kam's expression changes from one of benumbment to one of irritation. Peeved, he looks down at the stout geek and questions him.

"So how exactly did I rob you?"

The guy looks nervous and begins to stutter, "Well, uh, I mean, uh, you assaulted me!"

The security guard decides he's heard enough.

"Come with me, sir," he says, grabbing Kam's left arm just above the elbow.

The jerking move makes Kam drop his blunt. Shocked by the guard's brazen aggressiveness, Kam yanks his arm back.

"What the fuck is wrong with you, cuz?" Kam says, then delivers a crushing right cross to the guard's throat.

The twenty-eight-year-old was completely caught off guard and his larynx is punished for his stupidity. He falls to one knee, grasping his injured neck. Some people you just don't fuck with, and Kameron Brown is one of them. The nerdy narc is terrified.

"Punk-ass mothafucka," yells Kameron. Several club members turn to see the ruckus.

The guard regains his composure and struggles to his feet. Kameron stares at him like a ravenous jackal, and as soon as the guard motions toward him, Kameron quickly wraps his huge hands around the guard's neck and begins to squeeze the life out of him.

"I'll send yo mothafuckin' soul to heaven, white boy!" Kameron yells. The club's older members are utterly horrified.

"Someone should help that young man," some wealthy guy at a nearby table blurts.

The guard grabs Kameron's wrists in an attempt to break his grip, fighting for his life. But Kam's grip is too strong, and the guard's efforts are ineffective, as Kam runs off at the mouth in a devilish tone.

"I will light this bitch up like the Chinese New Year," Kam yells, still squeezing the guard's thick neck. "It will be January first in the year two thousand all over again, mothafucka!"

"Kameron," a voice yells. "Kameron!"

Kam looks up as the guard is on the verge of passing out. It's Brad. He saw the commotion from the fairway and now he's in a mad sprint to get to Kameron before he kills someone.

Kam sees Brad coming and releases the oxygen-deprived guard. He falls to the wooden deck and lies nearly motionless, minus the frantic heaving of his chest.

The nerdy guy quietly tiptoes away.

"Kameron, what's goin on, bruh?" Brad asks, intensely concerned. "What you doin' here?"

Kam fixes his collar and reaches down to retrieve his smoldering blunt. He takes a puff and walks closer to Bradley.

"Yea, what's up, Bradley?" Kam says calmly, sounding as if he wasn't just choking somebody. "We need to talk, dog."

As they both proceed to walk inside the clubhouse, a few guys run over to the guard to ensure he's alive and well. He would quit his job the next day; seven dollars an hour wasn't worth the permanent finger marks he will have on his neck for the rest of his life.

Brad heads toward the locker room to shower up and change his clothes. Kam follows closely behind, still smoking his shrinking blunt.

They enter the well-kept locker room and are surprised to see an elderly man, possibly in his seventies, wearing a black lace bra and panty set. He has one foot propped up on a bench, and he doesn't see them enter, so he continues to apply moisturizer to his thighs.

"Okay, that's wild," Bradley says.

"Dude, what the fuck kind of club is this?" Kameron inquires before bursting into laughter.

The man hears Kam laughing and quickly turns around.

"Oh, my. Uh, it's not what you think," he says, startled. The man hastily shrouds himself in a large towel, snatches his gym bag, and scurries off.

Kam simply shakes his head.

"What part of the game was that?" Kam jokingly asks.

Brad just shakes his head too, then walks over to his locker and opens it.

"Look, Bradley, I'm going to make this quick," Kameron says. "You need to either get the dope crackin', or come up with Jimmy's two-five, pronto, cousin. You feel me?"

Bradley takes off his shirt and grabs his soap and a towel from his locker.

"Look, Kameron, I'm working on it, man. Why do you think I was out here today? I need more bread. So get off my back, okay?"

Brad then sits on the wooden bench in front of his locker and removes his shoes and socks, followed by his pants and briefs, then wraps the towel around his waist.

Kam just smiles and tokes on his blunt. His diamonds are lusterless in the dim locker room.

"Okay, Bradley," Kam says. His deep voice echoes. "But don't come callin' me and Cicero when one of them fucking dagos is sticking toothpicks under your fingernails. We can handle ourselves. Can you?"

"Whatever, man," Brad tells him, then stands up. "I got my shit together. We're about to be billionaires." He slams the locker shut.

"All right, Bradley, do ya thang," Kam tells him, then he turns and starts to walk out, but pauses.

"Oh, and Bradley, if I get into some funk because *you* fucked up, me and you are going to have problems." He stops. "Well, you are going to have problems."

Kameron smiles and tosses the rest of his blunt to the floor as his text message communicator begins to vibrate.

"Stay safe, Bradley Micheaux," Kam tells him while checking his message. "I know vegetarian mothafuckas like you don't want no beef." And he walks away.

Silent, Brad slides toward the shower to cleanse his body and his mind.

✕✕✕

Back in his classic Chevy, Kameron waits outside the country club, rolling a new blunt. At this point everything is slower, but he thinks his senses are enhanced. His lips are dry and blackened from years of smoking, and his memory is not what it used to be.

Suddenly, a red convertible pulls up next to Kam's load with the top down and the windows up. The driver of the two-seater has smooth cocoa skin and long acrylic nails. She bats her fake lashes at him and grins.

Kam finishes rolling his blunt and just stares at the two ladies. The passenger then hops out wearing a short plaid skirt, her complexion milky and pale. Brunette hair and blonde streaks flutter in the wind as she runs over to Kameron's passenger side holding her skirt up so that it forms a basket.

Kam shows little expression as he reaches over and rolls the window down. The schoolgirl-dressed prostitute quickly dumps more than four thousand dollars in cash into the passenger seat. And without a word, she hops back into the red convertible just before the driver does a U-turn and vanishes toward the city.

Among his many pursuits, Kam also manages a few girls on the side. He smiles, flashing his baguettes, while reaching into the backseat and digging out a brown paper bag to put the cash in. It takes a few moments to emancipate the sack, which is stuck between a schedule of classes for Penn Valley and a *Murder Dog* magazine.

Going back to school has crossed Kameron's mind, so much in fact that he's considered taking some refresher courses and the Law School Admission Test. Nonetheless, he frees the bag and stuffs the illicit cash from pandering into it. The women risk their bodies and their health, yet Kam is without the pathos of the common man.

"Another day, another mothafuckin' dollar," he says to himself while counting through the crumpled tens and twenties.

Metal enters metal and sparks fly as the four fifty-four comes to life and the engine roars. Kam adjusts his mirrors and the rear tires eject gravel from underneath them.

Back en route to the hood, cruising north, thoughts of his mother and brother seep into Kameron's consciousness. Quite possibly a side effect of the weed, Kam begins to hear his mother's demanding voice.

"Kam! Kam! Boy, get yo ass up! You got to go to school today," Shirley would tell her fifteen-year-old son. "You done already missed two days this week."

Kameron recalls that's how he was wakened every day. Shirley's words were always biting. But her actions said more about the content of her character. For instance, Shirley's light-brown hair was always self-styled to save money. And she would typically buy her own clothes from thrift stores and secondhand shops, while spending more for her children's garments.

By the time Kam was a freshman in high school, his older brother and only sibling had already done ten years in Leavenworth, and the stress of the world had weighed more heavily than ever on his mother since then.

When the cops caught up to his brother with an arrest warrant on murder charges, Tre had a pound of weed and a half kilo of Peruvian flake. He got life without parole. The day when the judge read Tre's sentence, Shirley began what would be a life-long addiction to Valium and vodka. The combination would induce profound lows and bouts of depression that would last for months.

Driving steady with one hand on the steering wheel, Kam eyes the passing trees that line the road as his thoughts continue.

"Kameron, look, I'm working two jobs to send yo black ass to a good school, so don't fuck it up," Shirley would often tell her sixteen-year-old son as she drove him to the bus stop. He made average grades, but he was a standout in basketball and football, which would prove to be his only means of avoiding Tre's fate, or worse.

Kameron never knew his father. Twilight, as he was called for his dark skin, was killed by the KCPD in a routine traffic stop while Shirley was seven months' pregnant with Kam, and the family was forced to move to the Wayne Minor city projects on Twelfth Street.

It was in the projects where Kameron would get his hard-knock upbringing. He would get his first gun before he got his first pubic hair. Despite the temptations and despair surrounding them, Shirley was able to instill in her youngest child a strong survival instinct, as she worked her fingers to the bone to afford his Catholic school education.

Kam couldn't completely avoid the street life, however. When Shirley would pass out on the living room sofa, Kam would steal money from her pocketbook and roam the streets with other kids from similar homes and similar situations.

Well-oiled cornrows gleam in the sunlight as Kameron sparks a new blunt and chokes on it. He reminisces about those days, and recalls how he decided to attend a local college on a football scholarship. But Shirley would die from an overdose on the night of his high school graduation. It was a night she'd feared would never come for her son.

Overjoyed and relieved, she drank herself into oblivion. Years of writing letters to Tre and sending what she could for his commissary and books had taken its toll. So after Kam graduated, she apparently felt her job was done. The time had come for Shirley to rest.

Smoke leaves Kameron's lungs as he remembers finding his mother's body, sprawled out and limp, eyes bulging.

"Damn, Momma," he mumbles while driving. Tears escape his eyes and he quickly wipes them away.

"Ain't that some shit," he says out loud and sighs.

Needing a distraction, he turns up the volume on his stereo and hip-hop bass lines shake the rearview mirror.

"I stopped poppin' bottles with models on expensive-ass dinner dates. Instead I hit throttles and startle my enemies with infrared slugs through chest plates."

Kam would spend three semesters in college, but the call of the streets was too loud, so it was there that he returned. And it was there where he would hook up with his friend Cicero, to make a name and a living for himself.

"We avoid food poisoning at cheap-ass diners, we eat lobster tails in private jetliners with leather recliners. But we deliver shiners to knuckleheads as constant reminders, just because we in suits, don't mean we ain't grinders."

Vibrations from his phone interrupt Kam's thoughts. He checks the caller ID. It's the mother of his son.

"Hello," he answers, prepared for the drama.

"Kam, yo son needs some shoes," an angry female voice yells. A child cries in the background. "I told you that last week."

"I've been busy." He quite frankly forgot.

"Well, look— " the woman states before being cut off.

"Look, I'll drop off some bread tonight," he tells her. "Quit fuckin' buggin' me."

She begins screaming and cursing and he hangs up, tossing his accursed communicator into the passenger seat, disgusted.

"Why do I have to deal with this bullshit," he says to himself, as the rhymes continue.

"T.D. Jakes can't save us, we prefer snortin' cocaine and takin trips to Vegas. We used to earn slave wages, now we dump X and meth every time them white bitches page us."

Cornrows on his head rock back and forth to the beat, as moments of self-pity end and the unforgiving urban landscape reappears in his windshield. Kameron puts his game face on. There's work to be done. The time for tears and sadness has passed.

❊❊❊

Kam enters the city on Holmes Road and makes a smooth right on Seventy-Fifth Street, heading west. He gets thumbs up from other hustlers and waves from flirting women. They love his style. He's a bona-fide K.C. baller.

Kam is high as a kite, loving his life as bass lines rock. He cruises to Prospect Avenue, the city's ghetto thoroughfare, and turns north, nodding his head to the beat of hip-hop simply enjoying the weather, when his phone rings again. He checks the caller ID. It's Cicero.

"Yea?"

"What's crackin'?"

"B.I.Z. fanito."

"You went to the Bayou Classic?"

"Grambling won."

"Cool."

"Peace."

They hang up just as Kameron's Chevy is pulling to a stop-light on Thirty-Ninth Street, just a few miles from his apart-ment. He cracks the windows and sits in the turning lane with his blinker on. He waits at the stoplight, watching the neigh-borhood's disenfranchised residents going through their daily motions.

Homeless people wrapped in dirty blankets and crack addicts with blank stares and unkempt hair wander about. Aging grand-mothers with multiple shopping bags wait at the bus stop as Kam offends them with his abrasive rap music.

"We choose to abuse the families of our enemies, chop they nieces to pieces and get real low, use pillows to smother they mothers, grab the steel then blow."

At that moment, a beat-up red minivan pulls to his right and stops. A beautiful dark-haired woman sits at the wheel check-ing her makeup in the rearview mirror.

She's Italian, maybe Hispanic, and Kam glances over at her. He turns back toward the red light just as the woman in the minivan sticks a sawed-off double-barrel shotgun out the win-dow. Seeing it at the last minute, Kam ducks to his left as the beauty pulls the trigger in broad daylight. *Boom!*

Buckshot shatters his windows and sprays the interior; several pellets hit Kam in his midsection.

Injured but undaunted, Kam quickly reaches under his seat and pulls out a nickel-plated pistol.

"Don't fuck with Jimmy's money!" the woman yells, then pulls off through the red light swerving to narrowly avoid a collision.

"You stupid-ass wop bitch!" Kameron yells as he sits up and squeezes the trigger on his weapon. He rapidly fires seven slugs straight through his windshield at the minivan. *Pop. Pop. Pop. Pop. Pop. Pop. Pop.*

He's too late. The van is gone, and he has a dozen hot pellets in his body.

"Ah, fuck," Kam grumbles, gripping his side. He's only a few blocks from Truman Hospital, so he mashes the gas pedal and heads there in his damaged candy-blue Chevy.

Kam, fuming as he drives, talks to himself to take his mind off the pain.

"These fuckin' punk-ass dagos! These fuckin' dagos are gonna pay for this shit. That's real talk."

Bleeding and feeling weak, Kam reaches the hospital's ER, and luckily for him it's not yet overcrowded. A young physician fresh from his residency quickly sees Kam and removes the buckshot. No organs were hit, so within a few hours Kameron is patched up and watching reruns of *Seinfeld* in a hospital bed.

Later that night, recovered and seething, he makes a phone call while a tray of lime Jell-O turns warm next to him.

"Hello," Cicero answers his cell phone. He sits comfortably next to his chocolate princess watching DVDs on a plasma television in an upscale hotel room. It's 10:20 p.m.

"They got at me," Kam calmly says from the hospital room he's sharing with a flatulent gray-haired senior citizen. "Tried to smoke your boy, cuz."

"Where are you?"

"The nurse's office," Kam replies.

"Who was it?"

"Jose's peeps. It's about that scrilla. They sent a bitch after me. Can you believe that shit?" Kam says, sitting in his sheer hospital gown. "They probably found out dumb-ass Brad was fuckin' with other cats with long money, too."

His bearded roommate grumbles, then breaks wind and the smell is gut wrenching. It quickly wafts over to Kameron's side and he gets a big whiff.

"Damn! You stink, mothafucka," Kam yells at the old man. A thin transparent sheet separates them.

"Damn. Well, don't go to the game," Cicero advises. "Watch it at home."

Kam's voice turns angry.

"You know I'm a big fucking fan of the fucking Chiefs, dog. I gotta go to the game!"

Kam's roommate squirms and farts again. This time the stench is worse.

"Okay, I'm about to go get my fucking gun and shoot you in the face, cuz," Kam screams in his deep voice, flashing his diamonds and platinum.

The old-timer grumbles, then mumbles something under his breath.

"Okay. Fart one more time, mothafucka, and see if I'm playin'."

Cicero, who's resting in a luxury suite sipping a drink, chuckles, then pauses, as his chocolate princess in her T-shirt and panties slides down and begins to give him head. He somehow continues talking without missing a beat.

"Look, the franchise had a terrible draft, but we got some good prospects for the future," Cicero says. "Right?"

Kam thinks for a second while a discombobulated Kramer once again bursts into Jerry's apartment, then he answers.

"Yea."

"So we'll be all right. Get well. Then go to the crilla and chill. Get some pussy or something," Cicero says, as the beautiful face bobs in his lap.

Kam is slow to reply.

"Is that cool?" Cicero asks with his hand on the back of his girl's head, pushing it back and forth.

"Yea. Yea, all right. Holla," Kameron says, then hangs up, pissed and unable to respond the way he wants: with gunfire.

But Cicero knows how Jimmy operates. If he had wanted Kameron or any of them dead, they'd be dead. He just wanted to send them a little message. That's probably why Kam was shot with pellets used for quail hunting, and not kidnapped or tortured.

At this point, though, it's serious business, no more playing around. Cicero knows Bradley needs to come through on his end, or they are all dead.

Moments later, a phone rings.

"Yea," Bradley answers from his BMW, rolling south down Broadway.

He steers with his left hand as he dips his pinkie nail into a small auburn vial and scoops out some coke. The night is cloudless and beautiful. Stars twinkle everywhere. Bradley places his fingernail under his right nostril and takes a snort.

"When you gonna handle that?" Cicero asks, having just discharged a million potential children into the mouth of a beautiful woman.

"I'm glad you called. We're going to check things out in a couple days."

"Be sure you do, our friend is laid up in the hospital because of you."

"Oh shit, are you serious, man?" Brad sounds startled. His light gray suit fits to a tee. "Man, I'm on top of it. That's real."

"Dude, you're my boy. But you fuck this up, and I'll have a T-shirt with your picture on it."

Brad is silent as he makes a left on Forty-Seventh Street.

"Holla."

The line goes dead. Brad places his phone on his lap and takes a deep breath.

"Shit," he mumbles to himself as he speeds through a yellow light, thinking about his life and its fragility. He can only hope things go as planned with the product. If not, the next time he sees the Bayou may be from a small box labeled "remains."

Chapter 14

Chords from an electric guitar drill the eardrums of generations X and Y inside a dark inner-city night-club. The crowd moves like an ocean of humanity, swaying to and fro. Raves such as this can last all night long, but this one is just warming up. The band's shirtless drummer bangs away at the percussion instrument as he eyes a busty redhead jamming in the front row. The music blasts.

Outside, showers pour from the sky. Sweaty, rain-soaked mosh pitters make the center of the incivility resemble a whirling typhoon; they repeatedly encircle one another as if testing the manhood of their potential adversaries.

There is another test being conducted tonight, however. It is the test of a new, nameless hallucinogen. The test subjects have no idea what's in store for them.

Neon-green glowsticks wiggle back and forth for the acid and LSD users' enjoyment. Furry pink elephants wrestle with giant blue doves in their heads. Those just starting out sweat and grind their teeth off the E. Those who are more experienced chew bubble gum.

The rain sprays the city, leaving huge puddles on sidewalks and causing car accidents on westbound interstates seventy and southbound thirty-five. Phones at GEICO's downtown office will be ringing off the hook in the morning.

Suburban kids from well-to-do Johnson County, Kansas, often come to the Missouri side of the state line for a little fun and excitement and tonight is no different.

Fortunately for some, the Safe Drug Coalition has set up a booth in the Xcess Club's foyer to test for fake Ecstasy tablets, against the mayor's wishes, of course. Nonetheless, SDC has no test for the light-blue capsules that a resolved Bradley Micheaux will be trying out tonight. Needless to say, Brad's clinical trials are not FDA approved. And with a sinister character like Kameron Brown bearing down on him, the appropriate paperwork will just have to wait.

Raindrops pound the paint job of a small German-made four-door parallel parked in front of the club.

"Here, take these," Brad tells two young guys sitting in the backseat of his blue-gray BMW. "Only one per customer."

They both nod.

"Charge them twenty dollars per pill. If they bitch, go down to ten dollars. You got it?" Brad asks.

The scruffy-faced Jack Lee nods, as does his friend Collin.

"This is gonna be sick," Collin yells with excitement as he puffs a generic square. His voice is light and feminine.

"I know. Make a little cash. Maybe meet some sluts," Jack Lee says with a deep, more mature-sounding inflection. The twenty-year-olds begin to chuckle.

Brad just stares at them. Rainwater on the windows blurs the world outside the dark-gray leather interior.

"Look, be discreet, and be sure to watch their reactions," Brad instructs. "If anybody starts freaking out, get the fuck outta there. You feel me? I'll be waiting right here."

"No problem, dude," reassures Collin before taking another puff of his cancer stick.

"Dude, yea, we got this," Jack Lee weighs in. "Just chill out."

They exit the car and get drenched before reaching the nightclub's awning. They're carded by the bouncer then make their way inside, where a sea of bobbing heads greets them. Butterflies flutter in the stomachs of the X users.

Collin, the shorter of the two, wastes no time and immediately approaches a sexy five-foot-five blonde and her cute brunette friend standing near the coat check.

"Hey, what's up with you guys?" the fresh-faced Collin asks the two.

"Not much. Some bitch fucking elbowed me in the face," the blonde with straight, shoulder-length hair blurts. She thinks the young-looking Collin is hot, so she quickly responds to him.

"Damn, that's fucked up," responds Collin in his navy-blue sweatshirt still smoking his square. "Hey, you guys do X?"

He wastes no time getting right to the point, just as the house band's lead vocalist stage dives and is passed around the sunk-in dance floor like a living joint. Roped pacifiers dangle from the necks of white whirling dervishes.

"Yea, you got some?" the brunette asks. The club's music is loud. Curly locks hang just below the large gold hoops dangling from her earlobes.

"Nope. I got something better," Collin tells her. He tosses the cigarette butt to the floor and smashes it with his Diesel sneakers. Girls of European descent jounce through the populace with colorfully beaded cornrows, resembling Bo Derek.

"What? Coke? Coke's not better than X, man," the blonde interjects, rubbing her eye.

Collin grins.

"Fuck coke! This shit is new, and it's better than coke," says Collin.

The girls smile.

"This shit fucking rocks," he adds.

For years, Kansas Citians have endured being last to get new things: movies, clothing, music, food, soft drinks and even drugs. They always seem to hit K.C. last. So these young girls jump at the opportunity to try something new; to be the first. Even with a new drug, it's worth the risk.

"Hell, yea, I'll try it," the brunette says. Her tight little hips are hugged by her stretch jeans.

"Yea, fuck it, me too," the blonde replies, midriff exposed. "Maybe it will make my fucking eye feel better."

The bass guitar hums as Jack Lee leans against the wall with arms folded, watching his young partner-in-crime work.

The three walk over to a bar and purchase bottled waters to take the dope. Collin pulls three capsules from his jeans' pocket and the girls stare at them with suspicion.

"They supposed to be twenty bucks each, but I'll let you guys get them for ten," he says. They agree and each slide him ten-dollar bills from their tiny party-sized purses.

"Are you going to take one too?" the brunette asks.

"Hell, yea," answers Collin without hesitation. Rain can be heard striking the club's blacked-out windows.

The girls smile; that's good news. Mind-altering capsules grace tongues and natural spring water washes them down to be digested and absorbed.

Poorly lit, the nightclub is a cesspool of drug experiments and same-sex escapades. Many firsts have taken place at this midtown location, just to the east of the flat, western plains.

Bradley Micheaux sits in the parking lot in the rainstorm facing the nightclub's front door, simply thinking. He needs these drugs to work, to be effective, and to be safe. As he ponders a fallback plan B, six guys spill out of the club throwing fists and cursing like sailors. The falling rain immediately baptizes them.

"That was my girlfriend you were hugging, motherfucker!" a drunken brawny guy yells as he swings wildly, connecting several blows to the temple of a leaner, more inebriated man in a form-fitting white button-down shirt.

The fracas catches Brad off guard, so he scans the faces of the combatants to make sure it's not one of his boys. Brad sees it's three Mexicans and three white guys, but one just happens to be Jack Lee. He was somehow swept into the melee as the five others rushed past him. And none of them know him, so they all think he's with the other clique. Now Jack Lee finds himself in the middle of a drunken slugfest, and he is forced to throw punches at both crews.

Rain comes down on everyone. Fists fly. Soaked shirts rip and jaws are punished by flying knuckles. The large Mexican who started the shit slips to the pavement, and when he hits the ground, the two white guys begin delivering kicks from their Doc Martens into his fat stomach. Unbeknownst to him, his girlfriend had just returned from sucking both Caucasian dicks in the bathroom.

But the other two Mexicans think they're doing damage to the other clique's friend, when in reality they're trading blows with Jack Lee, an innocent bystander.

Brad's eyes go big when he recognizes the kid, but he's calm. Jack Lee grew up in an Irish household with four older brothers that were known around Kansas City as big-time bar brawlers. Jack Lee is a scrapper, holding his ground against two guys.

Jack Lee takes several shots to the face from the quicker of the two guys, but delivers a powerful body shot to the guy's kidney, and he buckles.

Grinning, Brad fires up a cigarette and watches from the safety of his Beamer.

Then *crash*.

While his boy was taking a body blow, the other guy grabbed a beer bottle and cracks it on Jack Lee's head, and he falls. Now the feet set sail, and Jack Lee is forced to cover his face and head.

Meanwhile Collin is inside, high as a stealth bomber.

"Two thumbs up!" Collin yells to the girls on both sides of him, and they all laugh.

"This shit is awesome," the blonde says. "I guess this is what a wet dream feels like."

They all laugh again.

Back outside, Brad sees Jack Lee take cowboy boots to the back and chest. He decides he needs to act, not because he's courageous, but because he knows it will guarantee Jack Lee's devotion.

He opens the car door and pops the trunk. Rain smacks his face and sullies his all-black Italian-tailored suit.

He moves his tennis racket and gym bag to the side and pulls out an aluminum baseball bat.

The guys kicking his friend don't see Bradley approach, but they would have surely run off if they knew the former college shortstop was armed with a metal baseball bat, of all things.

"Hey, what's up. J.L.?" Brad says. The guy nearest him turns around and Brad steps into the swing. The sound of the aluminum bat striking his cranium is similar to that of Tiger Woods teeing off on a five hundred-yard course. *Ping!* He immediately drops and blood pours from his busted head.

Unfortunately for his friend, there are no streetlights on the block, and with the darkness of the night and the pounding rain he doesn't see Brad.

But his midsection soon feels the full strength of a cleanup hitter as Bradley crushes his rib cage. The guy screams and grabs his side. Bradley strikes his body again and again, breaking his ulna, radius, femur, and several small bones in his wrists and ankles. The guy falls. Bradley stops swinging.

"J.L., I can't take you anywhere, man," Bradley jokingly tells his comrade, who is now soaked in blood and rain.

"Dude, fuck you," J.L. says with a grumble as Brad helps him to his feet.

The three Mexicans lay on the ground holding their injuries, as the other fighters bail.

Yet in club Xcess, a trio of young adults has stumbled upon the next big thing; quite possibly the Earth's next scourge. Tequila shot after tequila shot, their highs remain unchanged. They could drink fermented fruits all night and not feel any adverse effects.

"Barkeep! Barkeep!" Collin yells, grinning. His face is flush and rosy. "Is today your birthday?"

Screeching riffs dart unhindered into inner ears. The middle-aged bartender looks annoyed by the kids he knows are on something.

"No, it's not my birthday," the barkeep responds.

"Well, it's not mine either, but I'm going to party like it is!" Collin screams with gusto.

The girls giggle loudly. They're just as animated.

"Can I get you another drink?" the bearded bartender inquires.

Collin looks confused.

"Now, you *know* I want another drink," says Collin. "What kind of barkeep are you?"

The girls again burst into laughter, and at that moment, Collin's text message communicator begins to tremble on his hip.

"Whoa," Collin says, startled. He glances to the blonde.

"You are so nasty!"

She just grins. Then Collin looks down. "Oh."

He removes the device from his hip and reads the message: "CUM OUTSIDE ASAP. ROUND THE CORNER."

He closes the silver box and returns it to his side.

"Well, ladies, it's been real," Collin slurs. "But I gotta split."

"What? Hell no, man. The party just started," the blonde says as she sticks her tongue down his throat, tasting the Wheaties and milk he had for breakfast. They begin kissing wildly.

Jealous, the brunette stares at them and feels left out.

"What the fuck? You guys just gonna forget about me?"

Collin gazes over at her, then they begin swapping spit and increasing the likelihood of developing cold sores. But he suddenly pulls away.

"Look, I really have to go. But you guys rock! Write your numbers down and we can hook up real soon."

"Promise?" the blonde asks.

"I swear," he replies.

The girls jot names and numbers on napkins and send Collin off with more tongue and spit. Elbows fly into shoulders and chests as sweat circulates between hallucinating future doctors and lawyers.

Brad and J.L. sit silently in the Beamer down the street and around the block as Collin jogs out of the club and is immediately doused by the downpour.

He searches for the car then finds it and immediately hops into the backseat, soaking wet. A lumpy-faced J.L. turns to face him.

"Holy shit! Were you in a sky diving accident?" Collin says before rolling about in the backseat, laughing his ass off.

Brad looks away and cracks a small smile. The battered J.L. is unamused.

Still laughing it up, Collin adds, "Dude, you look like a big bag of smashed scrotums!" He giggles extremely loud, nearly losing his breath.

"Are you done, fuck face?" Jack Lee asks. "I might not look like this if you would have been around to help. Fucking prick."

"I'm sorry, dude. But I was conducting very important research," Collin weighs in, making his voice sound like a collegiate professor's.

"Yea, so how did it go?" Bradley asks.

"Hell, just look at me. I feel greeeat," Collin proclaims, swinging his right arm, sounding like that cartoon tiger. Serotonin swamps his brain.

"And it's not like X. It's a more focused high," he adds before leaning forward between the front seats and whispering. "And I'm not hot or dehydrated at all. And I'm not grinding my teeth. That shit is annoying as shit."

"Good," Brad responds, nodding his head with an intense stare. "Good. Let's go."

Rain pounds KC as the BMW's foreign tires cut corners and make headway back to Brad's lab. Driving like a man with much on his mind, Bradley has ignored an ailing J.L. in his passenger seat until a crocked Collin speaks up.

"Uh, J.L., do you want to go to a hospital or something? You look like pure D shit."

"Man, yea, I can take you by Jackson County General," Bradley offers.

J.L., holding a dirty towel to his bleeding forehead, raises an eyebrow and simply stares at Brad.

"Are you kidding me? I heard some doctor there cut this dude's nuts off, and he was only there for a flu shot."

"Ouch," Collin says, grabbing his crotch.

"Fuck that, just take me home," concludes Jack Lee.

Brad agrees and the tires spin on the wet asphalt.

As the triad cruises in the rain through the urban landscape of neglected tenements and hourly motel rooms, Collin is on cloud nine.

"Man, I am so ripped. I'm fucking weightless," Collin boasts of the drug stimulating his gray matter. His eyelids are heavy as he reclines in the backseat. "I'm so in touch with reality, I think I can literally taste life."

"Oh yea?" J.L. asks. "What's it taste like?"

Collin thinks for second, smacking his lips together. "You ever been punched in the mouth? Well, it tastes like that mixture of blood and spit. J.L., that taste should be pretty fresh in your mouth."

"Fuck you, ass wipe," J.L. retorts.

"Yea. Kinda like that, and soy sauce," adds Collin.

"You're an idiot," J.L. states, nursing a laceration above his eye.

But Bradley is silent, absorbing Collin's every word, every gesture.

"Dude, you need to put this stuff on the market, like, today," Collin asserts.

Brad laughs.

"You think so?" he asks, concentrating on the road.

"Hell, yea," Collin replies. "I don't know what the fuck you're waiting for."

Then a light bulb comes on.

"Man, you should just let me and J.L. push this shit for you. You don't need C and his boy."

"Are you fucking crazy?" Brad calmly asks. "For one, C is my boy. For two, I'm not trying to get killed."

"That's cool," Collin says excitedly, really not feeling him. "Fuck it, bounce. Leave the city. We can handle shit here and you can get shit moving in another state. Fuck it, overseas! Dude, I got some friends in Germany, and a fuckin' cousin in Brazil."

Brad's facial expression changes to one of contemplation. Damn, he never thought about that. Why not cut Cicero and Kam and Jimmy out of the loop? This drug would speak for itself. Word of mouth. He could be filthy rich without their help. What help would they really provide anyway?

Bavarian Motor Works passes a huge fountain of chiseled mariners riding horseback, facing all points of the compass. Tridents are at the ready, water spews from the mouths of their steeds, which are submerged in several feet of fluid being splashed by the night's raindrops.

"Man, I think Collin might be right," Jack Lee weighs in. "I know C is your friend, but fuck that. This is business."

Brad ponders the situation. He's already into Jimmy for two and a half million, and now he's borrowed another seven hundred and fifty thousand from Pendergast. Since Cicero would have to deal with Jimmy, Brad figures he can just pay Pendergast back and be out in time to catch *Carnival* in Rio.

"You guys are fucking retarded," Bradley says in his Southern Louisiana accent. "Let's get some breakfast. Cool?"

"Yea, that's cool," J.L. says.

"Word. I'm not even hungry, but I know that shit is going to taste good as hell," Collin declares. "I want some Belgian waffles with strawberries and whipped cream, and a big bowl of vanilla ice cream with hot fudge."

"Would you please shut the fuck up!" J.L. screams. "You're making my headache hurt."

Black tires slosh over wet asphalt as roots of deception begin to grow and take hold in Bradley's mind.

✖✖✖

Later that night, a twenty-one-year-old blonde and her twenty-year-old brunette friend would die in a head-on collision driving home from club Xcess. Going more than one hundred miles per hour in a Ford Mustang, the girls thought they were on a magic carpet ride. Strangely, even the dashboard crushing them felt good. The coeds were so badly mangled they would have to be identified by their dental records.

Chapter 15

Twin crowned maidens of the same royal bloodline face opposite directions while one lies upon the other. Together, they present a formidable front. It is the month of Julius Caesar, and he who controls their destiny chooses to sever the maidens' alliance, to the bewilderment of those in his company.

"I know this mothafucka is not about to split two queens," Cicero says from the end of the blackjack table. The décor of the casino is crude and tacky. The floor is smoky and filled with the usual degenerates and compulsive gamblers.

"The gentleman has twenty showing," the dealer instructs. "Sir, are you sure you want to split a twenty?"

In 1994, Kansas City's mafia families finally got what they wanted: Casinos. Five of them. No longer would they have to deal with the bureaucracy that Vegas had become. That desert pain in the ass could become a long-lost memory.

Since the year riverboat gambling graced the shores of the Missouri River, the number of households filing for bankruptcy quadrupled in the tiny midwestern market. After losing their cars and houses and family heirlooms, many gamblers simply stopped going. As a result, the area couldn't support five casinos and years later, only four remain.

"Yea, I'm sure. Split 'em," the gambler says, smoking on a square and sipping a rum and Coke.

Over fifty of Missouri's loosest slot machines line the vast and dense one-level playing area. Pink neon flamingoes jeeringly mock those seriously betting their lives away.

Cicero just shakes his head. He is a regular customer. He frequents all four of the boats, sometimes out of boredom, sometimes to win. Tonight he's in his usual spot at the Isle of Capri: the first seat on the dealer's left, where the initial cards of each hand will be dealt.

"I can't believe this shit," Cicero says. His pin-striped navy-blue three-button suit is flawless. And he's not alone in his discontent. Cicero has a seventeen, and the dealer has five showing.

The first card to the queen splitter is a three, and he waves the dealer off.

"Oh, come on," someone's grandmother whines. Her chain smoking has annoyed the hell out of Cicero all night. But she plays by the rules, and by sticking to the script, she's helped Cicero win two thousand dollars.

The dealer hits the other queen. It's a four.

"The gentleman has fourteen showing," the dealer states. "Would the gentleman like another hit?"

The non-gambler once again waves the dealer off.

"This is some for real bullshit," Cicero proclaims.

"Tell me about it," the guy next to him jumps in.

"Yea, hit me," the next man says. He's malnourished with a bushy, dirty mustache. The dealer issues him a nine, putting his total at twenty-six. Bust.

"Fuck me," he yells out, disgusted. "That was my four." Normally he wouldn't have taken a hit, but the genius before him broke every rule in the blackjack handbook. He had no choice.

The dealer continues dishing out cards to the packed table until he returns to himself. Bells ring and coins crash into metal trays. Cigarette butts litter the ornately patterned pink, purple, and sky-blue carpet. The island theme in Missouri is sickening.

"Dealer has fifteen," the blackjack pro states for his customers. Then a three springs from the deck. "Dealer has eighteen."

"Fuck," says the man after the splitter of queens. "That was my fucking four. I would have had nineteen." He stands and leaves the table, broke and sober.

The dealer collects Cicero's one-hundred dollar black chip as well as twenty fives and fifties down the table. He looks over at the table's asshole. The poor schmuck is so clueless he has no idea five other gamblers want to stick an ice pick in his chest.

The dealer once again hands each gambler a card, face up, with his first card face down. The second card comes around and at the end of the hand Cicero has several decisions to make.

A hand and wrist wearing a fake gold watch slides over the table.

"Insurance?" the dealer asks. There are no takers, so the hand slides again back the other way. "Insurance closed."

Cards slide under a tiny mirror fixed only for the dealer's eye. He checks it quickly, then move the cards back into standard playing position. He has a seven showing.

In front of Cicero is a sixteen. For him this is a no-brainer.

"Hit me," he confidently tells the dealer while sipping his cognac straight.

A five plops down perfectly next to his six.

"Twenty-one! Excellent hit, sir," the dealer congratulates.

"Good hit, man," the guy next to him reaffirms.

Roulette wheels spin and dealers in white shirts, black vests, and bow ties monitor their tables while black orbs above monitor the dealers. ATMs shuffle fresh cash to three- and four-time losers.

Tones suddenly emanate from Cicero's waistline and it catches the dealer's attention and he pauses the game.

"Sir, no phone calls at the table," he states.

"Yea, I know, hold my place," Cicero replies.

He stands and ambles away from the table and checks his phone's caller ID. The number looks familiar, but he can't recall whose it is.

"Hello," he answers. A slot machine shows three flaming sevens and the ringing and yelling cause him to strain to listen for the caller's voice.

"Hey, what's up?" a sexy voice says.

"Who is this?"

"Oh, you get big time and you don't recognize your sister's voice." Cicero feels relieved.

"Oh. Hey, what's goin' on?" he asks. He's more curious about her call than he is about what's going on in her life.

"Not too much. I'm going out to Charlie's for a drink," his sister answers.

"Oh yea?" he inquires.

"I sure am, and I just wanted to know if you wanted to meet me for a drink," Lucia says in a lovely voice. She then hears the ruckus of coins and eighties music from house speakers. "Where are you?"

"The boat. Where is Charlie's?"

"On Thirty-First and Main."

"When you goin'?"

"I'm on my way now."

Cicero checks his stainless steel timepiece. It's 10:48 p.m.

"Yea, okay. Let me cash out and I'll meet you up there."

"Okay, cool," Lucia says, sounding elated. "First round on you?"

Cicero laughs.

"Yea, okay."

"Okay, baby brother, see you up there."

"Alright, Lucia. See ya in a few."

They hang up and Cicero returns to his table only to find the table's fuck- up has finally left, and everyone, including the dealer, is happily relieved.

Cicero slides the dealer a fifty-dollar chip, then requests a rain check for his winnings so he isn't forced to carry nine-teen-hundred dollars in chips to the cash-out window. It's a safe move.

The dealer halts the game and motions to the pit boss, who approves the transaction. Cicero waits patiently, sipping the boat's cheap cognac while the small white slip of paper is inked.

"Double zero!" a nearby dealer shouts. That tiny ecru ball at the roulette wheel has skipped the red and black and has finally found the green and white ovals. It was long overdue.

But for the lucky bastard in the tight jeans with three five-dollar chips on the double zeros and two straddling the zeros, it was worth the wait. He was down a hundred but the seven-hundred dollar payout is enough for the old timer to cash out and buy a steak dinner at the local Waffle House.

Cicero ambles over to the window surrounded by brass bars and slides the gaming receipt to the cashier, who smells of cheap perfume and cigarette smoke. With a worn face and worn fingers, she speedily leafs through cash and slides it to Cicero. He rolls the money into a wad and slaps a rubber band around it.

Stepping over empty plastic cups and tubs meant for slot machine coins, he glides over to the escalator as bright lights flash and blink. The feet of the retired and those of drifters smack the carpeted floor in search of that one slot machine that's ready to hit. Fake palm trees and pink-and-blue island scenes becloud the sanity of those in search of instant riches.

Even when they win, they eventually give it right back to the boat. That's what gamblers do. They never know when to quit.

Cicero makes it outside and hands the valet his parking stub. The pimple-faced kid sprints over to the parking garage and moments later his new black Maybach appears. The insurance scam paid off, evidenced by the four plasma screens in the sun visors and headrests.

For twenty-five thousand in cash, young Jacque came through with two- hundred and fifty thousand dollars in bogus receipts for marble sculptures and original French and Italian artwork Cicero never purchased.

He hops in and notices his change from the center console is missing. Not wanting to be petty, he chalks it up and drives off on twenty-inch gold wire rims. They too were thrown in as part of his trumped-up claim with State Farm.

The nighttime air is chilly, but the cloudless sky allows every star in the galaxy to be viewed with ease from the flat plains.

Cicero cruises south in his six-thousand-pound beast, past the city's still-developing downtown. Years of town hall meetings and urban planning have produced very little inside the downtown loop, and after five p.m. the area is virtually a ghost town.

On top of that, underlying racism has thwarted efforts to establish a light rail system or subway: no one wants inner-city minorities having easy access to their suburban homes. The city's growth is at a standstill, which is why those eager to succeed either skip town all together or do as Cicero does, and hustle. Even if the town has little market value to legitimate corporations, it's a huge market for Coca and Mary Jane. Always has been, always will be. Cicero always knew: while some parts of the Fountain City are good for raising a family, other parts are good for raising a drug cartel.

He coasts fast and smooth as he drives south down Highway 71 in the owner-driver version Maybach fifty seven, sipping his glove compartment-stored cognac. His new chariot will surely ruffle the feathers of the city's envious motorists. On the dark empty highway, thoughts of his father drift in and out of his head.

Slow jams disseminate from the local radio station and filter through his high-tech stereo. Cicero wonders if his father had actually accomplished anything in life. He had made a name for himself on the streets, but would Antonio be content with that?

Cicero nears his exit from Highway 71 and makes a gliding slant to the right. He makes a smooth right turn at the light and notices a family of four stranded. Steam billows from the hood of their station wagon as the father of the family tries to flag Cicero down. His assistance is much needed.

Two small children sit huddled together in the backseat as Cicero ignores the father's plea for help and continues on to the nightclub to meet Lucia. He doesn't consider stopping for one second.

The neighborhood is brimming with the aroma of marinated pork ribs as he passes one of the city's oldest barbecue restaurant chains. He's been drinking all night, and the smell has him considering stopping and ordering a slab with fries and a strawberry pop.

Nonetheless, Cicero continues to head west riding steady and sure, surrounded by soft leather and beautiful wood grain. Twin turbochargers purr as he nears the club and begins searching for a parking spot.

"Why am I here?" Cicero says to himself out loud. This is not his type of scene, not his crowd.

He parks his Maybach a safe distance from the club and once at the door of the historic brick building pays the enormous amount of twenty dollars to get in.

"Is Marvin Gaye singing here tonight?" Cicero sarcastically asks the bouncer at the door.

"Nope. You got ID?" the bouncer asks after frisking Cicero. He presents his Missouri driver's license, then steps into the club. He's immediately struck by loud R&B tunes blasting from multiple speakers. The club is crowded with hard-working blue-collar guys, a few executives, and unemployed people who look like they just got off work, including Lucia.

Guys in suits sip on beers while others in expensive sweaters pop bottles of Moët at little tables with signs on them that say RESERVED.

The mood is festive. Lovely women with red skin tones in tight jeans and tight skirts giggle at silly jokes and make eye contact with potential suitors. Several stare at Cicero and smile, which he does in return to a couple who catch his eye.

A waving hand then appears from out of the throng near the bar.

"Cicero! Cicero! Over here, boy!" Lucia yells.

Cicero sees her and makes his way over to the bar where his sister is standing with a girlfriend of hers. Dance floor lights bounce off his bald head.

He cuts through a group of chubby women chatting, then suddenly feels extreme pressure on his right foot.

"Fuck!"

"Oh, my bad, player," a drunk guy apologizes after stepping on Cicero's loafers. His Cartier sunglasses are on the verge of falling off his face as he stumbles toward the dance floor.

Cicero's fingers curl inward and knuckles protrude. Cicero's pissed off but he refrains from flashing on the guy.

"It's cool, dog," Cicero replies. Jolting lyrics come across loud and clear in the romantically lit nightspot.

"What took you so long, boy?" Lucia asks as Cicero finally makes his way to the bar.

"How you doin', honey?" Cicero says before hugging his sister.

"C, this is Cheryl." Lucia points to a large Amazon woman.

"Hey, Cicero," Cheryl says with a huge grin. Her bright red lipstick and makeup are caked on and nearly offensive.

"How are you, Cheryl? Nice to meet you."

"Are you still single, wit' yo' fine ass?" Cheryl blurts in a raspy voice. She and Lucia have been drinking Long Island Iced Teas all night.

Cicero laughs. "Yes, I am single, Cheryl."

"And no kids, girl!" Lucia weighs in, lovingly rubbing her brother's arm.

"None that I know of," he quips, and the group laughs.

Cicero orders a cognac from the bartender, then scans the room for familiar faces. Even though he rarely goes to night-clubs, he knows many of the guys and women in here. In his younger days Cicero was always in the mix, but as he began to make more money, he didn't have time for parties, nor the anxiety associated with the city nightlife: carjackers, young hustlers trying to make a name for themselves, beggin'-ass females. Nevertheless, he is known around town for his gangster connections. Some consider it the ultimate feat.

"Hey, what's up, C?" a man dressed in an oversized black suit says. His hair lays flat on his head. Every tooth in his head is gold.

"What's up, man, how you been?" Cicero says.

"Just chillin', man. I heard you got a new Maybach."

"Oh yea? Damn. Where did you hear that?"

"Shit, you know Kansas City is small. Man, I heard those run like four-hundred thousand dollars."

Cicero laughs.

"Naw, man. It's nothing major."

"Damn, I heard that. Do ya thang."

Cicero smiles, then nods, as does the talkative man.

"Hey, this round's on me. What you drinkin'?" the guy questions, yelling over the loud music.

"Oh, just a little XO," Cicero says, then smiles.

"Cool. Hey," the guy yells to the bartender. "Let me get an XO!"

The busy bartender reaches up to the top shelf of the glass and mirror case behind him and pours the minimum requirement for a shot.

"That's twenty-five dollars."

"Damn! Cicero, you tryin' to get all my pocket money," the guy complains as he ruffles through his wallet. He reluctantly pays the bartender, leaving him with five dollars in his wallet. Cicero sees the five and chuckles under his breath. The club's loud music muffles it.

"Damn, C. You an expensive-ass date! I guess I'll be getting one Bud Ice and calling it a night."

Cicero laughs.

"Thanks, Kev, next round on me," Cicero says loudly over the throbbing rap music.

"Cool. I need it, too," Kevin replies. He's one of Cicero's occasional customers. They used to play sandlot football and three-on-three basketball together in his mom's neighborhood. These days, they sometimes meet, maybe once or twice a year, in secluded locations and exchange C-notes for nose candy. C is Kev's back-up connection. Kev normally fucks with the Mexicans on the west side.

As the night goes on, more and more people step inside the club, and more and more guys buy Cicero a drink: customers, other hustlers, and old friends from school.

"Oh shit, is that my boy?" a now drunk Cicero inquires out loud, looking across the room. His words reverberate off the nightclub's exposed burgundy brick walls.

The short pudgy guy in the white, long-sleeved shirt turns around and his cheeks go ear to ear, making his goatee curve.

"What's up, Cicero?" the short guy yells from about ten yards away. He drunkenly makes his way toward Cicero, bumping into people and spilling his beer.

"Where the fuck have you been, Fry?" Cicero asks his buddy as they hug.

"What's up, boy?! Man, I haven't seen you, in like, three years," Fry replies, still hugging his friend.

They both take a step back and look at each other. They spent some broke, bored nights together in college. But they also started hustling together in college.

"Man, I've just been layin' low, tryin' to handle my business. You feel me?" Cicero slurs, now holding a half-empty beer bottle.

"Yea, man. I've been in Houston, Las Vegas. You know I'm trying to start my own clothing line?" the stocky Fry says.

"Yea, I heard about that. How's that goin?"

"It's goin' cool," Fry says, putting on his serious face. "Right now I'm working on my marketing plan. The clothes are straight, it's just getting my shit in stores, you know?"

"Yea, I feel you. Keep at it, man. Let me know if there's anything I can do to help."

"No doubt, dude. No doubt. That's real talk," Fry states. He then glances around their nearby vicinity and inches closer toward Cicero's ear. The music is clamorous.

"Hey, dude, I might have beef up in here," Fry tells him.

Cicero's face goes from smiling to expressionless. He loves beef more than a Texas cattle rancher does.

"It's whatever. Just say the word," Cicero says before taking a small swig of his beer. "What's crackin'?"

"Nothin' for real, just this buster. It's over some old dumb shit," Fry calmly explains. "But I saw him when I walked in, and he was muggin' and shit."

A look is all it takes. The slightest glance can say a thousand words. Countless people in the city would fight, even kill, for their respect. Yes, over a look.

"Man, I got your back, you know that. It's whatever," Cicero says, then smiles. He and Fry shake hands.

The liquor has Cicero on edge, just like the hundred other men in the club. The wild west still exists.

"All right, dude," Fry says.

He then walks off to mingle and Cicero stumbles back over to the bar to have a seat. He orders a drink of water to dilute all the alcohol he has consumed tonight.

"*Shake somethin', dance a little bit. Shake somethin', dance hoe, you ain't doin' shit,*" the music blares. Gone are the days of Chubby Checker's "Twist and Shout."

Cicero sits at the bar with squinty eyes, saying hello to old flames and associates, when he eyes a woman with an Olympic body whose services he often employed when it was called for.

The beautiful twenty-seven-year-old waves and Cicero nods in acknowledgment. They choose not to speak to each other in public, but Cicero grins as he recalls first having sex with the young woman a few years ago, when he realized her vagina had to be the biggest he had ever been in.

Even the act of making love couldn't keep Cicero from thinking about business, which is why one week later the young lady had half a kilo of snow in her love box traveling from LAX to KCI.

Still sitting at the bar with a major buzz, Cicero notices Lucia across the crowded room arguing with her ex-boyfriend. It doesn't mean much to Cicero, however, because Lucia is always arguing with somebody.

But at that moment, her tall ex-man waves his fingers in her face, then walks away. Cicero can see his mouth clearly say, "Fuck you, bitch!"

Cicero has a gut reaction. His stomach tenses, as he watches Lucia storm through the crowded club toward him. Her friend Cheryl is nowhere to be seen.

Lucia, in a high-priced cream chiffon Chanel suit, reaches Cicero with a frightened look on her face.

"This mothafucka John just threatened me," she pants, nearly out of breath.

Cicero is thrown for a loss.

"What? Are you serious?" he asks with his deep voice.

"Yes! He said he heard I was talking shit about him to some other girls or something. And he said he was going to fuck me up. Cicero, will you go talk to him?" Lucia pleads. She's afraid.

Whether or not his sister was talking about this guy, to Cicero, it doesn't matter. He could deal with Lucia later. As for now, this situation had to be handled.

"Yea, I'ma talk to him right now," C replies.

He drops a fifty-dollar tip for the bartender, then stands with his suds-filled beer bottle and walks through the dancing and talking clubgoers. His pin-striped cobalt suit fits him well as the look on Cicero's face commands respect from everyone in the nightclub.

Lucia's ex-boyfriend is tall and dark as night, so it's easy to see his chocolate bald head ambling through the nightspot. Hours of drinking forces John to the bustling bathroom, as Cicero follows close behind him. Unfortunately for John, he's from out of town, and he has no idea who he's just threatened. Having only lived in the area for a year, John knows little of Lucia's younger brother, nor does he know he's in the club, and following him.

Hours of drinking have also intensified Cicero's self-diagnosed paranoid personality disorder, forcing him to retaliate against John quickly, without any thoughts of forgiveness clouding his rage.

John steps into the tiny, overcrowded bathroom and Cicero pushes in behind him.

"Hey! Hey, there's no room in here," a guy yells from one of the two urinals. The restroom is probably about ten feet long and five feet wide, but there are six grown men in it, waiting in line.

"You're all right, just hurry up," Cicero yells to the guy up front. Despite the frantic pace in and out of the restroom all night, the white tile floor is spotless and bright.

One by one, the guys piss and leave. By the time John makes it to the urinal, only he and Cicero are in the restroom.

Cicero thinks about his beautiful sister, and how this large dude threatened her. Cicero thinks about the look of fear on Lucia's face, and without a word, he puts all the force he can muster into swinging his chestnut- brown beer bottle into the back of John's bald head.

Crash! Glass shards scatter as blood immediately flows from John's dark head.

"Aarrgh! What the fuck?" John screams as he grabs his head, turning toward Cicero to face him. "What the fuck is wrong with you?"

Enraged, Cicero yells at the taller, bleeding John.

"Don't ever threaten my sister again, mothafucka!" Cicero proclaims before firing rights and lefts to John's face, connecting with each blow.

The fists flying at him stun the former college football player, but he's in phenomenal condition, which is why he's able to rush Cicero and completely lift him off his feet in a powerful bear hug.

"Fuck," Cicero yells as his back is forcefully thrust against a paper towel dispenser. Cicero continues to punch John right where the bottle struck him, deepening the gouge in his head and driving chunks of glass into his skull.

"Don't ever talk to my sister like that, you bitch-ass motha-fucka!" Cicero yells in John's ear, steady striking him in the back of his head with his right hand.

A crowd gathers outside the bathroom door and several men and women peer in.

"Oh shit!" one woman screams after seeing blood everywhere. In fact, there's so much blood flowing from John's head that he slips in it, and he and Cicero fall to the floor.

Cicero then wraps his left arm around John's neck, placing him in a headlock.

"You bitch-ass mothafucka," Cicero says while pounding John's face with his right hand. It sounds like a meat tenderizer strik-ing a slab of beef. John's nose is repeatedly hit as he regains his grip around Cicero's waist and once again lifts him off the ground, slamming his back into the sink.

The club's old security guard finally makes his way to the commotion in the restroom.

"Ya'll stop all that fighting now," he says with a Southern drawl before pulling the door open. "Holy shit!"

He sees blood all over the walls, floor, sink, and urinals.

The astonished security guard slowly backs up and closes the door and walks away, while Cicero continues to punch John in his face. John once again drops Cicero and they both fall to the floor. This time, John just lies there, holding his head. He's lost too much blood and he's feeling weak. Realizing John could die right here, right now, Cicero hops up and dashes out the bathroom, covered in blood.

"That's him! Somebody stop him!" a waitress yells out. Some-body goes to grab Cicero, but his loving sister is able to grab the person, and all three of them fall to the dance floor.

Then like an angel, Fry, in his white shirt, reaches down and frees Cicero.

"Get the fuck up, dude," Fry tells his friend as he pulls him to his feet. "Cecil is outside in his car. Come on!"

Fry leads a blood-covered Cicero through the crowd to the chilly nighttime air.

"Man, I was the one supposed to be fighting tonight," Fry jokes.

Once outside, Cicero sees his friend Cecil from college in his spotless Lincoln Town Car.

"Get in, dude!" Cecil yells from the driver's seat. Fry opens the back door and Cicero hops in as tires screech and the two are in the wind like tumbleweeds.

Back inside the club, one of John's lady friends grabs a towel and holds it to the back of his head.

"Somebody call an ambulance!" she screams. The bathroom resembles a brutal murder scene, which it could have been.

Lucia, seeing John is still alive, coolly makes her way to the back of the club and slips out a back door. She runs down an alley to her car, and calls Cicero on his cell phone.

"Yea."

"Are you okay?"

"I'm cool."

"Where you headed?"

"I don't know."

"Okay, well, what should I do?"

Cicero thinks for a minute.

"Just go home. I don't think he'll be bothering you anymore."

"Okay. Call me when you get somewhere."

"All right."

"Bye, baby brother."

"Okay, bye."

And he hangs up.

"Man, I was just about to park," Cecil yells to the backseat. "There was tight bitches in there."

Cicero laughs. "My bad."

"It's all good, fuck it," Cecil states. "I guess I just have to fuck my baby's mother again."

The two laugh as they run red lights on their way back to the hood. Cicero, full of adrenaline and liquor, glances down and realizes he only has on one shoe.

"Fuck. Ain't that a bitch."

"What?"

"Man, I lost my shoe in the club."

Cecil laughs.

"Fuck it. At least you ain't a blood donor right now like ya boy."

"Yea, you got that right."

At that moment Cicero's text message communicator vibrates on his hip. Somehow it wasn't destroyed in the alter-cation, so he opens the silver box and checks the message. It's from Olivia.

"HEY, WUT'S GOIN ON??? I HEARD BOUT WUT HPND. U OK??"

News travels fast and Cicero smiles. He loves how the peo-ple he shits on care so much about him.

"I'm okay. Will hit u back later. Stay safe," he replies to her.

"U 2. Lata," she texts him.

Cecil's Lincoln cuts corners and Cicero closes his communi-cator as his thoughts turn to Brad, hoping he's on top of their drug venture. They pass by a rundown factory and Cicero asks

Cecil to pull around back. The car enters the pitch-black alley-way and Cicero eyes a forest-green dumpster.

"Yea, pull up to that dumpster." He then jumps out the car into the frigid air and removes his shoe, socks, pants, suit jacket, and shirt, and throws it all in.

He comes back to the car with his cell phone and text messen-ger in hand wearing only boxers and a wife beater.

"Okay, let's go," Cicero says.

Cecil just shakes his head and chuckles as his car's rims rotate expeditiously, leaving black burnt rubber on the asphalt.

"Hey, man, you can take me in the morning to pick up my car?" Cicero asks, feeling funny in his underwear.

"Yea, I got you."

"Cool. After that I'll take you to Niece's for breakfast. Get you some pancakes. Cool?"

Cecil laughs.

"Cool."

✖✖✖

Later that night, after Charlie's has emptied out and Cicero is safely tucked in his bed, flight ensues through billowy evening clouds. It is intense and invigorating. The aviator joyously soars above the treeline without the aid of propellers or jet fuel.

His hands reach toward the icy rings of Saturn, as well as her moons Mimas and Dione. He sails through the indigo firma-ment. He is the envy of falcons.

This man in flight is Cicero, and he flies under the light of a full moon in a late-night dream. His black cotton T-shirt and white boxers blow in the breeze of atmospheric travel.

This dream is not new; he's had it many times. But his liftoff soon takes a harrowing turn when he hears howling close behind him. To his chagrin, three wolves are also in flight, and they pursue him with salivating mouths.

"Shit," Cicero says.

He dives at the speed of sound toward the Earth, yet the fanged marauders continue to gain on his position. Cicero's heart begins to race while he glides under power lines in this mountainous rural area.

The red sands of the desert are strangely foreboding as the wolves get within mere feet of Cicero's flesh. They eagerly wish to sample it.

Stars blink in the distance. He slides between cardinal red barns and silvery silos, but he can't shake the hairy dark-gray carnivores. In desperation, he decides to stand and fight, so he lands on the rooftop of an abandoned farmhouse. Acres of dead corn stalks wilt on the land.

He stands unscathed on the roof as he turns to face the predators, but they are gone. The night is silent and empty. Cicero glances to his left, then back to his right, when he notices food has appeared on a candlelit table for two.

He steps closer to the rooftop dinette as two opposing meals rest on gold leaf plates. Cicero inspects the fare. On the plate closest to him is a ripe Bartlett pear. But on the other saucer is a medium-rare filet mignon, plump and juicy.

Never one to pass up fine provisions, not even in a dream, Cicero moves to the other side of the table, where he takes a knife and fork in hand. He slices the succulent cutlet and proceeds to partake, but just before his tongue can taste the meat, he sees it has become infested with squirming maggots.

Startled, he drops the fork and knife and the wolves suddenly reappear, surrounding him. They stare at him with piercing yellow eyes.

Cicero tries to flee with outstretched arms, but his power of flight has vanished. *Canis lupis* drool as they advance on him and sink their teeth into Cicero's muscular legs and back. He screams, and there is a shrill ringing in his ears. The carnivores gorge themselves on his body as blood spews.

The ringing in his ears intensifies and he screams again upon waking up, alone in his bedroom, drenched in sweat. The ringing telephone is loud and lucid.

A bare-chested Cicero sits up in his bed.

"Fuck," he murmurs in a low voice.

Sweat rolls off his torso onto the black silk sheets. Yet another nightmare has disturbed his slumber, and the phone at his bedside continues to ring. Cicero gazes up at the large wall-mounted clock. It's 4:00 a.m.

Cicero reaches over and grabs the phone.

"Hello."

"You know a Bradley Micheaux?"

"Who is this?"

"He's gonna skip town with your money." Then the caller hangs up.

Cicero, left holding a dead phone, is without a clue as to who was on the other end. He returns the sleek black cordless phone back to its base and reclines in his king-sized bed.

He lies down and shuts his eyes. Cicero ponders the meaning of his dream, and the subsequent phone call. As he begins to doze off, he hopes peaceful sleep will come. He hopes... peaceful sleep...will eventually come.

Chapter 16

The solstice bids farewell and the equinox comes to pass. Life explodes with vibrancy, then diminishes as the Earth tilts on its axis.

Bradley Micheaux has been cranking out product by the boatload all summer long. It's gaining an intensely loyal fan base on the underground rave scene. Money is rolling in, but dissension is afoot. As the season of winter comes forth, so does discontent. A few months after that anonymous late-night phone call, a newly resolved Cicero has fresh insight.

"That's real, man. The truth always comes to light," Cicero tells Kam as they sit in a noisy restaurant. "Yea, man, turns out punk-ass Brad is planning to get low with the dope," Cicero continues. "Like, fuck us."

"Man, how you know?"

"Remember that white bitch I was fuckin' wit?"

"Yea, the little thick one."

"Yea, she knows his boys Collin and J.L., and they been runnin' they mouths and shit."

"You gotta be fuckin' kiddin' me, dog?" Kam says in his deep voice. "C, don't fuckin' play, man."

Cicero just stares at him. His expensive lime-green Australian-made sweater hangs a bit loose on him. Nonetheless, it coordinates perfectly with his lime-green ostrich boots.

"So this mothafucka is just gonna bounce?" Kam rhetorically inquires, wearing a sky-blue sweatsuit. "Okay, I'm going to twist his roof off. Fuck that. We still got about eight-hundred-thousand dollars to pay Jimmy back."

Kam hides his eyes behind light-blue rimless Gucci sunglasses, and he is so gung-ho it causes Cicero to chuckle.

"Hold on, man."

"Naw, dude, fuck that."

Vibrations on Cicero's hip make him pause and he checks his text message communicator. The message reads: "Where's da restaurant?"

He quickly types in: "On the corner. Forty-Seventh."

He places the device back on his hip and looks back up at Kam.

"No, seriously, I got more bad news."

"Dude, don't spoil my appetite," Kam says, but Cicero goes on as the lunchtime crowd picks up and the volume in the quirky restaurant increases.

"You remember when we met Jimmy at his spot?"

"Yea," Kam replies, his teeth glitter and sparkle.

"Well, you remember that cat that was with Jimmy and ya boy, Petey Pete?"

Kam holds back a laugh, at the same time bracing for the worst.

"Fuck. Yea, I remember him."

"Well, he was a fed."

"Fuck," Kam grumbles. A group of older businessmen in suits glance over at him, offended by his midday language, but Kameron ignores them.

"Yea, I know. My plug over at the FBI just told me that shit today. You know ole girl with the short hair that used to hang with my sister?"

"Yea, I remember her, but fuck that. That doesn't help us

now," Kam says sarcastically. His white-and-sky-blue sneakers begin to tap the hardwood floor in a now irritated state.

"I feel you," Cicero tells him. "So check it out," he says, leaning slightly toward Kam and lowering his voice. "I'm gonna bounce for about a week or two to lay low and figure out my next move."

Kam is without words as he fiddles with his place setting and spoon.

"Man, I suggest you do the same," adds Cicero, leaning back and raising his voice back to normal. "That's real talk."

"Shit. You think Jimmy knows dude is a fed?"

"Man, I don't know. I'm not about to call him and tell him," Cicero grins. "Fuck that. Our phones probably got more bugs than the projects."

Kam just frowns and shakes his head.

"Man, I ain't goin' nowhere, cuz," Kam asserts. "Shit, where would I go?"

Cicero just stares at him as he places his hand in his slacks' pocket and impatiently jiggles his car keys.

"Man, I'm out here funkin' with dagos, and duckin' and dodgin' the feds? Fuck that," Kam continues. "Man, I'm down to grind for mine! These mothafuckas act like we don't lay bodies out. Like we ain't 'bout that drama. Man, I've been known to dish out toe tags. It's whatever!"

Kam angrily throws his hands up, ready to accept all comers. His chest heaves as adrenaline begins to flow in his arteries.

At that moment, a perky young waitress walks up. Kam and Cicero immediately notice the top button on her white blouse is open, exposing ample cleavage. They both get in quick glances before she can get a word out. The move relieves some tension at their table.

"Can I take your order?" she asks in a sweet tone.

Kam, now calm, picks up the menu and looks at it for the first time.

"Yea, let me have the smothered grilled chicken sandwich with everything on it," Kam requests.

"Mushrooms, onions, and cheddar cheese?" asks the waitress.

"Yea. That's everything, ain't it?" Kam bitingly responds.

"Yes. I was just checking, a lot of people don't like the mushrooms," she answers. "You want fries with that?"

"Yea."

"And what can I get you to drink?"

"Let me get the house stout."

"Okay, great," the waitress says, penciling shorthand onto a tattered note- pad. "And for you?" she asks, looking at Cicero and smiling.

"Yea, I'll have the Caesar salad."

"Will that be all?"

"Yes."

"And to drink?"

"Water."

"Okay. I'll bring your drinks right out," the waitress says before walking off to the bar.

Kam looks pissed.

"A Caesar salad? You fag," he tells Cicero.

"Man, I need to eat healthier," Cicero explains. "Don't you know obesity is an epidemic?"

Unimpressed, Kam continues to press the issue.

"Water? Fuck, man, at least get a beer," Kam pokes.

"Man, fuck you," Cicero says leaning back, getting upset. "Don't worry about what I order, asshole. How 'bout that?"

"Fuck you!" Kam fires back, yelling and leaning forward.

Then they both stare at each other with intense eyes, both appearing seriously agitated. Several customers gaze at them as they lock eyes. The stress of their lifestyle has caught up to them, and Cicero's fingers begin to tap the white tablecloth while Kam's left foot speeds its non-stop tapping.

Then suddenly, Cicero smiles. Not that he's weaker, but he's more cognizant. He knows if they get into a fight on the Plaza, the police will be there in a flash, and will quickly take them to jail and begin looking up records and other things that don't need to be looked into.

"Dude, you need to calm the fuck down," he tells Kam. "For real."

Kam's face lightens. While they've never had a fight, this isn't the first stand-off they've had. And Cicero always seems to have the cooler head to end it, so Kam relents.

"Yea, you right," Kam says, relaxing and calming his busy foot. "Man, I've just been real fuckin' edgy lately."

"Getting shot tends to do that," Cicero weighs in. Foot traffic in oxfords and low pumps skirts past them in a rush, but they sit patiently in the restaurant with a functioning model train making rounds along the ceiling. They don't have jobs, so they sit.

"I know, man. And this new shit doesn't help," Kam insists.

Other oddities hang from the ceiling, such as brassieres and football jerseys, and French advertisements from the thirties and forties. Dames in yellow ankle-length dresses and pearls cling to bubbling beverages as they prance. Their smiles, dipped in bright red lipstick, are wide and stretching.

The waitress then returns with their drinks as firm legs sexily enter the restaurant's foyer, extending from underneath a snug black miniskirt.

Lana walks in with a bag of hot goods, and her striking looks attract stares from men and women. Her plump ass pokes out of her skintight black dress like a giant bee sting.

Cicero sits facing the door as always, something his father taught him, and he stares at her.

"Damn," he mumbles.

Kam turns his head in interest and his face wrenches.

"Shit," Kam mutters. Princess cuts on his sport watch reflect light from the restaurant's halogen bulbs.

Lana strides in and all eyes are on her and her skin tone, which is the equivalent of a steaming café latte. The conservatively dressed businesswomen are put to shame by her young fine body and garish confidence. Her auburn hair is untamed and wild. She is a caramel delicacy.

"I got that watch you wanted," she says as she smoothly slides into the cushy booth next to Kam, forcing him to slide over.

Lana has delivered on everything Cicero and Kam have asked for, and today she brings the crème de la crème: a Patek Philippe timepiece encrusted in nearly two hundred diamonds.

"Why you lookin' like a supermodel?" Kam asks Lana, flashing his oral baguettes.

Lana has an incredulous look on her clear skin. Her green eyes are stunning.

"Are you kidding me? This is the Plaza," she responds. "You have to look like you have money or they will follow your ass all around the store."

A five-carat tennis bracelet shimmers on her tiny wrist.

Cicero laughs.

"Hell, you give them a reason to follow you around," he says. They all chuckle.

"I know," the five-foot-three Lana replies, grinning, realizing the hypocrisy of her complaint. Her teeth are spectacularly white and straight.

She then reaches into her forest-green shopping bag and pulls out a maroon cube. She opens the box and all the light in the room is immediately drawn to the amazing platinum wrist-watch. It causes Cicero to squint. The time tracker is completely smothered in diamonds and sapphires from end to end.

"Damn," Kameron says in a drawn-out low voice. "That's a nice-ass watch."

Lana holds it close to the table so not to attract too much attention. Cicero just stares at it with a sly grin.

"Look at the price tag," Lana instructs.

Kam reaches into the box and flips the small white tag over and sees two hundred thousand and some change. But he remains calm.

"Yea, that's definitely a nice-ass watch," he repeats in the under-statement of the day. "I can only imagine what you did to get that joint."

Lana glances at him and smirks.

"Whatever," she says playfully.

Twenty-eight baguette diamonds hold down the face, along with eight sapphires the shape of spheres and three shaped like rectangles. The bracelet is set with one hundred and sixty-seven diamonds running the entire length.

Cicero ogles the perfection of the timepiece; its craftsmanship. He's awestruck. Another ninety diamonds somehow found room around the bezel. It's breathtaking.

"Yea, ole boy at the store said it's resistant to humidity, dust, and up to one hundred meters of water," Lana explains. "Something like that."

Cicero notices how the bezel is neither square nor circular. Rather, it resembles a ship's porthole.

"I can give you fifty later today, then fifty next week," Cicero says. "Cool?"

"That's cool," Lana says as she hands it to him under the table. Cicero tosses the watch back in the box and places the box in the forest-green bag.

"Damn, man, is time that important to you?" Kam asks with a chuckle.

Cicero thinks about his question for a moment, then answers, "Yea. Yea, I guess it is. You only here once, Kam. And after this, there's nothin' else, so every minute counts."

Kam shrugs off Cicero's comment and sneaks a peek at Lana's cleavage. Feeling Kam's eyes on her, Lana turns away from him in the booth.

"So did you guys order?" asks Lana.

"Yep," replies Kam. "Why? You gonna have a meal with ya boy?"

Lana looks at Kam and frowns.

"Naw, I got some shit to do," she states.

Cicero laughs.

"You mean you got some shit to steal," he says to her, mockingly.

Lana's full lips curl and she looks slightly offended.

"No. Actually I'm meeting my cousin," she states.

Their hurried waitress seems frazzled in the lunchtime rush as she stops near the corner of their table.

"Sorry, guys. Your meals are coming right up," she tells them. "Ma'am, can I get you something?"

"No, thank you," Lana says. "I'm not staying."

"Okay, your food will be right up," echoes the waitress, then she scurries off in comfortable rubber-soled shoes and black loose-fitting pants.

"Damn, I need to call my mom," Cicero says out of nowhere.

"Well, you two have fun," she says as she stands to leave.

Kam looks at her from head to toe and smiles.

"Hey, Lana, guess what Cicero ordered."

"I don't know. What, a burger?" she asks, adjusting the spaghetti straps on her tiny black dress.

Kam laughs, showing his diamond teeth.

"Hell, naw, this fag ordered a damn salad," Kam says with a frown.

Lana glances at Cicero.

"You on a diet?" she questions. "You look like you're in shape."

"Naw, I'm not on a diet," Cicero reluctantly answers. "I'm just watching what I eat. Is that all right with you, Ms. Lana?"

"Hey, live ya life," she says.

"Whatever," Kam blurts. "I'm watchin' you, Big C."

"Well, I'm out," Lana tells them. "Ya'll be safe."

And she strides toward the door, wild hair bouncing. And once again she attracts the eyes of both he and she, as young Ms. Lana exits the eatery.

Kam and Cicero receive their meals and begin to indulge.

"So, where you gonna go?" Kam asks, stuffing his mouth with fries. Later tonight he'll be brushing his teeth thoroughly with jewelry cleaner.

"Don't know yet," Cicero answers, not giving Kam any details. He figures it's better that way. No loose ends.

Kam's eyes squint.

"I figure I'll just lay low," he adds. "You know, just chill out. Spend a few days getting my shit together outta town. You should do the same."

"Naw, fuck that," Kam exclaims in his slow, deep voice. "I'm not into bouncing like that. I mean, I got money to get. I ain't worried about it."

Cicero leaves it at that. They finish their meals and wait for the check. Cicero drops one-hundred dollars for the food and the tip and they depart, going separate ways.

C enters the parking garage, then hops in his Maybach. The supple dark-blue leather happily greets him.

"I love this car," he says to himself, staring at the engagingly illuminated instrument panel.

The vehicle smoothly rolls out the garage and Cicero makes a left on West Forty-Seventh Street. The royal-blue sky is impeccable on this cloudless day. The temperature is perfect.

There's no music playing in the car, so Cicero is free to think, uninterrupted. He ponders Brad's intentions to basically fuck him and Kam. He thinks about how he and Brad were so close in college, and yet over time, have drifted apart. Struggling in college had brought them together, but once their struggles were over, Cicero thought, so were their commonalities.

Then his cell phone rings. His Maybach heads east, crossing Troost Avenue, KC's very own Mason-Dixon Line, as he answers the phone.

"Hey, what's up?"

"Not too much. I just haven't heard from you in a while," Olivia says in her eternally saddened tone.

It's true. Cicero has had no need for her, so he could not care less.

"Yea, I've been hella busy," he tells her. "How have you been?"

"Okay, I guess," she says, sighing as she lies in her bed staring up at the ceiling. Several bottles of medication line her bureau. She's taken her cocktail for today, and is feeling dispirited as usual. Fortunately, the nausea hasn't kicked in yet, and her occasional bouts of diarrhea have subsided.

"Oh yea?" Cicero says, unconcerned. "So what's new with you?"

Olivia sits up in the bed and crosses her arms and legs at the ankles. The white T-shirt and red shorts she has on fits her in a comfortably sexy way.

"Cicero, what do you think about me?"

"What do you mean, O? You're my girl. My partner. You know?"

Olivia doesn't buy that answer.

"No, Cicero. That's not what I mean. Do you care about me?"

Cicero exhales deeply. He doesn't want to have this conversation. He's been able to avoid this discussion since day one. He mashes the pedal in his Maybach headed toward the hood.

"Olivia, it pleases me when you're happy, baby. And that's all I can say. I want you to be happy."

Olivia pauses and her eyes go down. Her beautiful skin is freshly oiled and it shines as sunlight penetrates the blinds in her room. Her hair flows past her shoulders and down her back.

"You really don't care about me, do you, Cicero?" she asks.

Cicero is becoming fed up with this conversation. He has Brad to worry about, not to mention Jimmy and other shit. And he still needs to make travel arrangements. He simply has more important things to deal with.

"No. No, I don't give a fuck about you, Olivia. Is that what you wanted to hear?" Cicero flashes. "I mean, shit, I pay yo tainted ass to fuck mothafuckas I hate. Could I really give a fuck about you?"

Olivia is silent. A solitary tear descends from her right eye and lands on the corner of her mouth. She extends her tongue to taste it.

"Yea. I always knew that," she says confidently. "I always knew that. But I'm glad that you said it. Thank you."

Cicero looks at the phone, not believing his ears.

"You know, I thought you at least cared a little bit, but I guess not. You're an evil man, Cicero. But you'll get yours."

"Whatever," Cicero grumbles. "Are you done?"

"Yes. Good-bye."

And she hangs up.

Cicero glances at his phone, then tosses it onto the passenger seat. It's easy for him to degrade and abuse Olivia and have no feelings of remorse.

"I don't have time for this shit," he states in his deep voice. "Nasty-ass, stupid-ass bitch."

Cicero reaches Prospect Avenue, then stops at a red light.

"Where the fuck am I going?" he questions out loud.

He makes a sharp left into a gas station, then parks.

"Damn, that car is sick," a young cat with gold teeth yells. He and his boys jump into an eighty-six Monte Carlo SS and get low in a hurry, while Cicero places a fully loaded nine-millimeter on his lap. He knows how guys in this part of town get down, and he's ready for them.

Cicero glances down and checks his new Patek Philippe watch. It's 4:36 p.m.

"Fuck it."

He grabs his cell phone and calls information.

"What city and state?"

"Kansas City, Missouri."

"What listing?"

"American Airlines."

Moments later, Cicero Day has a roundtrip ticket to the Golden State. His flight leaves at 8:00 p.m. tonight.

He puts the pedal to the floor and burns rubber back to the west.

Cicero grinds his teeth as murderous thoughts scale hurdles in his bald head.

"This punk-ass mothafucka," he whispers to himself, thinking about Brad's treachery. His black Maybach glides like a daydream down the rugged pothole-laden street as scattered clouds begin to roll into the stratosphere above.

A certain Bradley Micheaux shall soon have an uninvited guest.

Stopping by his apartment, Cicero grabs a small black vial from a nightstand drawer and stuffs it in a tight black velvet bag. He then opens a safe under his bed and takes out ten-thousand dollars in cash. Rushing and nearly tripping over the black leather bench in front of his bed, Cicero also tosses a few sweaters, a suit, a couple pairs of slacks, some alligator boots and a pair of Italian loafers into a black suitcase before trotting down to the parking garage and hopping back in his sedan.

"Yea, Brad, I got somethin' for ya," Cicero says to himself as he starts his car. Then once again he's in the wind, cutting corners, on a mission.

Cicero navigates toward The Paseo, then heads north, crossing the Missouri River, toward the International Airport and the unsuspecting Bradley Micheaux's North Kansas City home.

✖✖✖

Cotton, silk, and wool blends twist and bend, misaligned and uneven. Cuffs touch collars. Zippers invite sleeves. Buttons long to be fastened. Boxer shorts crumple under the weight of dress loafers. Wrinkles feel at home on expensive trousers as toiletries are dumped on them, joiningthe fray.

A certain Cajun also has travel plans in mind, so he secretively throws his clothes and personals into a large dark-brown carpetbag. A similar bag rests next to it on the king-sized bed, stuffed to the brim with chrome-like discs containing little blue tablets, and the chemicals needed to replicate them. Documents with notes and formulas also lie in the bag, along with a hundred thousand in cash.

Brad, shirtless and wearing only faded blue jeans, leisurely ambles about his small, modernly designed bedroom grabbing essentials. He's unshaven, a bit scruffy looking, and his hair is unkempt.

Alternative rock vividly escapes a tiny high-tech silver stereo on a faux wooden shelf. The two-story home is neatly decorated with all modern furniture in pale sandalwood shades and grays and silvers.

His decision to skip town with his newly invented drug in hand while owing the mob money has stressed Bradley out, but as troubling as it has been, it is nonetheless the path he has chosen.

All the walls in his bedroom are a ghostly white, absent of color, with the exception of a wide abstract painting to the left of the doorway. Blobs of crimson and pumpkin quarrel as a long slanting streak of indigo fights for attention in its downward descent from left to right. For Bradley, the painting resembled progress, and man's ongoing struggle with himself, ignoring the possibilities of that progress.

Bradley zips the bag with his clothes in it and an artificial sense of relief overcomes him as he lies on the snow-white down comforter to rest his mind. He stares up at the blank ceiling and its recessed lighting with his hands behind his head. His bare feet caress the hardwood floor.

"This time next week, I'll be knee-deep in something Brazilian," Bradley says slyly to himself with a smile. "And that's real."

Knock.

Knock.

Knock.

Brad's heart jumps into his throat and he quickly sits up in the bed.

"Who the fuck is that?" he says out loud, perplexed and fearful. He walks over to a nine-drawer sandalwood dresser and pulls out a pistol.

Knock.

Knock.

Knock.

"Yea, I don't do unannounced guests," Bradley mumbles as he steps through his living room en route to the front door.

He steps to the left of the front door to look out the window and avoid any slugs or buckshots that may come right through the door.

Brad places his index and middle finger on one of the cream mini blinds and pulls it down, causing it to V. That's when he eyes Cicero's Maybach parked straight ahead in the street, black and glossy.

Brad then looks a bit to his right, and sees Cicero's broad shoulders standing at his front door.

Knock.

Knock.

Knock.

"Damn. What the fuck is C doin' here?" Brad whispers to himself.

Knock.

Knock.

Knock.

Unsure of what to do, Brad decides to stash his gun under a gray sofa cushion and returns to stand before the door.

"Yea! Who is it," he yells in a sleepy-sounding voice.

"It's me, man. Open up."

The latch turns and the doorknob does the same as the white wooden door swings inward and opens.

"Damn, man, what were you doin' in there? Jackin' off?" Cicero jokes with a wide smile on his face. A light breeze ruffles his expensive lime-green sweater.

In his hands is a plastic bag with two Styrofoam containers inside.

"I got lunch, dude. Let's chit-chat," Cicero tells him. Cicero's still not completely sure of Brad's plans, but he needs to find out, if he can, before leaving town.

Confused and anxious by Cicero's unannounced stop and cheerful demeanor, Bradley has no choice but to accept his offer and entertain him. As soon as Cicero leaves, he'll be on his way to a sunny beach to be besieged by the infamous Brazilian bikini wax.

"Yea, come on in, man," Brad says to his friend, and Cicero enters. As he comes in, Cicero quickly peers right into Bradley's bedroom and sees the two packed bags. Brad forgot to close his bedroom door, and that was all the confirmation Cicero needed.

Brad closes the door and glances over at the sofa cushion, which is now bulging and looking out of place.

Cicero walks in and heads straight for the island in the kitchen. The white tile blocks are clean and uncluttered.

"Man, you're gonna like this. It's from that one little Italian spot in Gladstone."

"Oh, okay, I wanted to check that out," Brad nervously comments.

"Yea, my dad used to take me all the time. It was one of his *favorite ristorantes*," Cicero says with an Italian accent and a smile.

"Cool," Brad says as he pulls up two silver barstools.

Brad checks Cicero's hands again, then looks at the island, and notices there is no red plastic cup present.

"You ain't drinkin' today, dog?" Brad asks his friend.

"Nope. Not today. I'm tryin' to live a little healthier," Cicero says as he removes the Styrofoam containers from the plastic bag. "I even ate a salad earlier."

Brad's eyes squint.

"A what?"

"Dude, don't start."

"Whatever, man. Say, you want something to drink?"

"Naw, I'm cool," Cicero replies as he hands Brad the container that was on top.

Brad opens it and eyes a delectable portion of fettuccine alfredo with grilled chicken and crushed white pepper. Two lemon wedges grace the right side.

"Damn, dog, this looks real good," Brad says. He struts over to a drawer and removes two forks.

"A, man, grab me a spoon too."

"All right," answers Brad.

They sit next to each other and begin to partake.

With the spoon in his left hand and the fork in his right, Cicero twists the fettuccine noodles in the spoon with the fork, then neatly lifts it into his mouth.

"Yep, this is some good shit," Cicero says with a full mouth.

"You ain't kiddin'. This is real good," agrees Brad. "Kinda spicy, though, for alfredo sauce."

Cicero slurps his noodles and glances over at Brad, who is eating slowly, as if thinking about something.

"What's on your mind, man?" Cicero inquires. "You look like something is bothering you."

"Ah, naw, man, I'm just a little tired, you know? Been busy with the product."

"Oh, yea. Man, that paper is rollin' in. Kinda slow though. What you think? I mean, what do you see us doing in the next few months?" Cicero asks with a smile on his face.

"Yea, we're just about ready to start expanding, you know. You know, hittin' Topeka, Lawrence, Warrensburg, and St. Joe."

Suddenly, Bradley begins coughing. He places his right hand to his mouth to cover it; he's never been a rude person.

"Damn, what's on this?"

"It's just white pepper, man. What, you can't handle it?"

"I'm cool, man. I just need something to drink, some fucking water," Brad says as he stands and walks toward the refrigerator, coughing more ferociously.

"Naw, dog, you know what? I don't think that's the white pepper that's causing you to cough like that," Cicero says as he continues to eat his meal.

Brad looks back at Cicero with one hand on the silver refrigerator door, still coughing. His eyes water and phlegm flies out of his mouth.

"Yea, man, I think that's that poison I put in your food," Cicero says, smiling.

Brad's eyes go huge and he drops to one knee and places his left hand on the floor to keep from falling.

"Why, C? Why would you do that?" Brad asks as he continues to cough and gasp for air. He glances over to the bulge in the sofa, but he lacks the strength to get there.

Cicero's smile turns to a menacing look, and Bradley comes to know the depth of his friend's wickedness. Remorse knows him not.

"What you mean, why? Because you tryin' to fuck me, Bradley, that's why. Next time you plan on skipping town with my money, and my drugs, close your bedroom door, dumb ass. You deserve to die for that dumb shit."

Fear rolls up into Bradley's heart as he continues to cough forcefully and his eyes turn bloodshot red.

"Oh my bad, there won't be a next time," Cicero tells him as he finishes the last of his fettuccine.

Then Cicero smiles as Bradley completely collapses to the kitchen's cold gray linoleum floor, his bare skin slapping it. Vomit oozes from this mouth. His toes curl with disgusting tension.

"Man, I have to admit I was a little nervous at first, because I forgot which one had the poison in it. That's crazy, huh? But thanks for figuring it out for me, dog. You are a good friend."

And Bradley dies. His breathing was restricted and his oxygen was cut off. His brain functions ended, then his heart abruptly stopped beating. The descendant of Acadians leaves the world of the living via toxin-induced asphyxiation, delivered by a dear friend.

"Rest in confusion, Bradley Micheaux," Cicero says before

grabbing both Styrofoam containers, forks and his spoon and placing them in the plastic bag.

He walks into Bradley's bedroom and grabs the bag stuffed with the dope and chemicals and the hundred grand.

He carries the satchel out to the living room, sets it on the stainless steel coffee table, and looks through it.

"Cool. I can give this to Jimmy and get back in his good graces," he says out loud. "He thinks the money has been coming in too slow; like we've been holding out on him."

Then he has a second thought.

"Shit, then again, I could give this to him and he can still whack me. Just for general purposes. To prove a point to his other lieutenants. Fuck that. Plus the feds are watching him. Fuck. Shit. What if Jimmy is *working* for the feds?"

Cicero grabs his cell phone from his hip and dials a familiar number. He checks his watch; it's almost 5:30 p.m., so it has to be someone fairly close to his location.

"Hello," a female answers.

"Hey, what's crackin'?"

"Not much, still with my cousin. We're actually in the movies," Lana says.

"A, I need you to meet me right now at that spot in North-towne," Cicero instructs. "It's hella crucial."

"How much you got?" Lana asks. Her talking during the movie is frustrating a few people near her, and her endearing older cousin looks upset and offended.

"I got you, girl. Just meet me in about forty-five minutes. I got something to do first. Cool?"

"All right, cool."

And she hangs up.

He places the phone back on his hip and walks into the kitchen, where Brad's body lies in an awkward dead man's position.

Cicero grabs a black plastic bag, then bends down and puts his arms around Brad's chest. He then lifts his body and drags it down the hall along dusty hardwood floors to a messy bathroom, and tosses his slender muscular corpse into the white porcelain tub.

Brad's arms land over his face, as if shielding his eyes from a stunningly bright light.

Water from the silver showerhead sprays at full force on his body, and Cicero leaves momentarily only to return with a large butcher knife from the kitchen.

He removes his sweater and his T-shirt and begins to dismember his former friend. He removes all of Brad's clothing, and is surprised to see his friend had three balls.

"What the fuck?" Cicero briefly chuckles, then positions himself to begin cutting.

Starting with the fingers, Cicero chops Bradley into bits and pieces. *Chop*. The left pinkie. Blood immediately flows. *Chop*. The right ring finger. *Chop*. He separates the ulna from the radius in Brad's right arm, slicing the sinewy flesh as blood squirts. Blood is everywhere, but the water from the shower helps to wash it down the drain. The stench fills the air.

Cicero starts to perspire as he gets to the larger bones in his legs, so he goes to Brad's basement in search of something more substantial. That's when he finds a hand saw.

"Yea, this will work," he says, staring at the blade. He looks over and notices there's no lab equipment. The basement is spotless.

"This asshole was really gonna fuck me."

Back in the shower, Cicero saws into Brad's muscular thigh, and into his left femur with conviction. The grinding sound is intense and nauseating, but he proceeds nonetheless. Specks of blood splatter on his face as he applies more pressure, using more strength.

"Fuck," he says out loud, nearly out of breath. He gags at the awful smell. He stands and walks unsteadily toward the medicine cabinet. Inside he finds a bottle of Old Spice, and quickly begins splashing it over Brad's body parts.

"Fuck," he mumbles.

Once Bradley's body is cut into manageable pieces, Cicero turns off the shower and tosses all the drained parts into a black trash bag, including Brad's severed head. The look on his face is one of utter horror.

Cicero grabs the head by its blond hair, holding it in his hands and staring at it with contempt.

"You pussy. When I go, I won't have a scared-ass look on my face." He carelessly tosses the head into the bag, then ties it up.

Cicero cleans off his body and face in the restroom sink with soap and steaming hot water.

"I hope this mothafucka didn't have any STDs," Cicero says jokingly to himself. "That's all I need."

Then Clorox, Ajax, and Lysol work to break down all the organic leftovers unseen by the naked eye. The household products work their magic as Cicero scrubs the bathroom clean. He's careful not to miss a spot. He even cleans old shaving cream and soil stains Bradley never got to.

He puts his clothes back on and checks his watch: 6:09 p.m. "Cool."

Cicero grabs everything he touched and puts it into another

bag, tossing in Brad's jeans and the food as well. He then searches Brad's house, high and low, for the million plus. He looks in closets, cupboards, under mattresses and floorboards. He finds nothing.

"Fuck."

He grabs a handkerchief from his pocket and wraps it around the doorknob as he closes the front door and leaves.

Without being noticed, he slides to his Maybach with the brown satchel draped from his shoulder as he places it and the two large bags in the spacious trunk.

Cicero starts the engine and mashes the gas pedal, headed toward the location where Lana awaits his arrival. On the way, he dumps Brad's body parts in the dumpster behind that little Italian restaurant in Gladstone. He honks the horn three times and drives off. That's the real reason Antonio used to go there: to dump bodies. Cicero was with him, many times. As Cicero heads to the airport, dense clouds glide into the skyline and the air begins to smell of rain.

Chapter 17

He stared at those hills for two weeks. He stood in his plush white robe, smoking cigars and sipping expensive cognac from his corner balcony at the Four Seasons on Doheny Drive. For two weeks, he ordered exquisite room service and gazed at the bright dots of light on the rolling hills just to his north. And now, for two days, Jimmy has been calling his cell phone. He hasn't answered. Is it a trap? The view of Beverly Hills and the west were tranquil and reassuring, before the last two days.

Now, paranoid, thinking Jimmy (or the feds) has caught up with him, Cicero thinks about what he told Lana as he heads to busy LAX. Wearing a baby-blue sweater, he passes countless movie billboards, advertisements and palm trees, all while his Middle-Eastern cab driver swerves in and out of traffic at a mad-man's pace. It is the month of Safar, and the seventy-two-degree California weather is perfect.

"In the event of a water landing, your seat cushion may be used as a floatation device," the television monitor smoothly explains after descending from the 747's ceiling.

As a forty-something beauty goes about asking the passengers for their beverage preferences, Cicero can't help but look outside the window at the baggage handlers, carelessly tossing luggage around as they laugh and crack jokes.

"Lana better not fuck me," he whispers to himself, stroking his bald head with a look of worry on his haggard face. He'd kept it brief. Told her only what she needed to know: hold this for me till I get back in town, don't open it, see you in a few weeks.

Quick and to the point. He knows he really can't trust a chick he first met while she was stealing. While in L.A., he recalled following her out of a store at Bannister Mall, and she thought he was security. That is, until he asked her how much she charged for her services.

"Damn," he says in a low voice from his window seat, realizing he may have made a major mistake. But there was little time to think; he'd had no other choice. The aircraft's four huge jet engines rev as the silver, red, and blue mechanical bird slowly and deliberately taxis to the crowded LAX runway.

The Wright Brothers smile from Heaven as the bird propels forward and thrust equals lift. The six-person crew and passengers take to the sky while Cicero requests the airline's cheap cognac.

The aircraft ascends above the oncoming clouds in a turbulent climb to thirty-thousand feet. The landscape below, now appearing like tan rectangles, squares, and blue circles, shrinks into the Earth's abyss.

The elderly woman seated next to Cicero nestles in and begins reading a tiny brown prayer book. Reading glasses rest unsteadily near the end of her nose while light-gray hair pokes out from under her bright pumpkin-colored hat. Cicero glances over at the old woman, peers at her reading material, then back out the window.

Red lights remain illuminated above each passenger's head indicating that seatbelts are still required.

He stares out the window with a smug look on his face at the ever-whitening nimbus and stratus clouds passing by at over three-hundred miles per hour.

"Heaven," he says mockingly to himself. The woman next to him hears his comment and looks over at the young bald man. She's on her way to visit her ailing sister in New Orleans, and she can't help but sense the negativity and urgency coming from the troubled soul next to her.

"How are you, young man?" the woman asks.

Cicero looks at her with a smirk, but Ruth always taught him to respect his elders, so he responds politely.

"I'm fine, ma'am. How are you?"

"Well, they say my sister won't make it past this weekend," she says while looking down at her tan wrinkled hands. The chestnut rim on her eyeglasses is thick. "So that's why I'm reading my prayer book."

Bing. The seatbelt light goes dim, and a middle-aged man with a ridiculously huge prostate jumps at the chance to drain his engorged bladder. He heads toward the rearward restroom while a frustrated mother takes her fussy one-year-old to the forward restroom for a diaper change and some baby talk.

Cicero looks back out the window at the seemingly endless blue sky, while two flight attendants make their way from the front of the plane with a cart full of beverages and snacks.

Feeling his contempt, the elderly woman digs into Cicero's heart.

"So do you pray, young man?" the woman inquires with a slight grin on her thin lips. Her lipstick has been applied unevenly.

Cicero turns back to face her, fighting his hardest to hide his agitation. As he begins to answer, a flight attendant steps into his view.

"Sir, your cognac," she says with a wide smile, handing Cicero a cup of ice and a small plastic bottle.

"Thank you," he answers as he tries to hand the flight attendant a nice twenty-dollar tip.

"Oh, thank you, sir, but we're not allowed to take tips," she tells him.

Unoffended, he stuffs the money back in his pocket.

"Miss, your ginger ale," the flight attendant tells the elderly woman.

"Thank you, dear."

Passengers chitchat with elation about their weekend plans in the Big Easy, and several kids whine as pacifiers and sippy cups fail to appease them. The plane's cabin is without a doubt energized.

Cicero pours the cognac into the short stout cup and the ice pops and crackles. He looks at his hands and briefly notices the calluses and embedded stains from gunfire. He pauses, then takes a swig from his libation.

"So, do you pray in thanks for your many blessings?" the elderly woman asks once again. Once again, she grins, affably.

"No disrespect, ma'am, but I don't know you. And I'm somewhat bothered by your question," Cicero says as nicely as he can. He takes a swig of his cognac and looks back out the window to the expansive blueness.

"Well, my sister used to say the same thing," the woman says looking at Cicero. Her hands gesture as only those of an elderly woman can. "Yea, we used to run down this dirt road barefoot. Just laughing and giggling. Life really wasn't that great back then. But you would never know by the way our teeth shone so bright."

Cicero glances at her once again, noticing how the woman's story seamlessly jumped to another topic.

"Yes, indeed. My father was a farmer, and my sister, she just didn't like going to church or reading her Bible," the woman says; the smile leaves her face. "Yep. And now, she's trapped in her own body. They say she can't recognize anybody but my brother."

Cicero swigs his drink, feeling neither joy nor pain from the woman's tale.

"Yep. And you don't want that to be you, young man," the woman says. "They says it's a medical reason for her illness. But I think it's God's way of punishing us when we do wrong."

She stares at Cicero.

"You know? When we don't heed His word. Especially when there are people in our lives that bring the Word, and Him, to our attention."

Having heard enough, Cicero finishes off his cognac and places the cup on the floor between his feet.

"Thanks, but my mother says the same stuff to me all the time," Cicero tells the old woman. "Life is too difficult and fucked up for me to ever think there is someone or something out there that gives a damn about any of us. Excuse my language, but I heard enough. So please leave me the *fuck* alone."

The elderly woman turns from looking at Cicero and goes back to reading her tiny brown prayer book, and says not another word to the young bald man until their flight lands in the boot-shaped state. Her wrinkled tan fingers ruffle the thin pages as she flips through the many prayers.

Green swampland comes into view as the metal bird begins to descend into what was once French territory.

Bing.

"The captain has turned on the fasten seatbelt sign," the lovely stewardess pleasantly mouths into a hand-held intercom. Her red fingernails are long and well manicured. "Please return to your seats and place your tray tables in their upright positions."

It seems fitting somehow that Cicero return to the state where he met Brad, where he learned more about life, and where he decided to hustle full steam ahead.

The plane smoothly touches down at Louis Armstrong New Orleans International Airport just before 4:00 p.m. It's late February: the Friday before Fat Tuesday.

The passengers deplane and Cicero enters the bustling airport. He eyes the elderly woman who sat next to him as she disappears into the crowd, carrying merely a small black purse and her prayer book. Cicero follows the signs to the baggage claim, carefully making his way through the throng of partygoers and local black Indians and coon-asses.

Eager college kids, returning crew members, and dirty old men hastily step through the airport on their way to bars, pubs, parades, and balls. They don purple, green, and gold beads and various doodads and odd knickknacks. The pace is frantic and electric.

Cicero grabs his black suitcase from the slowly rotating carousel and calmly walks toward the exit and a long line for a cab. His flawless platinum timepiece reflects the light of the sunny day in multiple directions off thousands of faces.

While standing in line holding his suitcase, Cicero eyes a celebrity rap star. Even though he isn't usually impressed by television stars or recording artists, Kansas Citians rarely see celebrities, so Cicero takes a moment to gander at the rare sight.

Flamboyance heaped upon flamboyance. Diamonds crammed against diamonds. Platinum entangled with platinum. The rapper, who calls himself Scrill, is overwhelmingly gaudy and flashy in his jewelry as he strolls from inside the airport out through the automatic sliding doors.

He usually travels with a huge entourage including a personal barber, a chef, and a Swedish masseuse, and innumerable flunkies and yes men. But today, the five-foot-six Scrill is with only a hired bodyguard and two flunkies. His dark-brown sunglasses are encrusted with yellow diamonds on all sides. And his mouth is actually the blueprint Kameron used for his platinum and diamond teeth.

"Damn, he's a short little mothafucka," Cicero says to himself in a low voice, gripping his solitary suitcase. People always look taller on TV, Cicero supposes.

A long black stretch limousine arrives just to the left of where Cicero waits in the slowly moving taxi line, and Cicero smirks.

"Shit, I could have done that too," he says out loud in an attempt to downplay the glamorousness of a limousine ride.

Cicero's face looks tired and beat as the twenty-year-old Scrill, dressed in baggy jeans, sneakers, and a Hank Aaron baseball jersey, nears where he's standing. At nearly five feet wide, his former-college-football-playing bodyguard walks toward Cicero in almost a straight line, right at him.

Unconcerned, Cicero notices the three hundred pounds coming toward him, yet he decides with his street mentality not to edge out of the bodyguard's way, who is now just three steps away. The black suit he wears clings tight to his back and bulging shoulders as the large man pushes Cicero in his back, shoving him several feet away.

"What the fuck?" Cicero yells as he looks back.

"Chill the fuck out, little dude," the bodyguard says to the six-foot Cicero in a deep menacing tone, with his right hand still on Cicero's baby-blue sweater.

The coffee-skinned Scrill and his two flunkies laugh at Cicero as the bodyguard opens the sleek black limo door for them with his left hand.

Never one to be disrespected, Cicero takes a step to the right and frees himself from the huge paw of the bearded body-guard, then turns to make eye contact.

Cicero stares the six-foot-four behemoth in the eyes, who unflinchingly stares back.

"What you gon do?" the bodyguard asks. His dark eyes are piercing and intense.

Cicero takes a quick survey of the area. No gun by his side. No car for him to jump in. No friends or family within five hundred miles. Way too much security presence. So he smiles.

"It's cool, dog," Cicero says with a grin, stroking his scruffy face with his right hand. His left grips his suitcase.

"Yea, I know it's cool," the bodyguard says loudly, as Scrill and his boys burst into screeching laughter. The giant slides into the limo and it lowers several inches due to the added weight. He slams the door as the black rubber tires spin and the group departs, leaving a fuming Cicero waiting in a long line for a cab.

Cicero grits his teeth thinking about what just happened, and at that moment, the skycap finally motions Cicero for-ward for a taxi of his own.

"Yea, last year's Zulu parade was fire, ya dig?" a disc jockey's voice blares from the taxi's radio. "And yes indeed, this year's will be like dat, fa sho!"

"Where to, bruh?" the native New Orleans cab driver asks his pissed-off fare.

"The Quarter," Cicero answers with a growl.

"You from Nawlins, bruh," he asks, looking in the rearview mirror, noticing Cicero's European facial features and abbreviation of French Quarter. Spent cherry-scented cardboard trees hang from the cigarette lighter near the radio controls.

"Naw man, just visiting," Cicero says, trying not to sound pissed off.

The yellow cab reaches the highway and heads eastbound on I-10. Cicero rides silently in the backseat of the spotless taxi, thinking about how he should have done something, anything, to hurt the dude that disrespected him.

Zydeco blasts through the Caprice Classic's shoddy speakers. Towering palm trees line the median of the highway. The reeking odor of swamp water, moss, and mud is everywhere.

The men travel from the western outskirts of New Orleans, passing colorful hotels, vast billboards, and various swamp life marooned on the side of the highway.

Out-of-state tags clutter the roadway as the cab driver weaves in and out of the congestion.

"See, bruh, it's like this every Mardi Gras," the driver tells Cicero. He has typical New Orleans features: thick lips, a square jaw, reddish-brown skin. He wears a stained white Mardi Gras T-shirt reading "Mardi Gras, New Orleans" in purple lettering. On the back, the shirt reads "Like a man" in gold lettering.

Cicero ignores the driver's comments and gazes out the window at SUVs with tinted windows and Volkswagen Jettas packed with pretty college girls. Breasts at the ready.

The zesty accordion-based Zydeco hits Cicero's inner ear,

transmitting the essence of the rudimentary Cajun instruments and the rhythms of the area's black Creoles. Cicero takes in the sounds and smells. He's not in Missouri anymore.

A cool breeze shakes the cab on the cloudless sunny day. Chalky white seagulls soar above, alone and majestic. The cab coasts over a high arching off ramp, leaving much of the traffic behind on their way to a shortcut en route to downtown New Orleans and the awaiting French Quarter.

The rear window on the driver's side is slightly lowered, allowing a thin gale to blow a circular wind to the other side of the cab, striking and tingling the back of Cicero's neck.

The disc-shaped Superdome stands out among the rectangular skyscrapers of the downtown N.O. This is a place where modern meets backwaters. And American urban decay taints Old-World European ways.

It's a peculiar and unique town, Cicero thinks to himself, as he peers at the cemetery to his right with its thousand or so above-ground mausoleums. Light-brown eyes look at Cicero through the oblong rearview mirror. The driver notices Cicero staring at one of the area's curiosities.

"Yea, bruh, the ground's too moist. Dem bodies, they wouldn't stay buried," the driver says with a laugh. An orangish-gold tooth covers one of his top front teeth. "No indeed."

"Yea, I know. I've seen 'em before," Cicero coolly responds. "Just can't get used to 'em. You know?"

"Me edda, bruh." The driver smiles, flashing his gold tooth, with one hand on the steering wheel. "Me edda."

The cab exits the highway and immediately hits traffic on Canal Street, which is lined with aged hotels and burnt-out retail shops, some of which have been refurbished, others of which have not. Nonetheless, all are full of tourists, or frequented by visitors with disposable currency to spend and waste.

"This is cool," Cicero tells the driver as they sit idle in the middle of the downtown traffic. He hands him a hundred-dollar bill for the twenty-five dollar trip and opens the door to get out.

The financially strapped driver looks at the bill and is stunned by the enormous tip.

"Well, well, where ya goin', bruh? You got a hotel room?" the driver inquires with a slight stutter, looking back at Cicero through the rearview mirror.

"Naw, I forgot to reserve a room, man," Cicero admits, grabbing his black suitcase from the floor of the backseat. "I guess I'll just try to find one."

Impressed by Cicero's generosity, the driver offers a favor.

"Naw, bruh. Check it out, my cousin Fleaurette works over at the Ritz at the front desk, bruh," the cabby says. "Tell her I sent you ova dear. My name Rafael."

Neutral ground divides the hustle of Canal Street as the traffic light ahead turns green and horns begin to honk at the taxi. Young guys and girls in green, gold, and purple masks cross the street in front of and in back of cars, stumbling in drunken stupors.

"Happy Mardi Gras, you bastards," one guy screams with both hands toward the heavens. His friends all laugh and tug at his shirt for him to follow them.

Cicero stands outside holding the cab door open, thinking about what Rafael has just told him as the honking horns grow in number and become louder in unison.

"I'm tellin' ya, bruh, it's a nice hotel," Rafael says. "And it's just right the way on this street. Dis Canal Street, bruh. Ya heard me?"

"All right, cool," Cicero finally decides. "Thanks, man." Then he slams the door shut.

"All right den, bruh. Remember, my family's name is Fleaurette. She just made twenty-six, she good people," Rafael yells as he mashes the gas pedal and skirts off to catch cars that were once right in front of him.

Cicero strolls south down the sidewalk on Canal Street through groups of men wearing rainbow-colored afro wigs and large plastic breasts. White sheets of paper with religious copy and party announcements litter the street and get trampled under the feet of the desirous.

Tonight, the king, queen, maids, and dukes of krewes and their captains shall prepare for spectacular float rides and masked balls. Some krewes will relish at the variety of performances to be held for them. For this weekend, they will be treated like royalty.

Cicero passes several narrow blocks, becoming disenchanted with his jaunt and the mostly intoxicated crowd. He stops at a red light as a light-brown trolley in nearly original condition slowly rolls past in the median. He peers to his left down Bourbon Street, and is overwhelmed by the sight of thousands of people walking, dancing, drinking, yelling, and flashing skin.

"Damn," Cicero says to himself out loud. "Mardi Gras is too wild."

Electrical pulses turn crimson to mint and Cicero again proceeds south on Canal Street, which in the eighteen hundreds was the dividing line between the French Quarter and the American sector of New Orleans.

A long line of shiny black limousines catches Cicero's eye and he realizes the Ritz-Carlton hotel is in his sight. A large royal-blue flag bearing a lion's head gently flutters in the delicate breeze.

"This better not be no bullshit," Cicero murmurs, thinking about what the cab driver told him as he lugs his suitcase.

A long line of bell boys and doormen in traditional garb and top hats rush back and forth in front of New Orleans' only AAA Five Diamond hotel. It is the best of the best.

The Old World architecture of nine twenty-one Canal Street blends the prestigious structure into its surroundings.

Cicero walks through the foyer passing oil paintings of French countrysides and ladies in waiting. He enters the lobby and is engulfed by classical furnishings and the wealthy fringe of Mardi Gras; a sight seldom seen by most Fat Tuesday revelers.

Before making his way to the front desk, Cicero takes a moment to bask in the elegance of the property. Places like this are why he hustles. He takes in the enormous flower display to his right. Orchids, daisies, azaleas, and palm leaves spring forth from a huge Italian-made vase.

"This is truly nice," Cicero says while gawking at the priceless antique credenzas, crystal chandeliers, and huge gold-trimmed mirrors in the lobby.

He steps left toward the front desk and is immediately stunned by the sight of a beautiful Louisiana native behind the long polished redwood counter.

She looks up from a computer screen and makes eye contact with him. Her ocean-blue eyes are stunning, providing a prominent contrast to her earthy, red-toned skin. A second woman, a leggy Czechoslovakian with streaky blonde hair, busily grabs paperwork and plastic room keys for impatient well-paid guests.

"Whoa. I hope that's Fleaurette."

Cicero reaches the counter and sets his suitcase to the carpeted floor and its intricate patterns of salmon paisley and sapphire and jade French crests.

"Hello, sir, how may I assist you?" the beautiful woman says.

Cicero glances at her nametag. It reads: Fleaurette.

"Hello, how are you?" he asks with a grin.

"Fine, sir. Are you checking in?" Fleaurette replies professionally without giving in to his flirting. Her natural eyelashes extend up to her eyebrows. Her teeth are pearl white and straight as an arrow.

"Well, you may find this kind of strange," Cicero hedges, "but your cousin said you may be able to hook me up with a room."

The five-foot-seven Fleaurette simultaneously appears confused and bothered.

"My cousin?" she inquires. Her Southern Louisiana accent is thick and sexy.

Cicero is instantly worried he won't have a place to sleep tonight. That he'll be forced to rest his head in some extremely suspect motel, or worse, somewhere on the repulsive New Orleans streets. But he doesn't panic.

"Yea, your cousin Rafael. He told me to look for the most beautiful woman at the Ritz-Carlton, and ask her to hook me up," Cicero says in his deep voice, looking Fleaurette in her amazing blue eyes. Her long straight black hair curls near the bulging breasts straining against her navy-blue pants' suit jacket. She smells of freshly cut roses and sweet oils.

She looks suspiciously at Cicero for having known her cousin's name and her accent really comes out.

"Raf don't never tell people to come here for me," she tells him with a slight smile. "You musta gave him a beaucoup tip, yea?"

Cicero laughs. His defined chest and shoulders fill out his baby-blue Coogi sweater, but it's been a long day. A long, annoying day.

"That's what he said," Cicero tells her.

She smirks, then begins typing in letters and digits into a hidden computer terminal with her curving, long, burgundy-painted fingernails.

"I really don't know why he told you that, we are fully booked," Fleaurette informs him while looking at the computer's monitor.

Sensing the impending bad news, Cicero reaches into his pocket and pulls out five one-hundred-dollar bills.

"Check it out, Ms. Fleaurette, if you can find me a room, I'll give you five-hundred dollars for being so helpful," Cicero whispers. "I'm telling you, I'd really appreciate all of your help if you could do that for me."

For a person making ten dollars an hour, a tax-free lump sum just to cancel someone else's reservation is a damn good deal.

"Okay," she answers without hesitation. "And your name?"

Cicero smiles.

"Cicero Day. C-I-C-E-R-O. And I'm paying in cash."

Fleaurette smiles and completes the transaction. Cicero slides her seven-hundred dollars for her trouble, and she flashes her beautiful white teeth.

"Thank you," she tells him as she passes Cicero his room key. "Just take the elevators down the hall to my left, up to the third floor, and follow the signs to your room. It's marked in the envelope."

Cicero grins. His craggy face is tired, showing the wear and tear of cognac, deception, and murder. And yet, Fleaurette returns the gesture in a way that only a Creole girl can.

Cicero takes the oak-lined elevator to his room on the third floor. He gazes down at the cocaine-white envelope for the room number: three sixteen.

After a few steps down the quiet, elegant hallway recently restored and renovated in undying Southern decor, the tan plastic key card slides into the black box near the brass door knob. A red dot diminishes and a green dot illuminates. *Clank*.

He turns the knob and enters the opulent executive suite, complete with rare China, complimentary cookies, an armoire-encased flat-screen television, and a fully stocked mini-bar.

Cicero steps into his large suite and the door slams behind him, causing a framed water-colored painting to rattle against the wall. The scene is out of Paris in the late seventeen hundreds. Raw life.

Cicero stares at the plush feather beds and duvet cover, envisioning what he needs the most: a restful night.

"Yea, I can deal with this," a weary Cicero mutters to himself.

A black suitcase immediately smacks the carpeted floor, followed by the baby-blue Australian-woven sweater. There is silence on the multi-line telephone; no pornography or e-mails being generated through the high-speed Internet access.

Instead, three-hundred-thread-count Frette sheets swaddle a man in deep, deep sleep. Cicero's eyelids are firmly shut. The room is silent and his body is still. The ruckus three stories below him fails to penetrate the exorbitant lodging that surrounds him. Tonight, Cicero Day sleeps soundly. Nightmares cannot find him this evening in the Bayou, dozens of feet below sea level.

Flambeaux carriers dance and whirl about on the dark night-time street as gawkers and drunkards clank nickels and dimes off the metal torches they carry. These descendants of slaves carry on tradition. The men who carry the torches for the parades traditionally lit the early processions before the invention of the light bulb.

But now, the gas-powered flambeaux torches burn below a slumbering Cicero, while thousands cavort and conjoin lust and liquor on the New Orleans pavement. They party throughout the night under the stare of a watchful full moon, dangling omnipotently in the clear sky.

Cicero sleeps for three days straight, only occasionally stirring or tossing about. For three days, he is without nightmares or dreams, or any painful memories. The drain of dismemberment, fermented fruits, lying, and stealing, have caused his body to shut down. For three days, he lies in a hotel bed, without waking, without seeing the sun.

Monday evening, long eyelashes grace a thick eyebrow. A cornea greets an iris, and light is reflected into the brain. The sense of sight is alive and well in one eye as it juts back and forth, helping the groggy brain to remember where it is. The same soon occurs in the right eye; the room is made more familiar to the decision-making organ of Cicero's body.

After three nights of comatose-like slumber, Cicero awakens. His eyelids painfully crack the green mucous foundation that has formed in the corners of his eyes. The joints in his elbows, knees, and shoulders snap with his first gingerly motions.

✖✖✖

"Oh, fuck," Cicero grumbles. The aroma of ripened shit escapes his dry, white-crusted mouth. It aches from thirst and non-movement.

Monday evening, the sun sets slowly in the west as the Mardi

Gras festival continues three floors below him and all around. Housekeepers have peeked at him several times over the weekend since the "Do Not Disturb" sign wasn't displayed. The first *mujer Cubana* almost called the *policia* at the sight of what she thought was a dead body. But Cicero's fingers twitched, and then his head turned under the feather comforter, so the NOPD was never notified.

"Fuck," Cicero moans in a deeper than average voice. The whites of his eyes are now the color of freshly churned butter, and they're bloodshot red with diverging veins.

Cicero sits up and places his feet on the intricately patterned carpeted floor. A pack of wild dogs greets the mailman in his stomach. He hungers for sustenance.

"Damn, I'm fuckin' starvin'," he says to himself in a groggy voice. Cicero slowly stands to his feet and is immediately hit with a dizzying head rush.

"Oh, shit."

He checks the tiny rectangular date box on the platinum, diamond, and sapphire-encrusted wristwatch he never took off. It reads: twenty three.

"Damn, I've been asleep for three days. I feel like fuckin' Rip Van Winkle," Cicero quips while sweeping the crust from his eyes with his right index finger. The little crystallized light-green chunks fall to the floor. One can only imagine how many light-green crystallized chunks have been ground into this room's carpet, Cicero thinks.

Cicero, still fully dressed in Friday's outfit, uncomfortably ambles toward his thick black suitcase. Brass latches slide outward and the case opens. He grabs his toothbrush and makes his way to the white marble-wrapped restroom. Gray arteries stretch throughout it. His finger flicks a switch and the instant illumination causes him to forcefully squint.

"Fuck, that shit is way too bright," grunts Cicero, before turning the light back off. *Click*.

He steps onto the white marble floor and leans over one of the double sinks, looking at himself in the large wall-sized mirror.

The lack of light helps to conceal the five lines that are developing on his forehead and under his light-brown eyes. The unkempt stubble on his head and face is beyond the trendy look. He now resembles a homeless man, a man with nothing.

The brass faucet turns inward and cool water flows in a familiar rushing cadence. Cicero wets his toothbrush, then realizes he has no toothpaste.

"Ain't this a bitch."

He thinks for a moment, then heads for the mini-bar, just as the sun bids adieu over the horizon and the noise in the streets seems to intensify.

Cicero returns to the bathroom and begins to scrub his teeth up and down, side to side, and back and forth, creating fluoride suds and bubbles of baking soda. He spits and rinses, then attempts the much-needed task of peeling his nearly adhesive clothes off.

They've been on so long, they're like a second skin. The cotton blends hit the chilly floor and Cicero steps naked into the marble white shower. The long brass handle rotates clockwise and cold, chilly, cool, room temperature, lukewarm, warm, and finally hot, steaming water spurts out.

Droplets pound Cicero's face as he closes his eyes and allows the water to penetrate his thirsty pores. He moans with delight at the feeling of a hot shower.

Cicero opens his eyes and takes the paper wrapper off the small bar of soap and firmly rubs it all over his back and arms. This is a cleansing he has longed for.

Cicero then places the soap back on the shelf and he rinses his body clean. Silence soon fills the bathroom as the waters stop running. Cicero steps out of the shower and places a terrycloth robe around him, wiping his size eleven feet on the plush rug in front of the designer toilet.

Moonlight sneaks into the executive suite, painting the French ambiance while he dresses himself in a black suit with a slightly lighter black button-down shirt.

"Damn, I need something to eat ASAP," he states as he leafs through the hotel's booklet of recommended dining. His stomach growls.

He hurriedly decides on one of the nearest restaurants, quickly grabs his room key card and exits his suite. The elevator glidingly carries him to the first floor where a throng of overpaid party animals jostle and joke among themselves. Cicero slides through them and out the large oak-and-glass doors.

Outside, foot traffic is thick with idiots and losers. Women of all ages with little to no self-esteem are everywhere; walking in tight bunches, surrounded by ogling and touchy-feely students and business owners.

"Show your tits!" is a mantra chanted over and over and over and over. It's heard mostly on Bourbon, but the other Rues also know the noise. Cicero avoids being hit by motorists and trampled by the N.O. mounted police on his way to Royal Street. Since the scene here is much less hectic than Canal and Bourbon, Cicero finds some relief from the tens of thousands he graciously blends into, yet wishes to momentarily escape.

At a restaurant to his right, a boisterous drove of blazers and foreign-made sweaters puff cigars and make informal contracts with Southern handshakes in a courtly setting.

Cicero steps inside the refined and painstakingly designed establishment. Over the years, it has become a cornerstone of New Orleans' exuberance and a leader in delectable Italian and Cajun fusion dishes.

A line of couples and quartets snakes from the host's stand to the sidewalk.

"Fuck this," Cicero decides.

He walks directly past the groups, attracting the piercing stares that only whites from the South can deliver. The busy blond-haired host, a descendent of French criminals, studies tonight's reservation list and fails to notice Cicero's abrupt advance to the front of the line.

"Excuse me, sir," Cicero states promptly with confidence.

The brown-eyed Cajun doesn't look up.

"Yea, we're all full tonight," he says effeminately, jotting check marks next to names like Toussaint and Rideaux. Smells of sizzling shellfish waft toward the door from the kitchen.

Softly and gently, two one hundred dollar bills float down the reservation list, stopping where the ink bleeds from the host's pen.

The twenty-nine-year-old host and his school loans endearingly look up at Cicero.

"Let me see what I have available, sir," he says with ardency.

The original Italian mosaic-tile floors remain immaculate as the sparkling stained-glass windows reflect the glow of detailed crystal chandeliers.

"Ah, yes. We just happen to have a cancellation. Are you dining alone this evening?"

Cicero grins. He loves it when money screams.

"Yes, I am."

"Excellent. Follow me then, sir."

Grumbles emit from the line behind Cicero. One older man in particular is irritated. His dark-gray suit is surprisingly well tailored and the gold nugget ring on his left pinkie is an eye-catcher.

"Say, chief, this guy just came from nowhere. Now we need a table, ya understand?"

His red face, fat cheeks, and white mustache give him a *Papa Noel* quality. But the young brunette filly under his arm helps dispel that notion.

"I'll be right with you, sir," the slim host says as he grabs a menu and the much longer wine list. "Follow me, please," the host instructs. The men stroll beyond photographs of celebrities, dignitaries, and duchesses that line the corridor walls.

Darkness fills the Bayou sky and sins and sins multiply. But young Cicero Day is now seated in a house that hedonism built, ready to fuel his famished frame.

He peruses the unique menu from his quaint candlelit table near the back of the dim restaurant. Cream-colored walls dotted with black-and-white photos provide a relaxing back-drop amidst the unfiltered white noise of drivel and prattle. Ubiquitous chatter and occasional outbursts of laughter remind Cicero that these days are festive ones.

Appendages, skin, and bones in a right-fitted shoe rapidly head skyward as his heel rolls smoothly on the tile flooring. Then the reverse occurs. His foot taps from sheer hunger. Water placed on his table serves as a resource to temporarily douse the flames of starvation.

Cicero considers the Gulf shrimp simmered in a spicy red gravy with Creole vegetables. He then looks over the crisply fried almond-crusted fillet of trout topped with sliced almonds and lemon butter sauce.

"Damn, that sounds good, but fuck that," grumbles Cicero.

He then glances past the poached chicken breast topped with baked ham over bordelaise sauce, but instead Cicero goes with the grilled filet mignon, topped with a rich béarnaise sauce.

"Sir, have you decided?" the young chipper waiter inquires.

"Yes, I have. I'll have the filet mignon."

"An excellent choice, sir. How would you like that prepared? I must inform you that our chef recommends medium rare."

"Really?"

"Oh, yes."

"In that case, I'll have mine medium well," Cicero chimes, bucking the powers that be. The waiter frowns slightly.

"Would you like something other than water to drink?"

"This water with lemon is cool for now."

"Okay, I'll have your order in a few minutes."

"Thanks."

Moonlight invades through large rectangular windows sectioned in nines and framed in oak. Chandeliers, ceiling fans, and recessed lighting adorn the interior as small palms stand along the walls. Tables are densely packed together.

The bouquet of grilled mammal flesh and decapitated crustaceans is deliciously alluring. It fills the restaurant and seeps into the wooden fixtures. Noise is everywhere.

Moments later, his dish arrives leaving vapor trails in its wake, resembling an artful snapshot from a cookbook. Presentation apparently is everything.

"Thank you," Cicero tells his waiter as he places the round plate on the pristine tablecloth.

"My pleasure. Can I get you anything else?"

"No. Not right now."

"Okay, sir. Bon appétit."

Cicero immediately digs in, slicing, forking, placing and chewing. Slicing, forking, placing and chewing. The tender cuts of meat are succulent. Saliva releases in his jaw at nearly torrential proportions.

A few patrons even silence their talking and begin staring at the carnivorous beast they see before them. In a matter of moments, the fare is gone, and the plate it arrived on is almost spotless.

The waiter happens to pass by and nearly loses his composure at the sight of the emptiness before the guest he just served.

"Wow! Is there something else I can get you, sir?" the waiter says without an inkling of a Louisiana accent.

Cicero dabs the corners of his mouth with the ecru linen napkin that accompanied his meal.

"Yes. I'll have a cognac, please," a satisfied Cicero states.

"Certainly. Do you have a preference?"

"Louis the Thirteenth."

"Coming right up," says the waiter as he scoops up Cicero's plate and utensils and whisks them away. A belly aches no more.

The waiter soon returns with a warmed amber-colored cognac in a fine crystal snifter.

"Thank you," Cicero says, gripping the two-hundred dollar shot of French ambrosia.

The matured potion tickles his taste buds and excites the palate as Cicero takes a long, prudent sip. It's quite delightful.

As he sits there, Cicero gazes across the clamorous room, trying to decipher certain conversations, or make eyes with a Southern belle who's lost her way. The lukewarm cognac seems to occupy a void in his bereft system, making him whole again. The nighttime sky is hauntingly inviting.

Cicero soon finishes his drink and drops three-hundred dollars for his meal and departs from the Quarter's upper-middle-class eatery.

Choosing not to partake in the night's revelry, Cicero returns to his accommodations at the Ritz-Carlton, strolling past pagans and idolaters, rummies and unofficial women of the night.

Once in his room, Cicero hangs his suit jacket in the cedar closet and slides over to the spacious parlor with the cushiony soft armchair adjacent to the bed. He rests his elbows on his thighs and leans forward, placing his face in his brown hands, ignoring the sight of the suite's fantastically high ceilings.

Muffled shouting creeps from outside into his room, as does the lunar gleam. The Cuban and Jamaican housekeepers were able to turn down the room and replace the linens and the fifteen-dollar tube of toothpaste from the mini bar.

The Ritz-Carlton's signature scent entertains his nostrils. And he gently leans back into the plush chair and closes his eyes, folding his arms against his chest.

Without words or further actions, Cicero slips into a deep sleep.

The sun is amazingly brilliant by the poolside. Cicero dons only swimming trunks as he reclines on a long chair made entirely of mint-green and off-white plastic straps. His skin is darker than usual, a golden tan.

Joining him are an unidentified man and woman. They appear to be a couple. They enjoy similar dark-red drinks with similar canary-yellow paper umbrellas. Smiles never once leave their faces.

The blue pool waters swoosh back and forth due to a steady breeze. Palm trees tower in the distance above the ranch-style home where the threesome are enjoying their day.

"This is the life," Cicero thinks out loud with his eyes shut.

But just as he does, the day's breeze turns cooler and large clouds sweep into the sky. Strangely, two clouds appear to clash. Like titanic feather-stuffed pillows, bumpy and rough to the eye, they bounce off each other with mammoth softness.

Cicero stares up at the collisions of the gentle giants as does the couple next to him. There are no other clouds in the sky except these two, and yet they manage to collide, like two rams butting heads.

The clouds are stationary against the breeze, and each time they softly collide, they recoil, then collide again. It's an extra-ordinary sight.

"Do you guys see this?" Cicero asks the couple, as he looks to the heavens.

"Yea. It's weird. These clouds are right above us just bumping into each other," the man says. "I've never seen anything like this."

He too is tan, but much thinner than Cicero is.

But the rarity of clouds fighting soon takes a backseat, when the cloud in the west is apparently defeated and begins to fall to the Earth.

"Oh shit," Cicero gasps.

The thick silvery gaseous mass plummets to the Earth with

extreme velocity. It's nearly a mile in length and about half a mile wide, and it appears to weigh immeasurable tons.

Cicero jumps up from his outdoor recliner as the falling titan gets closer and closer to smothering everyone in this part of the unnamed West Coast city.

Without giving them a chance to escape, the enormous cloud lands on Cicero and the sunbathing couple. Not incredibly heavy, the cloud has the weight of a king-sized mattress, but it is suffocating them.

Cicero struggles for air from under the vast cottony structure. He and the couple scratch and claw for each breath. It completely surrounds them.

Then, unexpectedly, the cloud splits and breaks in half, right over the pool. It splits, freeing all three of them from its stifling confines.

They gather themselves and stand to their feet, only to find an angel child sleeping comfortably on her belly inside the cloud.

Tiny white wings protrude from the small chubby back of a baby, whose head is down, corralled in her own arms.

"Oh my God, this can't be real," utters Cicero in shock and panic. The angel child wears a lavender linen cloth wrapped around its waist and midsection. The man and the woman gawk in awe.

"I can't believe this. That can't be an angel," the woman says. Without warning, the man reaches into the broken cloud and retrieves the angelic babe, who stirs at his touch.

He pulls the female child out. She appears to be around two years old. The man quickly sits down on the patio chair and as he does, the angelic child opens her eyes.

Her skin is the color of bronze, and her hair is a silky bright blonde. Her eyes are a radiant royal-blue, and she smiles at them.

The woman stares at the beautiful angel child and is struck by the facial similarities between the babe and Cicero. Then it hits her.

"This child is an angel, Cicero," the woman exclaims. "This child is your daughter."

Cicero is stunned and yet, an uncommon emotion he's never felt overcomes him. He feels blessed.

And then he awakens, still fully dressed, lying in the armchair with his black ensemble and Italian loafers on.

"What the fuck did that mean?" Cicero rhetorically questions his dream. "That shit was crazy."

The intrusive morning sheds natural light on the suite's exquisite interior. Awakened and stirred from his dream, Cicero stands up and stretches his arms and legs.

"Fuck," he grumbles, scratching his crotch and yawning, looking scruffier than ever. He unbuttons his black shirt and tosses it on the still-made bed and grabs a lemon-yellow short-sleeved sweater from his suitcase.

A sweeping second hand politely passes earth-made treasures on his platinum watch. It's a little after six a.m. Many of last night's partiers are still in the streets, just now making their way to hotel rooms and friend's floors.

Cicero peeks out the window of his corner suite.

"Look at these idiots," he states. He then slides away from the window toward the marble restroom where he thoroughly brushes his teeth in a rapid vertical motion. Water fills the basin as he spits, rinses, then repeats.

Once his teeth are polished, Cicero changes his pants, socks, and shoes, opting for a more casual look with his gator boots. He picks his room key up from off the nightstand and begins to head for the door when his cell phone rings, playing a familiar rap tune. He quickly grabs it from his hip.

"What's up, dog? Why you awake so early?"

Hip-hop blazes from the other end as the caller begins to cough profusely.

"A, man, that bitch is tryin' to leave town with our shit," Kameron says in a low, raspy, weed-affected voice.

Cicero feels his heart pounding in his chest, and he is speechless. He knew he'd made a mistake.

Kameron laughs. It is a chuckle of disappointment.

"So how did she get it anyway? What's up with Mr. Micheaux?"

Cicero is silent, and Kam recognizes the meaning.

"Oh yea? Like that? Oh well, fuck him," he says from the other end. "Anyway, that bitch is running her mouth about bouncing to Atlanta, dude. I guess she tried the shit and fell in love with it," Kameron says with a giggle, before inhaling a mouthful of cannabis smoke. "Yea, cuz, runnin' her mouth. What you want to do?"

Kameron marinates on his futon, staring blankly at his massive Samurai portrait, smoking his breakfast.

Cicero turns cold.

"Man, I'll be there Wednesday evening. Don't tell anybody I'm flying in. Keep an eye on ole girl, but I want to look her in the eyes before she tastes eternity. That's real talk."

Kameron smiles. His eyes are narrow and tight.

"That's what I'm talkin' about. Not a problem. See you then, dude. Be safe down there, cuz."

The call ends. Cicero stares at his cell phone momentarily, then returns it to his waistline. He makes his way to the elevator and down to the lobby, passing the gargantuan floral arrangement on his way out of the hotel.

The stench of piss and vomit persists on the warm February day, as C walks deeper into the Quarter in search of breakfast. Groups of twos and threes help each other stay upright in a fight against firewater and ale. While walking up Canal Street, Cicero happens upon a young college kid intoxicated beyond all U.S. legal limits, passed out facedown on the filthy curb. Digested chunks of corn cling to the side of his mouth and slowly ooze down his chin.

He's wearing a University of Southwest Louisiana sweatshirt. His sandy-brown hair is dirty and messy. Cicero gazes at him with a frown, then he chuckles.

"Damn. Better you than me though."

Right at that moment, a stray mutt scampers up and begins to sniff the kid's ass, which is partially exposed by his sagging Eddie Bauer khakis.

Cicero continues to walk, looking back at the kid and his new companion, when he bursts into laughter.

"Life is fucking stupid," he says, smiling nearly ear to ear.

Once on Bourbon Street, the smell of French toast enters the aromatic battle with urine and liquor. The mixture is strange and almost sickening to a starving Cicero, but he presses on to find the location of the more attractive scent.

A few couples sit outside at a sidewalk café. Tiny wood tables and chairs match the oak brown windowpanes divided into sixes. Soft canary-yellow siding contrasts with the traditional colors of the Quarter. Cicero eyes the couples enjoying crepes and fresh strawberries and carafes of orange juice and decides that's where he needs to be.

He crosses the street, stepping over broken purple, gold, and green beads, empty white paper cups, and numerous leaflets in reds and blues announcing everything from parties downtown to church services in Lake Charles.

The café is quaint and alive with the chatter of the ornery. Cicero slides in and seats himself at a small round table, quickly grabbing the thin menu stuck between the salt and pepper shakers. One yellow rose sprouts from a tiny white porcelain teacup at the center of his table.

He gazes at the simple menu, then peeks briefly over the top at the rose, noticing it hasn't been dethorned. He ignores it and sighs, returning the menu back to its space between the salt and pepper.

The waitress then sluggishly ambles over, trying to smile and not appear as if she was out until just one hour ago, which she was.

"Good mornin'. Can I get you a drink?"

Her hair is pulled back in a rough and hurried bun. Her blue eyes are thick and puffy.

"Yea, water with lemon. And I'll have the French toast."

"Anything else?"

"Nope."

"All right. It'll be right up."

"Thank you."

Cicero sits scanning the few other tables and persons seated at the sidewalk café. He thinks for a second about Lana but decides not to ponder the situation, which would only enrage him. Old beer and puke stink the atmosphere of the Quarter, as trampled doubloons lie crushed and even more worthless on the black asphalt. Other favors of amber plastic and gold paper, inscribed with various krewes' insignias, and names, add to the waste in the street.

On this Lundi Gras morning, a Kansas City native assesses eating food at a modest restaurant in New Orleans, Louisiana.

"Here's your water. Your French toast is almost ready," the waitress says.

"Thank you."

Cicero takes a sip of water and sees his tired waitress has forgotten his lemon.

"Of course," he grumbles. But he's not in the mood to bring it up, so he sips more water, while a shouting match intensifies over his right shoulder.

Upon their table rests a circular cake of purple, green, and gold. "Look, if you want to fuck the bitch, then just fuck her," a woman with straightened hair screams. It's dyed the color of a bright California Merlot, and her nose, eyebrows, and lips are pierced with rings of silver and studs of twenty-four-carat gold.

"Man, why are you wiggin' out? You said it was cool, like, fucking five months ago," her companion states. His arms bulge out from under a semi-small T-shirt, yet he is portly and fairly unattractive. Thick black-rimmed spectacles sit on his face, inching down his thin nose.

"Fuck off! I bet you guys fucked the other day when I passed out on the couch," she says, again screaming and attracting the stares of other groups and individuals at the outdoor eatery.

The stocky man frowns, as his left hand begins to fiddle with a fork. It wiggles rapidly between his index and middle fingers as his face shows he's becoming more and more agitated each second she scowls at him.

"I didn't say that shit when you fucked my brother," he loudly retorts.

"Damn," Cicero says to himself in a low voice.

The woman appears shocked. Her lips, with their dark-blue lipstick, open ever so slightly. A ring in the middle of her bottom lip begins to quiver.

"What? What are you talking about? I never slept with—"

"Shut the fuck up! You're such a fucking liar. You fucking whore!"

Suddenly, the man jumps up and jabs his fork into her collar, causing the restaurant's patrons to gasp and causing her to yelp in pain. Blood flies from her thin body.

"What the hell are you doing, man," a young waiter yells as he rushes over to stop the guy from killing his untrue girl-friend. He jabs the fork into her neck over and over again before the waiter can grab him and wrestle him to the ground.

Cicero sits watching, sipping his water, as the two squirm on the banquette. He could easily stop the skirmish, but he chooses not to intervene.

"This is tight," Cicero says with a smile, enjoying the show.

Police are quickly on the scene. The bleeding girl turns pale, holding her neck with a wad of bloody-red napkins. The wait-ress kneels next to her, praying she doesn't die.

"It's gonna be okay. It's gonna be okay," the waitress repeats, as tears roll down her face. She strokes the bleeding girl's hair.

Infused cinnamon and berries from the King cake decorate the man's black T-shirt as the police handcuff him and lift him off the ground. Moments later, paramedics arrive and whisk

the bleeding girl away for treatment. Several undesired punc-
ture wounds ventilate her bleeding throat.

The waitress, in a stained white Polo shirt, stands in near
shock with her right hand over her mouth as the ambulance
speeds off.

"Excuse me, is my French toast ready?" Cicero callously asks.

The waitress turns to her left to face him. She wears a look
of disgust.

"Coming right up, sir!"

She returns with a plate of three dense slices of brown, egg-
soaked bread lightly drizzled with powdered sugar and smothered in fresh strawberries and fresh strawberry syrup. She
throws it on Cicero's table, causing the yellow rose to shake.

"Thanks," he says without becoming angry. The waitress turns
to leave and slips on the woman's blood, nearly losing her
footing and falling.

He immediately digs into the food on his plate. Slicing the
fluffy French toast and depositing chunks into his mouth, chewing his food thoroughly before swallowing.

The Vieux Carre is now still, and Cicero enjoys his meal,
thinking about his plans for the day and evening. A knife scrapes
a plate and a fork assists. Platinum and diamonds sparkle on a
wrist in the early morning light as it penetrates through the
swamp gases of the Big Easy.

Chapter 18

About nine-hundred miles away, intense dark eyes covertly watch the townhouse of a young slumbering feminine creature.

Smoke escapes out the window of a beat-up Buick Regal. This is the car that Kameron uses when he doesn't want to be recognized. Everyone in Kansas City, Missouri, and Kansas knows his classic Chevy and his big black truck. So he crouches low in the plush, velvety, burgundy interior of the light-gray Regal.

Lana's east-side block is silent on this Monday morning. A few young professionals arise and prepare for work, some skipping breakfast, others skipping showers.

The new town homes where she lives are spectacular. Fresh white siding, forest-green rooftops, vaulted ceilings, and recessed lighting can be found in each of the identically cloned units. Spacious garages contain brand-new SUVs and convertibles. All lie smack dab in the middle of the ghetto, where Kam is comfortable.

He inhales deeply, chest expanding, capillaries engorged. His diamond-encrusted mouth is polished and bright.

"Yea, you done fucked up, little girl," he says to himself, voice raspier than ever.

Sticky dew clings to individual blades of grass, as ants march toward fumbled candy two by two. They're unaware they live in a high-crime urban area, so they march on.

The flick of a switch and the introduction of brilliant electricity disturbs the darkness in Lana's house.

Kam tries to quickly perk up to get a better look, but he does so slowly. Cornrows line his head flush and neat in intertwining pairs. Opaque round glass, once his eyes, reside inside his dome.

Shadows are cast on cheap plastic mini blinds as movement occurs in Lana's bedroom. Her French-cut lavender panties and lace brassiere are a man's dream come true. Kansas City has never known such flawless skin, or such supple lips.

The Kohler knob rotates in the restroom with the help of a caramel-wrapped hand. She sighs.

"I got a whole lot of shit to do today," Lana says to herself while removing her unmentionables. Her wild amber-colored curly hair barely budges when the hot water hits it.

Streams of steamy moisture roll down her perfect, young face as she lathers her loofa sponge with a perfumed shower gel smelling of jasmine, licorice, and fresh mint. A drought strikes the showerhead and Lana dries herself, then quickly dresses.

Outside, Kam continues to choke on his dwindling blunt when a powdered and perfumed Lana emerges from her front door. Her black form-fitting skirt hugs her round hips as the silky red shirt on her back dips low and flows. The ants momentarily stop and look.

"Damn, that bitch is bad," Kam mutters in his deep voice, as if seeing her for the first time. Then he perversely laughs and says, "I should rape her mothafuckin' ass, for real."

She slides down her stone-paved walkway to the new champagne convertible sports car in her driveway. The compact two-door chariot is sleek and smooth, the product of tireless Japanese engineering and compulsive perfectionism.

On. Off. The taillights briefly glow as she disables the alarm system and unlocks the door from the keychain in her tiny hand. The engine purrs and white rear lights are activated when she reverses out of the driveway and into Kansas City's empty morning streets.

Kam tosses his roach out the window and follows close behind in his under bucket. Not too close though, so as to avoid raising Lana's suspicion. He knows she is street smart; the type to constantly check her rearview mirror. THC clings to his cellular makeup as it has for many years. To Kameron, the moving world looks blurry and slow.

He follows Lana west along Forty-Seventh Street, lifting his left wrist and checking his black-and-gold numberless timepiece. It's 8:30 a.m. Hate festers in his mind.

"Where the fuck is yo' stupid ass goin'?" he grumbles about Lana's route toward the Plaza. They pass a homeless couple pushing a shopping cart and holding hands on Troost as they exit the black side of town and enter the white.

The homes instantly grow larger. Property values miraculously rise, as if levitated by the realty gods. Black rubber grips the asphalt and twists backward, thrusting forward.

"And, flu, zim, today, up, oyals, look, yea, oh no, then they," the radio spits while Kam twists the knob.

"You might want to dust those barbecue grills off. Expect the high today to be eighty-five degrees," the KPRS DJ gushes. "That's right! Eighty-five. Tonight's low will be around seventy. It's gonna feel like summer in February in the city today!"

"Damn. That's some tight shit," Kam blurts to no one, then chuckles. "It's got to be the end of the world."

Summer weather unexpectedly materializes in the month of black history.

Lana coasts across Maine and Broadway, venturing into the

luxurious Country Club Plaza on the posh western side of town, where days earlier she met with Kam and Cicero. The young lady and her tail travel past block after block of classical Spanish architecture, mosaic teal tile, and spewing fountains. Kameron follows like an unseen rook, positioning himself for checkmate.

She makes a left on Wornall Road, then a right onto Ward Parkway before stopping just in front of a quaint and exclusive luggage shop. Most of the Plaza's posh businesses are closed, minus a few coffee spots and stores where employees are setting up for the day.

Kam parks his Regal near the corner on Wornall, across from Williams-Sonoma, and watches Lana climb out of her coupe and knock three times on the glass door of the luggage store. A petite man in an English-tailored suit soon ambles over gingerly and unlocks the door.

"Hey, girl. Damn, your hair looks good. Come in, come in," he says in a high-pitched feminine tone.

"This fag," Kam growls with disgust, slightly leaning forward in his car to enhance his view around the corner.

The man's suit is the fine color of dying daisies. His dark bald head resembles a piece of melting fudge in the humid air.

"Girl, we gotta hurry up. My manager called and he is on his way! He wasn't supposed to be here today."

"Boy, calm down. It is gonna be okay. I'll be in and out," Lana calmly tells her nervous accomplice in her sweetest voice. "And I know you like it in and out."

He laughs. "Girl, you are crazy! I'll be right back."

She patiently waits by the polished oak counter as Chauncey scurries to the back room to grab some merchandise for her. The small shop is lit by gold and crystal chandeliers and is home to only seven pieces of luggage. Each represents wealth and the designer's full line. If a customer wants more, a customer orders it.

Chauncey returns moments later pulling a huge Louis Vuitton trunk with brown and flaxen LV wheels on the end.

"Look, girl, the two Louis suitcases and the tote bag are inside."

"Great," Lana says as she reaches into her hot-pink canvas handbag and pulls out a thick rubber band-wrapped wad of tens and twenties. "So I already gave you half, here's the other half." And she hands him three-hundred dollars.

"Okay. Shoot, that's what I'm talkin' about." Chauncey quickly takes the money with his left hand and stuffs it into his pocket, and they walk out the store together.

"Yea, girl, just let me know next time you want the hookup. See, all our stuff is insured. So if somebody steals it, or if it's damaged and a customer returns it, we just write it off, and no one misses it."

"Yes, Chauncey, I'll definitely be seeing you again," Lana states with a smile, flashing her perfect white teeth. She remotely pops the trunk and Chauncey lifts the Louis luggage and places it in the empty space.

"Well, that's cool, girl, but you know I need you to do that thing for me, before my manager gets here."

"Oh, yea. Boy, I almost forgot too."

With that, Lana opens her passenger side door and pulls out an old bulky red and brown wrench.

"Yea, I got this from my brother," Lana says, looking at it as if admiring the craftsmanship. Chauncey eyes it too, and says, "Yea, that's cool. That will work."

Lana takes a quick look around, then grasps the heavy wrench tightly and swiftly bashes Chauncey in the head with it. Blood squirts out his cranium and runs profusely down his face, dripping on his suit.

Kam sees the incident and is stunned. "Oh shit! This bitch is crazy. Fuck this. I will shoot this cute bitch, like, so fast."

"Damn, girl, you did that like you hate me," exclaims Chauncey, holding his head as blood trickles through his middle and ring finger. "But that's cool, it's got to look real."

Seeing the two still talking, Kam catches on to the ploy, and he laughs.

"Oh. These two here are wild." He chuckles, then focuses on Chauncey's bleeding head. "That mothafucka is an idiot. I can't wait to tell C. There's got to be a better hustle than that!"

The two partners in crime share a few more words before Lana smashes off and Chauncey passes out from blood loss.

Still laughing about the ridiculous event he just witnessed, Kameron follows Lana along the winding and elevating Ward Parkway near the Kansas state line.

He trails about six car lengths behind her, with a silver Benz station wagon between them, as his thoughts begin to veer. The weed in his system has Kam in a daze heading south, passing the old money of Ward Parkway.

He eyes the fifty- and sixty-room mansions that line the wide immaculate roadway divided by bubbling fountains and dedicated statues. Tennis courts, indoor swimming pools, guest houses, and servants have all been passed down from Kansas City's first ambitious robber baron whites to today's elite bloodline.

The weed causes Kam to think in strange ways, and his thoughts soon become philosophical. "Even their laziest mothafuckin' family members, and shit, can live life to the fullest," he mumbles, then laughs. But the thoughts don't end there.

Seeing these enormous red brick and gold stone estates on spacious, bright green acreage with groundskeepers and electronically timed sprinkler systems, Kam ponders the American system.

He thinks about how whites often argue that in today's world, all people are equal, which may legally be the case. But the written codes fail to capture many of the practices, and never will they make up for the unleveled playing field. Kam laughs to himself.

"This is some bullshit. These fuckin' laws. These fuckin' honkies got a three hundred-year head start, and shit," he says, talking to himself like a mental patient. "That's like makin' the Chiefs stay in the locker room while the Chargers put fifty points on the board."

"Then you tell the Chiefs, 'Play ball,'" he says with a radio announcer's voice. Then he chuckles. "Fuck that." He laughs again. Drivers in cars next to him gawk at this psycho with braided hair and platinum and diamond in his mouth talking to himself.

"White people are a fucking trip." He chuckles again.

Kam laughs again as he cruises slowly, well below the speed limit. This time the laugh is with a hint of cynicism.

"They got a real big fucking head start on us, cuz." He laughs, then his thoughts stray further. "I really don't know why there are any poor white people. What's their excuse?"

He finally focuses his attention back on the road, and Lana's Lexus is nowhere in sight.

"Aw, fuck."

The rolling plant-coated hills of Ward Parkway conceal her vehicle, but Kam is able to catch a glimpse of its sleek taillights about a mile ahead of him.

"Shit." He smashes the gas pedal and promptly gains on her.

The coppery coupe eventually passes Eighty-Fifth Street and makes a left into Ward Parkway Mall. The stores are about thirty minutes away from opening but dozens of elderly mall walkers have already started their laps.

Lana navigates her coupe around to the south end of the mall and Kam keeps a safe distance behind in his beat-up Regal. The mall's entrance is bare and beckons Lana to enter. She parks and steps out of her convertible carrying a large paper shopping bag, and glides into the mall as the automatic doors slide apart, making way for her thieving highness.

Kam parks on the west side of the mall where the early morning sun causes the one-level building to cast a vast shadow. He's just close enough to see the front end of Lana's drop top.

He sits in his car motionless, listening to the Isley Brothers on cassette. Feeling his high coming down, he checks the pockets of his blue sweatsuit, but finds nothing. Birds chirp from nearby trees, signifying the glorious coming of a new day.

Kam checks his ashtray for roaches and remnants of old joints, but his search is futile.

"Oh, this is some bullshit," he says in his deep voice, diamonds shining. Not one to be deterred, Kam checks his messy, paper-stuffed glove compartment for some type of mind-altering substance, when he stumbles across some tiny round purple pills.

He grabs the three light-violet pills and stares at them. "What the fuck is this?" Unsure but willing to find out, he quickly pops the pills into his mouth and swallows them.

"Oh, well, hopefully I won't die," he mutters with indifference. Within minutes, black butterflies sprout from his Regal's upholstery, and his windshield sheds liquid metal tears.

"Oh, ain't this a bitch, this is Jesse's shit. Fuck," he says of some hallucinogens left in his car by one of his Mexican friends. The plush seats begin to foam like Alka Seltzer tablets and the aroma of freshly bottled Sprite fills the air.

"Shit. I gotta ride this shit out. This is some bad timing," Kam acknowledges. Then he hears a voice.

"This ain't bad timing. Quit being a pussy," the passenger seat yells. Kam quickly turns to the right and sees the headrest on the passenger seat looks just like his incarcerated brother. "Look at you, all high and shit. And you stink. Gimme a sandwich!"

Kam leans back away from the chattering seat, only to feel the seatbelt trying to arouse him by blowing in his ear. "A, seatbelt, chill out, cuz," he whispers.

"Dude, where's my motherfucking sandwich? And no goddamn pickles this time," the seat demands in a demonic tone. "The world is topsy-turvy and no one wants to die."

Kam's breathing becomes deeper and his heart rate intensifies. He's slowly losing it. Sweat beads on his forehead and rolls down his face and goatee.

"I gotta ride this shit out," he says, panting. Mushrooms bloom from the floor and tiny elves and frogs frolic in lily fields in the backseat.

"Yea, ride it out, asshole. Ride it out! Yee-haw," screams the passenger seat.

Kam closes his eyes and sweat continues to flow down his face before he passes out in his Regal in the empty parking lot of Ward Parkway Mall.

XXX

Birds chirp again and Kameron stirs. His mouth is dry and his eyelids are heavy and tightly closed. But his body stirs and he awakens. The parking lot is still empty, but it's now ten hours later and his Regal is the only car in the pitch-black parking lot. Lana is long gone.

"Shit." It's the only word he can muster. He sluggishly regains his faculties and turns the key in the ignition, revving the engine, then smashing the gas pedal back north to his midtown apartment.

He does about ninety down Ward Parkway when his cell phone rings.

"Yea," he answers abruptly.

"Hey."

"Yea, what's up?"

"What you doin' tonight?" his baby's mother asks.

"I don't know. I got shit on my mind right now."

"Well, I was gonna stop by for a little bit, maybe cook something."

"Yea, that's cool."

"Where you at?"

"I'm on my way home right now. When you comin' by?"

"I guess in about an hour or so."

"That's cool. I'll be there."

"Okay. I'll see you then."

"All right." And Kam snaps his phone shut, tossing it into the now silent passenger seat.

XXX

Beads, trinkets, toys, aluminum doubloons, plastic cups, necklaces, dolls, and other throws litter the black pavement.

Cameras flash in the foreground and in the distance, capturing exposed breasts and genitals. Cicero mixes in with the jam-packed crowd of thousands on the New Orleans Rue. He wades through ankle-high rubbish, sipping a cold beer. The triad of green, purple, and gold adorns everything in sight under the bright full lunar orb.

Flash. A coed of simple beauty lowers her halter top in the summer-like weather, in exchange for worthless baubles from a total stranger.

"Thanks, honey! You sure earned these," the guy says to her before kissing her on the cheek.

"Thanks. Have a good Mardi Gras," she drunkenly replies as her girlfriends hand her her yard-long strawberry daiquiri. Her upper body is weighted with layers of intricate crap and doodads.

Cicero takes it all in, strolling down the street, when he notices his boots are covered in a revolting dark-brown muck.

"Fuck. Why did I wear these," he laments out loud. The perpetual motion of the multitude prevents him from wiping them. Catholics and atheists alike gather in the Big Easy to drink themselves stupid, see some skin, and hopefully have unprotected sex with someone whose last name they don't know.

Twenty-year-olds in LSU and Ole Miss T-shirts carry massive alcoholic drinks just like those in Southern and Grambling shirts and hoodies. Cicero steps through while drunk and sober women caress his bald head and make eyes at him. He stares back as a crackle of thunder bursts through the sky.

"Whoa! God don't like this down 'chere, shan," some drunk

Cajun slurs, bumping into Cicero. He looks at the local as if he's got shit on his face.

"Fuckin' idiot," Cicero says in a low voice.

"Hey, don't make love, I mean, don't make war, make love," mutters a cute blonde with a nice buzz. Looking up, she gazes into Cicero's eyes as her half-sober friend clings to her arm trying to pull her up the Rue.

Her looks and her spirit catch Cicero's attention, and hold it.

"So are you the love ambassador?"

"Yep. You wanna open up some negotiations?" She flirtingly motions. Her bright blue eyes beckon.

"Look, let's cut the shit. I got a suite at the Ritz-Carlton. You comin' with me?"

She thinks for a moment and can't resist Cicero's bluntness.

"Yea, let's go."

Her brunette friend angrily protests but the blonde pulls away from her grasp.

Cicero turns with his blonde date following and is about to head back to his room when a dazzling rainbow catches his eye.

Sparkling, shining prisms snatch energy from available light sources and toss it back to the world. The diamonds hang from the neck of a rapper with a familiar face.

Cicero stares as he stands between his two flunkies and his massive bodyguard.

"Man, it's some bitches out here," Scrill expresses with joy, exposing the brilliant diamonds and platinum in his mouth. He wears sunglasses with reflective lenses. Girls wave at him and others run up to get hugs, only to be thwarted by his hired protection.

"A, ya'll, I got to piss. Those grenadine Zimas are running

through me," the rapper tells his crew, which is preoccupied by the groupies and free-flowing liquor.

"Yea, that's cool, man. Don't get lost," one of his boys yells above the noise of the Quarter as he fondles the breast of a young Scrill fan. His bodyguard has a face full of saggy breasts and doesn't hear the rapper make his Johnny-on-the-spot announcement.

Seeing the rapper walk away, alone, Cicero unceremoniously calls off his date, to the chagrin of his new lady friend.

"Hey, do you have a cell phone?"

"Yea," she slurs, swinging her long straight hair back over her shoulder.

"Well, give me your number. I'm gonna call you in a few minutes. Is that cool?" Cicero says, looking directly into her eyes.

"Oh. You don't wanna hook up? You're gonna stand me up?"

"Naw, not at all. I just need to do something."

The shouting in the streets reaches a fever pitch when the Playboy girls begin flashing their silicone from one of the Bourbon Street balconies. Cicero's girl raises her voice so he can hear her.

"Okay. Just be sure to call me."

"I will."

She types her number into his cell phone and hands it back to her suitor.

Meanwhile, the short millionaire rap superstar sneaks off to an alley where a few drunken stragglers stumble through. Afraid to just whip it out and piss, Scrill looks for a darker, more secluded spot, as the sounds of Bourbon Street lessen. He is unaware someone is close behind, watching his every move.

A large navy dumpster nearly wedged between two of New

Orleans' oldest shotgun houses seems to offer Scrill what he's looking for. It's an alley known to be the home of several ghosts and phantoms.

"Yea, that will work."

He skips over a puddle of rain runoff and spent beer, causing his large platinum chain and medallion to smack his bird-like chest.

His back is to the dark alley as he faces the blue dumpster. He unzips his baggy jeans and releases his urine. It flows down the rancid asphalt that has seen piss for at least two centuries. His sunglasses reflect the river of waste coming from his body.

"Ah, I needed that," he exclaims.

Once finished, he shakes, then zips his baggy jeans. Scrill turns to leave the alley and is stunned to see a bald man standing just a foot away, staring at him with intense eyes.

"Yo! What the fuck is your problem, man? Don't be sneaking up on people like that!"

Brash, the short rapper pushes Cicero in his chest and tries to walk off, but Cicero quickly grabs him by his loose basketball jersey and forcefully thrusts his back into the metal dumpster, causing a loud crash.

"Help!" the rapper screams. His award-winning songs often include lyrics of murder and strong-arm tactics, but in reality he's a punk from the suburbs that had only been in one fight in his life, which he lost. The hubbub of Mardi Gras is too thick for his pleas to be heard.

Cicero leans his two-hundred-plus pounds of body weight on the much smaller man, then places his right hand over the rapper's mouth, preventing further screams.

"Remember me from the airport? You thought that shit was funny, didn't you," Cicero grumbles in a low voice. Tears well in Scrill's eyes and his heart pounds to be set free.

Cicero leans in closer, nearly putting his mouth on the terrified rapper's ear, as Scrill struggles in futile gestures to wiggle free.

"I got a rap for you, big Scrill," Cicero whispers, then mockingly starts to rhyme: "You should stay in your place, it would be more nutritious."

The rapper squirms even harder, and Cicero continues.

"Your life ends tonight, revenge is so delicious."

Still powerfully pinning him against the dumpster, Cicero swiftly clutches the rapper's platinum chain and wraps it around his neck, pulling it skyward with his left hand. The resplendent noose gleams in the moonlight.

The small man panics and struggles with all his strength, but it's not enough to free himself. Veins pop out on his neck and forehead. Reflections of Cicero's scowling face bounce off Scrill's designer sunglasses, warping his assailant's fine looks.

His eyes bulge bloodshot and wet. Cicero pulls the chain higher and harder, preventing any air from entering the star's starving lungs. He fidgets, and fidgets, until he suddenly collapses to the filthy street, lifeless. *Carne levare.*

Cicero releases the chain and stares at the rapper's cold body, as it lies in its own piss.

"You weak bitch. Talk shit now."

Partying voices become louder so Cicero acts fast. He lifts the wide lid of the dumpster, then picks up the rapper's dead body and throws it in, tossing it amongst the other flamboyant rubbish of Mardi Gras. He gently lowers the lid and hurriedly leaves the wrought-iron balconies, shuttered windows, and stucco of the Quarter, under the cover of darkness and ruckus. He escapes being caught *en flagrante delicto*.

That same night, he packs his suitcase at the Ritz and hops in a taxi bound for the first flight to Kansas City, Missouri.

Cicero will not see the finale of Mardi Gras in the Crescent City, the symbolic last day of depravity before Ash Wednesday and the beginning of Lent. His decadence and transgressions go on without a metaphorical day of closure, as he zooms 25,000 feet above the country's midsection.

Chapter 19

Once the product began selling, every Saturday at noon Brad would drop money off to one of Jimmy's restaurants in the River Market area. In turn, he would walk out with a nice to-go box of pasta primavera, passing by Amish and Vietnamese merchants.

But for three weeks, no deliveries have been made. Certain people of Mediterranean descent are becoming more than anxious, as feathers fall delicately from the ceiling in Kam's loft. Hollow orbs jettison among time and space.

This phenomenon transpires as brain cells buy the farm in Kameron's head and he puffs a cigarette dipped in embalming fluid. The formaldehyde rivals peyote and even mescaline in its hallucinogenic potency, but it makes Kam no difference. He's depressed. Not only did he lose Lana, his drug connection in Canada needs him to come ASAP, and he can't.

Flames crackle in his fireplace and water trickles down the large stone fountain in the corner.

Various drugs befoul his system. Kam has called Cicero's cell phone all night, but he still hasn't heard from him, and his nerves simply can't take it. Tonight, he's wasted off every opiate and stimulant available in the eight-one-six and nine-one-three area codes. Chemicals contaminate his mitochondria.

Tiny feathers the color of warm oatmeal float about.

Water runs in the kitchen sink and long painted fingernails make dishes clatter. The mother of Kam's son prepared a meal earlier that evening, and now she washes the dishes. Black roots interrupt her dyed blonde hair, as her full-figured physique bursts out of blue jeans.

Then the phone rings.

Kam, lying on his futon, ignores the ring.

"Kam, get the phone," Keisha demands.

Dazed, Kam leans over to his left and fumbles for the loft's cordless phone. Calls to his home are rare, so he struggles to find the phone as it rings and rings.

"Kam, pick the phone up," Keisha yells again from the kitchen.

"Hello," he answers. His voice is dry and rough.

"Hey, you fucking piece of shit, Jimmy wants his money," a man's voice says.

"What?" Kam slurs. He's groggy and his mind isn't clear as he stares up at the ceiling with nearly closed eyes. "Who... who the fuck is this?"

"Jimmy wants his money, cocksucker."

Kameron laughs, flashing his diamond-rich teeth.

Some of the orbs Kameron sees are idle, while others scoot in awkward directions at varying speeds. These orbs exist in a different dimension, so they never mingle with the feathers, which continue their nonstop descent from on high.

"Who is it, baby?" Keisha asks, now drying the dishes. "Is that Yolanda? She said she was gonna call."

The drugs have altered reality for Kameron and his thoughts are impaired as he wipes saliva from his mouth.

"Hey, fuck you, cuz," Kam tells the guy on the phone. "This is Kameron Brown, you fuckin' wit. You think you scare me? You don't scare me, mothafucka!"

The rushing waters in Kam's fountain sound like a tidal wave to him, pounding the beach in his thoughts. Serotonin and dopamine socialize in his brain's avenues and causeways as the deep voice on the phone laughs.

"Oh it's funny," Kam questions, becoming angry. "I'll take on your whole army, mothafucka."

"Baby, who is that?" questions Keisha, concerned. Gold outlines one of her front teeth.

With that, Kam leans over and pulls a semi-automatic pistol from under the futon and cocks the hammer back.

"I got heat for bitches like you."

"Yea, you're gonna need it, cocksucker," the man says, laughing.

"Oh yea! Oh yea! Mothafucka, I'm a gangsta," an enraged Kam yells in his deep voice as he wobbles and rises to his feet. "I'm a fucking G!"

Laughter spills from the phone.

Keisha walks from the kitchen and sees Kameron drunkenly wielding the weapon, and she panics. His drug abuse has caught up with him.

"Oh, my God. Baby, put the gun down," she pleads with both her hands in the air. "Kam, put the gun down, baby."

But the chemicals circulating in his body mute her words.

"You mothafuckas can't touch me! Ya'll mothafuckas can't take me out," he screams into the telephone. "I'm the only mothafucka that can take me out! You hear me, bitch? I'm the only mothafucka that can touch me."

"Kam, please stop," Keisha begs. Tears now run down her face, smearing her heavy mascara. "Please, Kam. Stop it, baby."

The man on the phone once again bursts into sadistic laughter, further angering a deranged Kam.

"Oh, it's funny," Kam rages. "I'm the only one that can take me out. I'll take my own self out! I ain't scared!"

He quickly puts the shiny black pistol to his temple and pulls the trigger. *Bang!*

"No! No!!" Keisha screams, still standing in one place, unable to move. Her hands cover her face.

Chunks of gray matter and bone fragments splatter the white futon as Kam's frame quivers and the pistol drops harmlessly to the floor. With one shot, he put himself to rest.

Hearing a woman's screams on the other end, the man on the phone calmly hangs up.

"Oh, my God! Oh, my God," Keisha stutters. She drops to her knees, about five feet from Kameron, and tears flow freely from her big brown eyes.

Kameron Brown's body is motionless and bleeding. He dies with his mouth open, exposing his precious smile in a final show of distasteful irony, so full of luster, and yet lacking life.

Crime scene investigators will determine narcotics and hallucinogens induced his suicide. It is indeed a dreadful end to a sad and tumultuous life. He was just a young man.

Chapter 20

The next morning, Cicero sits in his living room in his black blazer and slacks, anxiously calling Kam's cell phone and his house phone without getting an answer. His powder-blue shirt fits impeccably.

He sits, frustrated, wondering about the whereabouts of his friend, and the drugs he entrusted to Lana.

"Fuck this," he mutters. He grabs the keys to his pearl-white SUV (finally out of the shop) and decides to drive to Lana's townhouse. He's either going to wake her up with a pistol to her face, or wait for her to show up and torture her ass.

The weather is unbelievably summer-like. It's so hot, in fact, that the schools, unprepared for the hot ninety-degree temperatures, are closed today.

Cruising on his mammoth gold monster tires, Cicero once again sips cognac from a red plastic cup, with a nine-millimeter handgun resting comfortably on the passenger's seat. He pushes a button and the radio comes on.

"The high today will be around ninety five, but expect some spot showers early today," the DJ says. "In other news, award-winning rapper Scrill was found dead in New Orleans today. Officials haven't commented on how the rapper died, but sources say foul play is suspected. We'll keep you posted on the latest developments."

Cicero laughs as he turns the radio off. His cell phone rings.

"Hello," he angrily answers without looking at the caller ID.

"I just wanted to say good-bye," Olivia says over the phone in her unique, silky sad tone.

Speeding eastbound on Forty-Seventh Street, Cicero recognizes her voice and he's curious to know why she's called.

"What are you talking about, O?"

"I'm flying to Atlanta today in an hour to start my life over, and I just wanted to say good-bye. Can you come over and say 'bye before I leave?"

He quickly recalls Kam mentioning Lana was going to Atlanta. Cicero pauses. Even though he never introduced them to each other, Lana and O could be working together, he thinks. So he decides to go to Olivia's to find out. She's so sappy and emotional, he reasons, that she could be unknowingly dropping the dime on Lana's little getaway plan.

"All right, Olivia. I have something to do, so I can't stay long. But I'll be there in about ten minutes. Is that cool with you?"

"That's fine, C. I'll be here."

He hangs up and cruises on the empty Kansas City streets, passing fixed old schools and their raggedy counterparts.

At that moment, his cell rings again. He once again answers without checking for the caller.

"Son?" Her voice is soft and calm.

Cicero pauses.

"Hey, Mom."

"Your sister and I have been trying to reach you. We were worried about you. You didn't answer your cell phone."

"Hey, well, there's no need to worry about me. I've just been handling business," he says, sounding callous. His truck humps through an intersection.

"Handling business? I had a dream about you last night. It was so horrible, Son. You were in a lot of pain."

Cicero pictures his mother stroking her Bible or reading a passage as she talks and the thought irritates him.

"Mom, I know you care about me and I appreciate it. Everything is good. But I have to get ready for a business meeting so I'm gonna call you back in a few minutes."

The phone is silent.

"I'll try to stop by later today."

"Later today?"

"Yes, Mother. Later today. Okay? I'll call you."

"Okay, Son. I love you."

Cicero ends the call and shakes his head, refocusing his mind on his next moves.

Youthful laughter bellows throughout the neighborhood. Green maple and sycamore trees line the street on either side.

"Car!" a girl yells, forcing the kids to stop their game of double Dutch in the street.

Cicero squeezes his large SUV into a tight parking spot two houses down from Olivia's grandmother's. He exits the white iridescent SUV with his red cup and strides up the sidewalk, interrupting a lively game of hopscotch.

He climbs the stone stairs and glances over at the early budding flowers in Juanita's garden. As he looks over at them, the front door opens, and Olivia steps out in a yellow dress with her purse slung over her shoulder. Her long black hair is beautiful and her eyes appear unswollen for the first time in a while. Cicero stares at her and wishes she was clean. Disease-free.

"Hey, C. My grandmother is in the house. Can we talk around back?"

"Yea, that's cool, but I can't stay for long. I got some things to handle."

"Okay. I understand."

They walk around to the back of the house, into the alleyway where the neighborhood's residents keep their trash and discarded items.

Olivia's long, firm caramel legs shine in the sunlight, and Cicero stares at them. As he does, he doesn't notice Olivia pulling a handgun from her purse. She turns around and the sunlight hits the barrel. Cicero sees it and is shocked, but not overly surprised.

"So what's up with that, O?"

She points the barrel at his chest, holding it merely inches from him. Unfazed, Cicero takes a sip of cognac, briefly looks down at the barrel, then raises his head to stare her in the eyes.

In his sincerest voice, he whispers, "Do it."

Energy applies pressure to the crescent moon, and the minute mallet strikes the casing. *Bang!*

Compressed gunpowder explodes, ejecting one round from within the weapon's belly. It spins clockwise until it exits at nearly the speed of light, then penetrates the skin and ribs of the fearless Cicero. He doesn't flinch.

Blood spurts out. Cicero's body falls in the dirty alleyway, and lies twitching, and without breath.

Olivia solemnly strolls back into her grandmother's home through the back door and into the living room. She grabs her cell phone and dials a number. A man answers.

"It's done."

"Good," says Jimmy before he hangs up. He takes a sip of his vodka tonic and looks over at the government informer, who's managed to keep his identity hidden.

"That's that," Jimmy says, setting his glass down and briefly reflecting. "Yea, he earned a litle. But fuck that. I wouldn't take that type of disrespect from a full blood. You think I'm going to take it from a fuckin' half-breed? Now I get my dope, then I get my money."

Now clenching the murder weapon in her delicate hands, Olivia sits on the plush light-brown couch, and without a tear in her eye, she smoothly turns the gun to her abdomen and places it against her dress.

Heat once again flies from the barrel and singes the yellow dress as it passes through. Olivia's body collapses forward onto the floor.

Having heard both shots, Juanita hurries down the stairs. The shots sounded too close, and she is fearful.

"Olivia, did you hear that? Are you okay?" Juanita asks. Her flower-embroidered housecoat flows and she makes her way down the stairs to the first floor.

The grandmother enters the kitchen and sees the back door is open. She peers outside and sees Cicero dying, his body lying awkwardly on the black pavement.

Juanita's pulse quickens and her breathing becomes frantic as she turns and proceeds toward the living room. She places her right hand on her chest; her heart pounds with anxiety.

"Olivia, honey, are you okay?" Juanita questions aloud.

Then she sees her. Juanita's heart jumps into her throat and her stomach cramps; nausea ensues. Juanita eyes her granddaughter's bloody, still body.

"No," she screams at the top of her lungs, causing pigeons to disperse from the roof.

Juanita begins to cry, and quickly reaches for the black cordless telephone from a living room end table.

"Nine-one-one, what's your emergency?" a woman says, sounding like a recording.

"It's my granddaughter, she's been shot," Juanita frantically explains to the operator.

"Okay, we have your address, ma'am. An ambulance is on the way."

"Oh, God, thank you. Please, please hurry."

And Juanita hangs up the phone.

Now wailing inconsolably, she runs toward Olivia's blood-drenched body but pauses. She stares at her granddaughter's tainted blood and is momentarily fearful of becoming infected with her incurable disease. Shame suddenly overwhelms her, and she flings herself on top of Olivia's bloody body. Oxygen-rich red blood cells stain her floral housecoat.

"No," Juanita screams once again, gripping Olivia's limp body. A gaping cavity occupies the space that a child would never know.

"It's gonna be okay, baby," Juanita pleads, squeezing her granddaughter's bleeding body, rocking side to side. Tears stream down her aged tan face.

Juanita breathes erratically, wrinkled callused hands rubbing her grand-daughter's pretty face. Olivia's skin is now pale and colorless as blood leaves her frame.

"My poor baby. It's gonna be okay. An ambulance is comin', baby," she says, crying. "God will keep you close to him. It's about faith, baby. It's all about having faith."

Olivia's breaths are short and shallow. She clings to life, yet it begins to elude her grasp.

The grandmother stares at the dying body she holds, then she gently lays Olivia on her rug. Sadness overcomes her, that is, until she hears the sirens blaring. Juanita realizes her address is incomplete on the outside of her home, so she decides to meet the paramedics outside.

Juanita prays for Olivia, rubbing her hands together and mumbling. She opens her front door and steps outside into the hot air. Children's laugher immediately fills her ears, yet it doesn't comfort her. Her granddaughter may be gone, but hope remains for tomorrow's dearest. And that thought helps warm her.

Innocence is at play. Hopscotch and double Dutch entertain the neighborhood youth. Tag has yet to fall off the map. It remains a boy's way of expressing his feelings for a girl without being sentimental.

So Juanita sits on her porch with the siren's volume increasing, observing the ever-changing world through time-tested eyes. She has been a witness to riots, space travel, and now quite possibly the suicide of her beautiful granddaughter.

She's seen the persecution of quadroons and conversely, the invalidation of HIV being an evil person's plague or a gay disease. She knows it can affect the ambitious, as well as the God-fearing. She sits on her porch with her arms folded, tears flowing down her wrinkled face. A white-and-red ambulance speeds eastward toward her home.

The sunbeams try to fight through darkening clouds. Yellow rays of light strike the pavement on what would be considered by many as a beautiful day. Clouds then begin to gather from the west. The clouds loom above, watchful, as an ambulance approaches.

And yet, down an alley where vermin reside, and slime and sludge congregate, lies a dying shell. The clouds open and it begins to rain on the dying shell of Cicero Day. His eyelids flutter as blood flows from him in the pouring rainstorm.

Maroon solution flows down the side of his face in a slow waterfall of wretchedness.

Even after the children have made mad dashes to steps, stoops, doorways, doors, foyers, and elsewhere to avoid the run, burgundy life force continues to pool just beneath its reluctant spring. The stray yellow beams of light have been overwhelmed by the dark-gray coming of the rain.

Midnight-colored trousers, also of the Italian peninsula, rest unsettlingly comfortable on the drenched and ever more dampening pavement. Cicero's slip-on onyx loafers lie fixed in a conflicting state, pointing directly at one another in a supple and unsightly way.

The rain pounds it all as his black blazer functions as a colander for Heaven's tears. Angels weep for him.

His earth-tone hands and fingers, furrowed by the wetness, twitch in awkward positions.

A controlled commotion is heard inside Juanita's home as paramedics scramble to save Olivia's life. They are able to stop her bleeding, yet the wound is described as serious. She is on the verge of dying.

Cicero, while losing his own fight with death, can hear the paramedics scrambling to save the woman who shot him. And for a brief moment, hope enters his mind. All is not lost. Even in his sleep, the young Cicero never appeared so at ease. So to save his energy, he closes his eyes.

All things urban are flushed toward him in the downpour. Thunder crackles, and blood gathers, and then is dispersed by the rain into several streams that flow down the black glossy alleyway in an artistic display.

But hope has arrived for Cicero. All is not lost.

Chapter 21

Chances for redemption often come in varying forms. Sometimes, the chance for a new life comes in the form of a stranger's words. It sometimes presents itself in a dream, or as the love of a mother. The chance for a new life can also come from a near death experience. A close brush with mortality can often shake the bones of the relentless, compelling them to surrender their ways and pursue a more fulfilling life.

But from somewhere, strange screams echo throughout dark caverns. The stench of shit and rotten flesh is thick and ubiquitous. There's no escaping it. Shrieks of horror fill the ears of others who yell out. The sounds of pain are strangely harmonious and innately unsettling.

Peering down from a rocky cliff, naked souls can be seen tumbling and intertwining among one another in disturbing perpetual motion. Their mouths emit woes of unending sorrow. Their bodies flop in a boundless lake of fire. Nude men and women wail in utter agony at the top of their lungs.

This place is Hell, and the lava is a flame that does not consume. In this place, the pain of unrepentant sinners is eternal.

This is the place where Cicero's soul resides. The paramedics did not reach him in time. Olivia's life was saved, but poor Cicero was not fortunate enough to make it. Not blessed enough for a second chance. No. His soul now stands naked in a dirty, waist-deep jagged pit. His eyes open, and he finds himself surrounded by demons. They are ungodly creatures. They cackle at him and hiss with a cobra's revulsion. Oh, the horror.

They are black shadows, evil fumes. They moan. Their appearances mock all that God has created. They mimic nude women. They are ghastly. They screech and shriek like hyenas.

Cicero's soul is silent and petrified. If he could piss on himself, he would. If he could run, he would try.

One wields a sword of flames. He speaks with a human voice. It mockingly sounds like Antonio, the one Cicero so cherished in life. It speaks to Cicero's terrified soul.

"Welcome, Cicero. We always knew you would come to reside with us!" The demons laugh. Vomit of human bowels spews from one demon's mouth onto Cicero's face.

Flames arise, burning his flesh down to the bone. But not destroying it. The stench is that of a crematorium. Burnt flesh and shit. Cicero's soul screams in agony and the demons cheer, jumping up and down and yelping in joy.

The thought of an eternal soul never crossed Cicero's mind. He was simply too busy chasing money and trying to be the next Antonio. The next don.

Unfortunately for him, Hell's minions knew of Cicero, and the welcome mat to Hades had awaited him for quite some time.

The Deceiver of Men had expected Cicero's presence for many moons, and the fallen angel greeted him with the promise of unending flames and torture.

At a young age, Cicero gave up on the premise that there were forces greater than he. He disregarded the value of humanity, and the belief that powers in the universe could punish or reward the decisions that he would make in life. Those choices would ultimately determine his eternal fate.

And this, above all else, was his tragic flaw. As the flames arise from the hole his soul is once again engulfed in fire, but not consumed.

Cicero's soul yells out.

The wicked spirits roar and snort. Maggot-filled feces fall from their backsides. Maggots and blood leak from between the mocking female legs.

"We have such torment to show you, Cicero," a mischievous imp states. "You will come to know misery like never before, son. *Capisce?*"

The other condemned miscreants chuckle and howl. Cicero's feet are charred in the fiery geyser.

"Why?! Why?!!!" screams Cicero's soul. Defecation fills his nostrils and sickens his soul, causing him to regurgitate gallons of cognac and bile, burning his throat beyond belief. All around him, souls bleed and cry and wail over and over and over again.

Cicero screams. It is an unheard cry, in this, the beginning of a cycle that shall never end. The fires of Hell shall burn him for all eternity, forever and ever, without refrain.

About the Author

Che Parker has worked as a crime and politics reporter and staff writer covering national health care issues and Capitol Hill hearings. He is currently a graduate student at Johns Hopkins University. He works in public relations and lives in Alexandria, Virginia. Visit the author at www.cheparker.com or email cheparker@hotmail.com

Q & A *with the Author: Che Parker*

Q: Is Cicero a completely made-up character, or is he based on someone you know?

A: He's a combination of people, but there are many elements of his character that are completely fictionalized. He's a combination of a few people I know and grew up with in Kansas City. None of them, though, are that heartless (I don't think.) He's also kind of a symbol that some hip-hop artists "claim" to be: the smooth gangster. But he's educated, too. I think that makes him even more sinister. He had other options, other opportunities, but he still chose to be a cutthroat.

Q: Why is Cicero biracial? Does the racial mix bring something to his character? And why Black and Italian?

A: That goes back to the whole mafia, gangster appeal. We often see movies like *The Godfather* or shows like *The Sopranos*, and we see an "Italian" image of gangsters. There's obviously some truth to that, but it's also a stereotype. Real gangsters come in all forms: Jewish, Chinese, Black, Irish, Latino. You name it. But then you bring in guys nowadays who try to emulate that "gangster" image, and they get it wrong somewhere. They're sloppy. They look like criminals. They're not smooth. I think the character of Cicero is the best of both worlds. He brings the two worlds together, so to speak.

Q: Cicero wears designer clothes and alligator boots, and drives a vehicle that cost $100K. Why does he drink out of a red plastic cup?

A: [*Laughs*] Well, you have to realize, where Cicero grew up is the inner city, not the suburbs or the rich part of town. Carrying around a red plastic cup is pretty standard for a real drinker. Plus, I think that adds to the irony. He'll have a hundred-dollar drink in a ten-cent cup.

Q: People tend to believe that people who are void of emotion, morals, and empathy have some dark thing that happened in their childhood that contributes to this. You wrote of one incident where Antonio nearly beat a man to death, which Cicero witnessed. How much, if any, did this event contribute to Cicero not having a conscience?

A: I see this event, in and of itself, as being monumental to Cicero as a child. Before this, C is a good kid, although he is mischievous as well (as noted by the items hidden under is mattress). He is also obviously born with a few mental defects, which I mention briefly as being a personality disorder and being anti-social. In other words, I think this event kind of gives Cicero the "green light" to be bad and to have no guilt about it.

Q: Cicero is an educated man, holding master's and bachelor's degrees. With all of this education, shouldn't he have come in contact with moral lessons in life? Aren't our universities charged with producing well-rounded, as well as well-educated, people?

A: When I initially wrote TTF, the plan was to make this part three in a four-part series. The next one I wanted to write was going to be C's childhood, probably from grades seven to nine or ten. After that, the next novel would have been his college years. And this still may come to fruition. To answer the question more accurately, Cicero definitely learns a lot of lessons in college, but he ultimately learns how to better control people, a Machiavellian education, if you will.

Q: Most villainous characters in novels are bad from page one, helping the reader to identify them and dislike them immediately. Cicero's character starts out being almost likeable, then, page by page he changes. With the strong religious influence of his mother, the reader feels he will find the correct path. Were there signs, real, imagined, or implied or suppressed memories that the reader doesn't see coming to the surface that doom this character?

A: I tried to sprinkle in a few hints that he needed to change his ways or risk suffering the consequences. Obviously his mother played that role. Olivia played that part to some extent. The woman on this flight to New Orleans. And definitely his dreams and his mother's dreams. So yes, Cicero has plenty of opportunities to change his ways.

Q: Lacking in morals, Cicero is true to his friends as they are to him. This bond seems to be more than "honor among thieves;" would you explain this?

A: C is definitely someone who values loyalty. For example, once he learned of Brad's deceit, that was it. No second chances. Kam is loyal to the end, and even in the second-to-last chapter, Cicero is frantically calling him, trying to reach him. There is definitely honor among thieves, and with that comes a level of respect from other characters who briefly appear (during the club fight scene, for instance).

Q: Cicero's mother prays for him. Do you believe in the power of prayer?

A: Yea, I believe prayer can change things. But I also think the person being prayed for has to want change, or at least make some type of effort to change their ways. We get none of that from Cicero. He's consistent in that way. Even when he is facing a loaded gun, he doesn't flinch. But as we see, his unwillingness to change is his undoing.

Q: What makes *The Tragic Flaw* different from other crime novels?

A: I tried to add different elements that your typical crime or street novel might not have. Elements of religion and the supernatural, almost science fiction elements. That and the educational background of the characters. Almost all of them went to college, except maybe Lana and Lucia. Not sure it's all that different from other books. I just tried to give the subject matter my take, my spin, if you will.

Q: The obvious moral to *TTF* is wrongdoing will be punished. Is there a deeper message?

A: Not really [*laughs*]. I think that sums it up. I think we live in a culture that says "live fast and die young." You know, "eat, drink, and be merry." But at the same time, I think there are consequences for those actions and we have to be prepared for that as well.

Q: All of the characters in *TTF* are interesting in their alliances. Will there be more novels to explain in depth, for example, Olivia's devotion to Cicero, in spite of her instincts that he really doesn't care about her?

A: Yea, as I mentioned earlier, the plan was to show Cicero in college, mostly grad school at this point, when he meets Olivia. C actually thinks Olivia is beautiful (there are hints of this throughout *TTF*), and his initial thoughts of her are those of attraction. I'm still toying with the idea of a setting, which college campus where they meet. Could be in Louisiana, could be Atlanta, or maybe D.C.

Q: Kansas City is allegedly a mafia town; have you ever experienced or heard of any "Family feuds"? What is your knowledge of the mafia based on? And why use Kansas City, as opposed to Chicago or New York, as the backdrop of your novel?

A: I was born and raised in Kansas City, Missouri, and when I was growing up, you would hear all kinds of stories about mafia violence, families battling, real stuff, real violence, shootings, bombings. A lot of it occurred in the '70s in the River Market area, just north of downtown, and even earlier. You would hear these stories a lot. As I got older, I actually met a few people with "family" connections. My father went to a Catholic High School and he had a lot of friends who were Italian, so there were all these stories that would float about in my family. I could drop a few names, but I won't do that. Many people I've come across have seen murders, have helped the mob dump bodies (and that was their sole function). At one point my aunt dated a known mafia hitman, unbeknownst to her, of course. And it's not like the movies, at least not in Kansas City, which may have been unique. People of all races played their part. It wasn't just an Italian thing. Blacks, Irish, all types were involved. Even all the way back to Tom Pendergast in the '20s and '30s, Kansas City was known to have mafia activity. Yea, it was *real* deep in those days. None of this really comes out in *TTF* because C is really an outsider, for all intents and purposes. There was a scene involving Cicero's father where I mentioned a "family" name in the book. A connection of mine in Kansas City read that and suggested that I remove the name, for my own benefit [*laughs*], which I did. But there's definitely the chance that any one of these guys from Kansas City's past could be the subject of a future project. I've also been approached by that same Kansas City connection to write about some real events that took place in his family, which would be an amazing story. But I think we'll have to wait and see. There's a lot of possibilities.

Q: Cicero thinks Olivia's plot in life is unfortunate and not deserved. Yet his feelings for her are "matter of fact"-like. Is there a reason why his attitude toward her is that of a hired "ninja," making light of her situation?

A: This is a subject that I didn't want to take lightly in the book. To me Olivia is the most human character in *TTF* (Her life may be the subject of my next book.) I initially wrote this piece with some ignorance of AIDS and HIV, but that ignorance works well in Cicero, I think, which is key. He involves her in these trysts because it's some "sick shit" to do. And that makes sense coming from a character like him. In the big picture though, I would like for this to generate more dialogue about preventing disease and living healthier lifestyles in the black community. There's WAY more that can be done, especially for the younger generation coming up now.